ADVANCE PRAISE FOR
MISSIONARY POSITION

"Five romantic, exotic, and erotic stars." **The Book Enthusiast**

"Funny, sexy, and super-entertaining!" **Vilma's Book Blog**

"Brilliant, magnificent, Best Book of 2014!!!! Reading Selah's story made me realize age is just a number." **Books and Beyond Fifty Shades**

"… a captivating story about life, love, supernova hot sex, and an exciting and unintentional quest for self-discovery." **Nestled in a Book**

"Engaging, pulled me right in… I loved the twists… the sex scenes are layered with passion, lust, and ultimately love." **Shh Mom's Reading**

"Reading Missionary Position felt like taking a fabulously sexy vacation." **Ficwishes**

MISSIONARY
POSITION

Daisy Prescott

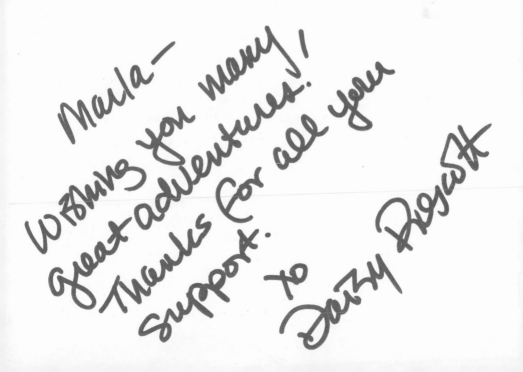

Marla—
Wishing you many!
great adventures!
Thanks for all your
support.
to Daisy Prescott

ISBN: 978-0-9894387-8-0 (paperback)

Cover Design by ©Sarah Hansen at OkayCreations.com
Front Cover Photo: Yuri/iStockphoto
Editors: Melissa Ringstead at There for You Editing;
Jenny Sims at Editing4Indies
Interior Book Design: Angela McLaurin at Fictional Formatters

ALSO BY DAISY PRESCOTT

Geoducks are for Lovers

and

Ready to Fall

To the Doers of Deeds

"Love never loses its way home."
~Proverb

ONE

"You should meet my brother."

I had been picked up many times in airport bars, but a brother set up was a first. Not that I expected the woman sitting next to me—with her glass of Pinot Grigio—to be the type to hit on strange women, but this was JFK. A crossroads of world travelers meant anything was possible. We'd been sitting silently next to each other at a sushi bar, poking away at our phones when our identical orders of spicy tuna hand-rolls were placed in front of us. She initiated a conversation and we fell into an animated discussion about the delicious merits of quality sushi.

Married? Never. Her? Divorced

Kids? No way. Her? A thirteen-year-old daughter.

From? Portland. Her? Chicago. Her accent told me she wasn't born there. I guessed someplace like Scandinavia where they bred supermodels.

The typical questions of where we were headed and sharing our woes of travel followed. I liked her.

"Is your brother in Dubai?" I asked. Anita had shared her excitement over her upcoming week there. I admitted it sounded glamorous and far more luxe than my travel plans.

"No, Dubai is for business and a little fun. My brother's in Amsterdam, where I'm from. You did say you're going to Amsterdam, didn't you?"

Dutch. I was close. Must be all the cheese. Or chocolate.

"Oh, right. I'll be there for a week before my work takes me to Ghana."

"Are you a missionary?" the athletic blonde asked me.

"A missionary in Amsterdam? Is anyone that much of a masochist? I'm not even a fan of the missionary position."

She spit out her wine. Wiping her chin with a napkin, she gathered her composure. "I thought perhaps you planned to visit Amsterdam to sin a little before doing the good work in Africa. Isn't that what most Americans do there? Meddle with the best intentions in the name of a church?"

I blinked at my bar mate. "Not a fan of religion?"

"I grew up in the Netherlands. Churches are for tourists in most towns."

I laughed. "I think I'll fit right in there. To answer your question, I'm a professor. My sabbatical is taking me to Amsterdam, and then on to Accra to study the female form in Ashanti sculptures."

"You study naked women?"

"Not only women. I'm an equal opportunity nudist. I mean I study the human form across cultures. Nothing against the penis, but it's hard to represent one in all its glory without it seeming silly or grotesque." I giggled, and Anita did, too. "I prefer female bodies in art with all the beautiful variation."

She blatantly swept her gaze over my body, from my messy, dark bob down to my overnight flight outfit of an open cardigan over exposed, but tasteful, cleavage, down to my yoga pants and comfortable but not fashionable flats. Maybe she was hitting on me. I straightened the scarf around my neck.

"You really should look up my brother." She tapped her phone, bringing it to life. "I'll give you his information. Text him. He'll be perfect company while you're in Amsterdam." Out of her designer bag, she pulled a business card and an expensive looking pen, which she used to scrawl a name and number on the back of her card.

"Your brother's name is Gerhard?" I failed to fully stifle my snort. Get hard. Gerrharrd. Gerhard would make the perfect name for a scoundrel pirate. I'd have to remember it for my next pirotica novel.

"I know. Isn't it the most uptight name? I wish I could say it doesn't suit him, but he can be a complete prat sometimes."

The garbled voice of a boarding announcement broke over the speakers. She glanced down at her watch.

"Oh, my flight's boarding. Call Gerhard. I think you'd have fun with him."

"Didn't you just say he was a prat?"

"Sometimes, but women seem to love the bad boys, don't they?" She gathered her things and left a sizable tip on the bar. "Great to meet you, Selah. Best of luck with your sabbatical."

I smiled at my new supermodel friend. If her brother shared her genes, maybe I would look him up when I arrived. "Bye, Anita."

"Say hi to Gerhard for me." With a sparkling white smile and a wave, she disappeared into the crowd of travelers.

What an odd, yet friendly, woman.

I spun her card on the bar. Anita Hendriks, management consultant. She had the same last name; the brother part could be legit. Gerhard, though. Get harder. I giggled and finished the last of my saketini. Scrolling through my mental file of lovers, aka The United Nations of Peen, I realized I'd never slept with a Dutchman. Maybe Gerhard could check off an item on my fuck-it list.

BEING A PROFESSOR might sound glamorous and interesting to some, but for me it meant having to fly coach on international flights. A window seat earned me a place in a slightly higher level of hell than a middle seat or the row right next to the bathrooms where the seats didn't recline. Still, it was hell nonetheless.

The crush of summer tourists filled the flight to capacity. College backpackers, stoners, and shifty-eyed men populated the plane. I doubted they would be seeing any Van Goghs or Rembrandts.

I wanted a cigarette. Damn quitting. Stupid aging and health. I reached into my bag for a piece of nicotine gum. Over the past three months, I'd managed to wean myself off cigarettes, deliciously comforting, soothing, invigorating, cancer-causing cigarettes. After smoking for decades, I missed the habit of it. At least flights were smoke-free these days. Otherwise, I might have been tempted to stand in the smoking section and acquire a contact nicotine hit.

Groggy after a sleep-aid induced nap, a gray sky greeted me when the plane landed at Schiphol Airport. Even in summer, Amsterdam had more rain than my beloved Portland. And cooler temperatures, I realized as I wrapped my scarf tighter around my neck. The variation in climates meant I had packed for three seasons for two countries. Ghana promised to be hot, humid, rainy, and dry, but never cool.

At immigration, Anita's business card fell to the floor when I reached for my passport. The man who picked it up and handed it to me looked half my age, which meant he was young enough to be one of my students. This reality didn't stop him from brushing against my side and flirting with me while we waited in line. With his guidebook opened to "cafés" I knew the type of adventure he wanted. Been there, smoked that. Before he could continue his attempt to flirt or ask to share a cab into the city, I brusquely thanked him and moved forward to the immigration agent.

Sitting in the back of a cab slowly making its way through morning rush hour into the heart of Amsterdam, I pulled out Anita's card with Gerhard's name on it. I admitted I was more than curious. After the attentions of the much younger man in line, I wondered how old Anita's brother was. It would be crazy to call him. Anita was gorgeous, and if her brother swam in the same gene pool, chances were he was just as tall, blond, and athletic. Everything I didn't typically find attractive. Although I shut down Backpack Romeo in the airport, these days my type meant anyone with a pulse, single, and not looking for a housekeeper. Viagra optional. I took pills to sleep and had a wee nicotine addiction. Who was I to judge the need for a little blue pill?

My fingers flicked the card to the beat of a techno song on the radio.

Anita wasn't a friend or even a friend of a friend. What would I say? *Hi, I thought your sister tried to pick me up at a sushi bar at JFK, but turns out she wanted to set me up with you.*

No, that wouldn't work.

Hi, your sister gave me your number. I've never had sex with a Dutchman, so I'm calling you. Are you up for some Flying Dutchman action?

No. Wasn't the Flying Dutchman some haunted ship doomed to roam the oceans forever? Maybe I could ask Gerhard.

Jet lag forced a yawn from me. After stretching my arms and rolling my neck, I tucked the card back into my purse. No need to rush things.

First things first. Coffee and something made of ninety-percent butter. Maybe some cheese. Followed by chocolate.

Maybe some *bitterballen.*

I snorted. I might have been too old for college backpackers, but my sense of humor still lingered around that of a fourteen-year-old boy.

Amsterdam, I'm coming for you.

You too, Gerhard.

"Enjoy the champagne," Mr. Navy Suit said, returning his attention to his companions.

I'd been summarily and impressively dismissed with a single "darling". Typical.

I spotted one of the curators across the room. Her stylish, yet simple maroon dress and sensible shoes were an island of comfortable familiarity in a sea of ostentatious display.

After greeting me warmly, Martha commented, "I saw you chatting with one of the men from TNG, our sponsors." She gestured to Mr. Navy Suit's group.

Of course the suits were bankers. Business men, especially wealthy ones, were so very, very not my type—even less my type than backpacking boys who could be in boy bands. My first college lover became a wealthy banker. I guess at one point they might have been my type. Briefly. Really only the one time.

"If I'd known, I would have flattered him more." I smiled at her.

"By the way he looked at you when you walked away, I think you made a very good impression." Martha laughed.

Interesting. I glanced at the group and found a set of stormy eyes meeting my own. I raised my glass and mouthed, "Thanks."

Mr. Navy Suit smiled with closed lips and raised his own glass. I noticed red talon woman had left. Even knowing I'd never see him again, it made me happy she wasn't his date. Or worse, his girlfriend. Such a cliché.

Martha and I chatted about Ghana and my project at the national museum. She was optimistic about my sabbatical research and encouraged me to promote my name with TNG for additional funding. After I rolled my eyes and joked about having my hat out for donations, she made a point to introduce me to several suits, sadly none of them was Mr. Navy. I scanned the room for him, but he'd disappeared. Poof. Like Cinderella.

A glance at my watch informed me I was about to be late for my drink with Gerhard. I hoped the bar had food. Two glasses of champagne into the evening and I hadn't eaten since an early lunch. Yikes.

After quick double kisses to Martha with a promise to keep in touch from Ghana, I rushed outside to find a taxi to the hotel.

Ready or not, Gerhard, I'm coming.

THREE

THE ELEVATOR DOORS opened on a high floor to reveal a twinkling view of Amsterdam in the dusky evening light. I stood for a moment near the entrance. Rich brown leather chairs, cream accents and flattering lighting gave the bar the look of a men's club. My glance moved around the room, which was sprinkled with men in suits and chic women, not a backpacker in sight.

Nor did a single man in a suit appear to be Gerhard; not unless he had become much, much older than Anita, or had brought a date with him. I debated between taking a table near the windows or a seat at the bar where I could watch the elevators. I chose the bar. While I waited, I could chat with the bartender, easing the awkwardness of this blind date feeling over something which wasn't a date.

A handsome young man wearing a crisp, white shirt rolled to his elbows and a black vest greeted me, placing a napkin and small bowl of bar kibble on the cool marble in front of my stool. Bless him. I ordered a dirty vodka martini and inhaled the bar snacks. The bowl was empty before the bartender finished making my cocktail. It was a very small bowl. Tiny.

My stomach no longer empty, I took a sip of what was possibly the best vodka martini ever and moaned, not loudly, but loud enough the bartender smirked.

"Enjoying your drink?"

I turned toward the voice.

Stormy Seas.

"Hi." Mr. Navy Suit glanced between me and the bartender, waiting for me to respond.

"Of all the gin joints," I mumbled to myself.

"Kiss me as if it were the last time," Stormy Seas quoted my favorite line from *Casablanca*.

I blinked at him, speechless.

"Let's try again." He smiled down at me. Even on my perch on the barstool, he still towered over me. "Hello."

"Hi." My brain still worked.

"Are you alone?" He gestured to the stool next to mine.

"Yes. No. I'm meeting someone."

His smile tugged at one corner of his mouth.

"American?"

"No, he's Dutch."

He chuckled. "No, I meant you. You don't sound Dutch."

"It was my accent that gave it away? Not my dark hair, olive skin, and Lilliputian height?"

"You're sitting down."

"Oh, right."

"So you are American?"

"Yes. And I'm guessing you're Dutch."

"Was it the accent?" he mimicked me. His eyes sparkled like sun on dark water.

"That and the package."

He coughed. I tried not to look at his crotch after my word slip, but failed. Unfortunately, I couldn't see anything. Bastard suit jacket.

"I meant your height and overall Dutchness."

He bit his bottom lip and nodded for me to continue.

"You look Dutch. Tall, fair, blue eyes. Add some wooden shoes and a pointy hat, put your finger in a dyke, and you'd be straight out of a children's book."

I had said finger and dyke in the same sentence to Navy Suit. I hoped he didn't catch it. By the way his eyes bulged, obviously he did.

"You must be Selah," he stated, shaking his head with a chuckle. "Anita told me you were funny."

I choked on a sip of my martini and tried to swallow. "What?"

"You're Selah, yes? Anita met you at JFK?"

Mr. Navy Suit was Gerhard. Holy fucking gene pool.

Thank you, Anita.

"I am. You must be Gerhard."

Something flashed behind his eyes and then he nodded. "Yep, Gerhard. That's me."

Regaining my manners, I extended my hand. "Selah Elmore, nice to meet you."

"Gerhard Hendriks." His large hand wrapped around mine in a firm grip. With formalities out of the way, he shrugged off his suit jacket and loosened his green silk tie before sitting down and ordering a gin and tonic. Silver ball cuff-links embellished the cuffs of his dress shirt. Mr. Hendriks was such a suit.

"For the record, I'm only half Dutch."

"What's the other half?"

"American."

"Really? But you have a Dutch name and accent," I stated the obvious. Go me.

"Want to see my passport?" He smiled. "My mother is American, and I went to school in the States. My—" The bartender interrupted him when he set down a gin and tonic and another bowl of delicious kibble. Gerhard took a sip and then continued, "Anita lives in Chicago now."

"And you?" I asked.

"Here for now."

"For now?"

"I travel a lot for work. Amsterdam is home, but otherwise I'm a nomad."

Sexy nomad. Images of Lawrence of Arabia came to mind.

"What about you, Selah Elmore?" My name sounded different, exotic, on his tongue.

"What about me?" His charming Dutchness charmed me stupid.

"Where do you live?"

"Portland. Oregon. Not Maine."

He nodded. "I've been to Maine, but not the other Portland. I went to college in Boston."

There was something distinctly Harvardian about him. "Harvard?"

His smile broadened, revealing straight, white, ridiculously gorgeous teeth. "How'd you guess?"

"There's something about people who attend Harvard."

"What?"

"They have names like Gerhard and wear expensive navy suits." I grinned back, testing the flirting waters.

"I'm a stereotype? Are you trying to catalogue me?"

"Stereotype? I don't know you well enough to say, but I do enjoy cataloging things. Blame my job."

He scanned my red jersey dress and narrowed his eyes. "You don't look like the banking type. I'd guess collector or curator since I first saw you at the auction reception."

He did remember seeing me there. Sitting up a little straighter, I mentally preened.

"Art history professor, but you were close."

"Ah, it all makes sense now."

"It does?" I sipped my martini and then nibbled on one of my olives.

"Why you were at the reception. African art professor?"

"No, the human form. Mostly how female nudity is portrayed across cultures."

He paused with his glass near his mouth. "You're an expert in naked women?"

I nodded, watching his reaction.

"Huh." He swallowed. "Who knew such a job existed."

His response was typical, making me laugh. "Jealous?"

"A little. My work involves no naked women. Although, sometimes there are naked breasts." His eyes met mine.

"In banking? You mean when you take clients to strip clubs?"

"Now, now. Don't start with your stereotypes again. Who said I was a banker?"

"I assumed."

He smirked.

"Yes, I know. Ass-u-me. You were at the reception tonight and someone pointed you out as part of the TNG group."

"Because I was standing with a group of bankers doesn't mean I'm a dull number cruncher."

I couldn't tell if he was teasing, but I felt like an ass for putting him in a box. "So what do you do?"

"I crunch numbers." His face remained blank for a moment, then his eyes crinkled and his lips twitched.

I smacked his arm where it lay on the bar. "You do not!"

"I do in a way, but no, not really. I work for another area at TNG."

"One that requires you to travel."

"Yes, in fact I leave for a conference in a few weeks. Enough blabbering about me, what are you doing in Amsterdam?"

I told him about my week here, and plans in Accra for the next six months.

His smile returned. "You'll love Ghana. It's Africa for beginners. Stable, peaceful, and almost everyone speaks a little English."

"You've been?"

"I had an assignment there three years ago. In Accra."

"I'll be staying in Accra! Mostly. I want to visit the North and see some elephants."

"You have to see the elephants. Also, eat *joloff* and *kelewele*. Watch out for the palm wine, though; it sneaks up on you."

Tall, gorgeous, charming, worldly? Bless you, Anita, patron saint of blind dates.

"I can't wait. I have oodles of *Out of Africa* fantasies running through my mind."

"Lion hunting?" he joked.

"No, a hot alpha man washing my hair. Duh." I rolled my eyes.

"The naked women expert dreams of being seduced in Africa? I'm sure that can be arranged." His eyes met mine, and we locked stares for a moment. I couldn't read him. Maybe it was a Dutch thing.

"Africa, Amsterdam. I'm easy that way." I smirked at my own word play.

His eyes searched my face for a hint of joking. There wasn't one.

He straightened his shirt cuffs. "You're a funny bird."

"I'd say so. Given I'm not a bird at all." I smiled at him.

He studied my expression, considering me for a moment.

"Anita said you met at the sushi bar in JFK." His face exhibited his doubt in my taste and sanity.

"We did. I see you judging me. Normally, I'd be sitting in judgment, too. Sushi. Airport. Eating raw fish in advance of a long flight. However, it's good quality sushi, and surprisingly delicious."

"I'll have to believe you and Anita."

"Next time you're at JFK, try it. Trust me."

"Trust you? I don't know you."

"Then trust Anita."

He blinked at me and his eyes flickered with some emotion I didn't understand. "Do you like sushi? It wasn't some sort of dare you lost with a friend?"

"Absolutely love it. I'll miss it in Ghana."

"Ghana is known for many things, but sushi isn't one of them. You should eat sushi before you leave."

"Is that an invitation to dinner?"

He played with the edge of his cocktail napkin for a moment, a smile playing at the corner of his mouth. "Yes. We should have dinner. Do you have plans for tonight?"

I checked my watch. It was close to nine, but unlike home, people here didn't eat until later. "Can we find a table somewhere?"

"We can get one downstairs. One of the best sushi places in Europe is in this hotel." Gerhard waved the bartender over and they had a quick conversation in Dutch before the bartender walked over to the phone behind the bar. He returned and they spoke for another minute. I understood nothing.

"We're set for 9:30. Another cocktail?" He smiled and pointed to my empty glass.

With a few words, Gerhard could make a last minute reservation for us at an amazing sushi restaurant. Suit or no suit, Gerhard was quickly becoming my favorite person on the planet.

We spent the next half hour chatting about Ghana, art, Amsterdam, and Boston. His arm drifted behind my shoulders and rested on the back of my stool. A delicious soap or cologne scent tickled my nose. Another point for the Dutchman. *Damn if he wasn't winning me over, regardless of being so very not my type.*

When we stood to walk down to the restaurant for dinner, my head came up to his bicep—his very shapely, nicely defined bicep. I could climb him like a tree if I were a koala. Lucky marsupials.

His hand warmed my lower back as he guided me through the bar and remained there in the elevator as we descended. The size of his hand made me feel petite in the best way. I shivered at the idea of his fingers other places on my body.

"Cold?" he asked.

"Not at all. I was thinking of your hand on my back."

"My apologies. Too familiar?" He removed his hand and leaned against the wall.

"Maybe, but that doesn't mean I didn't enjoy it." I met his eyes.

He broke eye contact and swept his gaze up my body while rubbing his thumb over his bottom lip.

He nodded but didn't speak. The elevator doors opened to the lobby, and whatever he intended to say, or not say, was lost.

Despite his teasing me over airport sushi, dinner tasted incredible. Beyond the airport variety, I'd eaten excellent sushi more times than I could count, but nothing came close to this meal. Everything tasted like it descended directly from sushi heaven and each dish resembled tiny sculptures. No spicy tuna rolls here. I didn't bother asking what I was eating after the first course. I didn't care. My normal squeamishness about texture and taste disappeared into a hedonistic frenzy of flavors and sensations. It felt like having an orgasm for the first time.

Gerhard laughed at my moans of delight while we ate. I teased him about letting his hair down when he took off his tie.

"I can't remember the last meal I enjoyed this much," I said when the last of our plates had been cleared from our table.

"You certainly enjoyed yourself. I worried at one point the waiters might have thought some hanky-panky was happening under the table the way you moaned and squirmed."

"Say it again," I demanded.

"Say what?"

"Hanky-panky."

"Heynkay-peynkay."

"Your accent is stronger when you say that. It's adorable."

"Adorable?" He arched an eyebrow. "Really? Kittens and baby bunnies are adorable. Bankers and number crunchers are 'boring stiffs' I think is what you said."

"Fine. Not every number crunching banker is a boring stiff. Neither are all Gerhards." I smiled at him.

"Thank you."

"You're welcome. Honestly, I've had a wonderful evening. Much better than spending it at some café with backpackers."

"You don't seem the type to hang out with backpackers and stoners."

"Maybe twenty years ago, but not now."

He subtly worked his jaw side to side. "Twenty years ago I was fifteen."

Well, that answered that question.

"Twenty years ago I was twenty-three," I stated, holding his gaze to gauge his reaction.

He blinked, but didn't react or make a joke about older women. "Then we're both too old for silly things like disco clubs and sleeping on trains."

I raised my nearly empty wine glass for a toast. "To being too old for silly things."

He clinked my glass and said, "But doing them anyway."

I laughed in response and tapped his glass with mine a second time.

Funny how if I thought I'd never see someone again, I acted more myself, more free than at home where I might run into them at the store in my saggy yoga pants and Sunday sports bra.

I said yes when he asked me out for dinner the next night.

And the one after.

Amsterdam became more interesting than old paintings, canals, and the possibility of death by bell-ringing bicycles.

FOUR

"MMM, GERHARD."

I squirmed and fisted the pillow, cracking open my eyes. Early morning light sliced along the edges of the blinds in my hotel room.

The things that man could do with his hands.

Too bad it was only a dream. He made the perfect pirate, all Norse God and fair. I let my mind wander through the images of my dream. Each one could be a scene in one of my nom de plume romance novels.

Thor on the high seas. Breeches unlaced, broad, hairless Scandinavian chest bared under a faded and tattered uniform jacket, and legs for days ending in boots, big boots, very big boots covering his very big feet.

After a quick debate, I grabbed BOB instead of my notebook. The scene could be saved for later.

Damn Amsterdam and its Dutch charm.

I fell backward into the pillows, letting my hands wander as I mentally thanked Betty for adding batteries to the bag the other day.

Where was I? Right, Norse Gods. Pirates.

Gerhard.

I STOOD AGAINST the back wall in the auction room—my favorite spot to watch the bidding. Some people liked to sit up front, but serious bidders preferred to be in the rear or side of the room to observe their competition. Not that I intended to bid—the estimates were beyond my price range—but I was happy to observe.

Martha gave me a little wave from her position on the right side of the room, near the banks of phone bidders. I cautiously waved at her, making sure the auctioneer didn't take my gesture for a bid.

The energy in the room simmered and heated up occasionally, but it never reached anything close to the bidding wars of contemporary or modern art auctions. Today's auctioneer charmed and worked the partially full room the best he could.

My phone rang. The man next to me scowled despite speaking loudly in German on his own phone. Returning his scowl, I silenced the ringer and dashed out of the room to answer it.

"Morning, Selah," a man's voice greeted me. I glanced at the screen where Gerhard's name was displayed

My mouth fought to resist breaking into a schoolgirl's grin.

"Morning. I'm at the auction," I explained, even though he didn't ask what I was doing.

"I know. Look behind you."

I glanced behind me, and then returned to the auction room, scanning the crowd until I located his familiar sand colored hair sitting in the last row on the far side. Today's suit was gray and stretched across his broad shoulders, accenting them in a way that shouldn't be allowed in polite company.

"What are you doing here?" I asked, standing still and making eye contact with him.

"Come sit with me," he whispered.

I didn't move from my spot.

"Come. Sit." He patted the empty seat next to him and ended the call.

My feet obediently followed his command until I sat next to him.

"Hi." His tone was hushed.

"Hi—" Enthusiasm made my voice too loud.

"Shhh!" an octogenarian in the row in front of us turned and hissed. The thin, bony finger she held to her lips ended in the sharp point of her blood red nail.

I raised my eyebrows at Gerhard, who stopped his laugh by biting his thumb. His shaking shoulders gave him away, though.

Tempted to stick my tongue out at Madame Shhusher, I instead leaned closer to Gerhard, inhaled his spicy scent, and repeated, "What are you doing here?"

He shook his head and wrote on his catalogue: *"Bidding."*

I took his pen and replied: *"For work?"*

Another shake of his head. *"For my father. He collects."*

Son of a collector. Not only did he make money, he came from money.

"May I?" I softly asked, gesturing at the catalogue. He had noted the sale price for several pieces and had drawn a circle around an upcoming lot, an Ashanti comb from Ghana. A woman's head and chest, including pert gumdrop boobs, were carved above what resembled a large hair pick. Valued in the low thousands, it was impressive. I pointed at the picture and gave it the thumbs-up.

He smiled and flipped a couple of pages forward, pointing at a color photo of a group of sculptures of women, their breasts a fascinating depiction of the effects of gravity. He waggled his eyebrows at me.

I snickered like a teenage girl passing notes with the cutest boy in school. Damn him.

No hissing, but we did earn another dirty look over the shoulder, which only made me snicker again.

Gerhard's hand wrapped around my wrist to calm me. It had the opposite affect; my pulse fluttered.

Madame Shhusher and the room faded away, leaving me fixated on his warm skin pressed against mine. His fingers tightened slightly and released.

His lot came up for bidding. This wasn't his first auction. He waited until the frenzy at the front of the room slowed, and bid with a subtle flick of his paddle.

The way his wrist controlled the paddle did things to my pulse and stomach, which would appall the dowager in front of me.

The auctioneer tapped his gavel and called out Gerhard's number as the winner.

"Congratulations!" I said, loudly.

"Shhhh!"

Gerhard laughed and grabbed my hand. "Let's get out of here."

We stopped at the desk to arrange delivery of the sculpture. I listened to him speak Dutch to the employees, charming them with his charms.

Bright sunshine greeted us when we walked outside.

"Do you have plans for lunch?" he asked, stopping when he stood a step or two below me, making us the same height.

"Aren't we having dinner tonight?"

"We are. Let's do both." He grinned at me.

"Don't you have to work? Auctions and lunches aren't exactly bankers' hours."

"Are you looking for excuses to say no? Am I overcrowding your schedule?" Worry darkened his happy expression.

"Not at all. I have nothing for the next two days until my flight. I just—"

He interrupted me. "Then say yes."

"Yes. But you didn't answer about your work."

He walked down the street and clicked the alarm on a black BMW sedan. I fell in step slightly behind him; my traitor feet would follow him anywhere.

And we hadn't even had sex.

The image of him holding his paddle popped into my mind.

Yet.

"… I'm not starting my next project for a few weeks." While I was thinking about paddles, he'd been speaking.

"What?"

"What what?" He tilted his head to look down at me.

"I missed what you were saying."

"Is it the accent again? It's stronger when I'm home." He gave me a small smile. "Sorry. I was saying as much as you cling to the notion I'm a banker, I'm really not." He bumped his shoulder with mine. "And my schedule is loose for the next couple of weeks until I start a new project."

"Ah …"

"Ah?"

"Got it. Where are you taking me to lunch?" If Gerhard wanted to bump shoulders with me and take me to lunch, who was I to say no? My mother didn't raise a fool.

"IT LOOKS LIKE a propeller penis. Or a penis jet, which most planes look like anyway."

"You're very articulate. And perhaps a little obsessed?" He smirked at me. The sun faded his eyes from blue to gray.

"Stop. Look. Really look at it. Vertical, rounded top. Classic representation of the human phallus." I flashed a grin at him. "Better?"

"It's a windmill, not some sort of Dutch inferiority complex made of wood."

"Who said anything about inferiority complexes? I certainly didn't. Interesting you would mention size envy." I pursed my lips together to maintain my serious expression.

We sat at a picnic table in a beer garden flanking the only working windmill within Amsterdam city limits.

Gerhard leaned back. "I guess from this angle, and with your perverted mind influencing me, I can see your point." He nodded, and then rolled his eyes. "Also, I think you've had too much beer."

"And cheese!" I speared the last cube on the plate between us. With the cheese clamped between my teeth, I grinned at him.

"Sexy. You American girls have all the tricks."

I chewed and swallowed. "We do. Songs have been written about our wiles."

He surprised me by singing lyrics from a Lenny Kravitz song. His singing voice resonated low and gravelly. Some might say it was pure sex. Some would definitely say that.

The contrast between the sex falling from his lips and his uptight suited appearance confused me. After a few hours with Gerhard, I failed at my attempt to categorize him. American men were easier to label and decipher, almost simplistic in their "type". And for most, food, ego stroking, and sex—not necessarily in that order—would keep them happy.

Gerhard would not stay put inside his uptight banker box.

I wondered if he ever lost the suit. Would I recognize him wearing jeans and a T-shirt?

I bit my lip. Jeans, T-shirt, or nothing.

I wanted to have sex with banker Gerhard. Maybe sex would solve the puzzle. He probably enjoyed being tied up and called baby.

I shuddered.

"Cold?"

I blinked a several times, clearing my head. "Maybe." A cloud moved in front of the sun and the temperature dropped. I grabbed my sweater out of my bag.

"You won't be needing a sweater for a while." He gestured to my sweater.

"I know. I'll miss the gray and the rain, but bring on the heat."

"You say that now. Wait until you're tired of the sticky feeling of mosquito spray, sweat, and dirt."

"Well, when you put it that way, it sounds lovely." I turned and smiled at him. "What do you miss about Ghana?"

"The people, mostly. My friends there. The mangos. The way the waves assault the shore."

"Sounds exotic and slightly dangerous."

"It can be. Don't be lulled into thinking the same rules from the States, or here, apply there. Promise me you'll play it safe. No 'I am woman, hear me roar' nonsense if you're dealing with police or the government. It's a land of chiefs and clearly defined roles." His expression was serious.

"I'll behave. This isn't my first trip outside the West."

"Where else have you been?" His voice revealed his interest.

"Vietnam, Chile, Costa Rica, Thailand, Cambodia …" I listed some of my more exotic destinations.

"Impressive."

"Thank you, Mr. World Traveler. What about you? Where's your next assignment?"

"I'm supposed to be based in Kenya for a month. I think. It might change." He stared out across the semi-empty beer garden.

"Kenya? We'll be on the same continent."

"Africa's a big place."

"True. But it will be nice to know I'll have a friend on the same continent."

"Is that what we are? Friends?"

"In twenty-four hours, what else could we be?" I held my breath waiting for an answer. I typically wasn't this woman—the woman who waited for the man to pursue. If I wanted someone, I had them. One word to Rob, the boy band backpacker, and he would have followed me home, but I didn't say the word. And here I sat, waiting for a man wearing custom tailored suit trousers and expensive black leather shoes, who was so very not my type, to chase me. Or at least confirm he was interested. He flirted. We bantered, but he hadn't made a move. Not even after dinner last night. I received a hand on my back and a polite double-cheek kiss when he escorted me to a taxi.

He interlaced his fingers and stretched out his arms, exhaling. "Sure. Of course." A little smile tugged the corner of his mouth, but his eyes didn't sparkle.

Wait.

Could Gerhard be gay?

I mentally replayed our time together. There was flirting and the aforementioned banter, but my friend Quinn and I had the same thing in spades, and he was most definitely gay. Quinn didn't make my thighs clench together. Unless I was trying not to pee from laughing.

Color me officially confused.

Meticulously dressed. Fancy shoes.

Tingles on my skin when he touched me or stared at me with his stormy sea eyes.

I looked down at his long fingers. Well-groomed nails. Metrosexual?

Would it be rude to ask if he was gay? Nothing compliments and says 'I want to have sex with you' like asking about sexual preference.

If I didn't want to have sex with him, I would ask.

Why would Anita, patron saint of superior genes, want me to meet her gay brother?

One word: Ghana.

He'd been there and would be a good resource.

Of course.

This wasn't a romantic set-up.

Suddenly, the beer, sun, and cheese caught up to me. I closed my eyes. After a few breaths, I opened my lids and sighed.

Gerhard stared at me funny.

"Tired?" he asked.

"Exhausted. I think jet lag snuck up on me. Or there was alcohol in our beer."

He chuckled and offered to give me a lift to my hotel for a much needed nap.

Once in my room, I found my moleskine notebook and made a list of things I knew about Gerhard.

Turned out, I didn't know very much at all.

Confused and frustrated, I fell onto the bed fully dressed and gave into beer and dairy sleepiness.

Gerhard Hendriks was a Dutch enigma, much like the Flying Dutchman.

I HAD A nap, a shower, and a new outlook on Gerhard.

We had now.

I was leaving; he was leaving. I wouldn't spend the next thirty-six hours stewing. I didn't stew. I wasn't a stewer. Not over men.

Forty-eight hours of going with the flow. I would be Selah Elmore, flow-goer.

I admitted when I first woke up, groggy from another Gerhard, Norse God pirate dream, I thought about emailing Anita and asking about his preference for teammates when playing hide the salami, but while showering I decided it would be weird and desperate, and anti-flow-going.

Instead, I would put on my lady pants and enjoy the company of a handsome man without wondering what it would be like to get in his pants.

It would be a first in a long time for me.

I loved getting inside men's pants.

Sighing, I dressed in a pair of black trousers and a flowy tunic decorated with a peacock pattern. Mature, classic, and flowy—very me.

My plan crumbled when Gerhard showed up wearing jeans and a navy polo shirt. If possible, he looked better in jeans than he did in his suits. Gone were the polished banker shoes, replaced by gray Vans. A classic tank watch decorated his wrist instead of the cufflinks I wanted to undo with my teeth.

I was in trouble.

When he warmly greeted me with the double cheek kiss, his five o'clock shadow scraped deliciously across my jaw.

Big trouble.

My cheeks heated and I resisted the urge to try for the triple kiss, planning to miss his cheek. Of course, before I could pucker up, he pulled away, complimenting me on my shirt.

Regaining my composure, I thanked him and asked, "Where are we going?"

"To eat a multitude of foods you won't be able to find in Ghana."

"I approve of your mission."

He smiled at me before licking the corner of his mouth. "What mission would that be?" He raised his eyebrows.

"The feed Selah all forbidden foods mission."

"Ah, right. Well, next stop on the food mission, the traditional *Rijsttafel.*"

"Sounds very Dutch."

"It means 'rice table' and it's Indonesian. How do you feel about spicy?"

"Love a little spice," I flirted.

"Good," he replied, giving away nothing.

Dinner equaled a table full of small dishes, most of which were spicy, saucy, and delicious. Pickles, various sauces, veggies, and mysterious condiments filled the bowls crowding any remaining table space not occupied by our wine glasses. It was a feast.

A feast of confusion.

Yep. Still no clue.

We flirted and talked. His eyes twinkled, and my cheeks hurt from smiling.

And still no idea.

It didn't matter. I had one of the best nights in memory. I laughed, he laughed. I snorted, he laughed harder. I spit spicy *sambal* into my napkin, and he almost spit out his water. The restaurant had cleared out when we finally paid the bill.

Stumbling outside, still laughing, I rubbed my belly and called uncle. "No more. No more food. No more laughing. I can't take any more."

Gerhardt wiped a stray tear from his face and nodded silently, his shoulders shaking with laughter. "Okay. I admit defeat."

I pulled a tissue from my purse and waved it, which only made him laugh again.

We were punch drunk on each other, walking crookedly down the sidewalk, gaining odd looks from fellow pedestrians.

After a handful of minutes of silence, broken only by the occasional residual giggle or snort, I realized we were walking in the direction of my hotel.

Perhaps I was about to solve the mystery of Gerhard and what got him hard.

FIVE

THE SAYING ABOUT assuming and asses rang true again.

Good news, turned out Gerhard was straight.

Bad news, I found out at the airport.

After our walk to my hotel, I failed in my mission. I, Selah Elmore, writer of erotica, expert in naked humans, chickened out.

I decided I didn't want to know.

We had a connection and not enough time.

I'd had years of no connections. Online dating, speed dating, mixers, bar pick-ups, grad students, divorced, widowed, perpetually single for obvious reasons … I had a long list of no connections. Sex? Easy. Having the ability to put up with someone enough to have a relationship? That was the part I could never seem to figure out. Or want. Friends in marriages and long-term relationships always talked about the work which went into keeping love alive. Blech.

I had enough work.

I had enough distractions.

I didn't have enough of whatever I had with Gerhard.

He walked me to my hotel steps, double-Dutch-kissed me goodnight, and confirmed dinner for the next night. He didn't push or ask to come up. Neither did I.

Younger Selah yelled at me for cock-blocking us. What was the point of traveling the world if it wouldn't include international relations? What happened to adding Holland to the United Nations of Peen?

Gerhard happened.

Damn him and his perfect suits.

I sat in the departure lounge and thought about him. Every tall blond man earned a double-take from me, followed by disappointment each time.

For our last dinner, we ate all of the cheese in Holland. Fried, baked, aged, fresh—the many faces of cheese. It was gluttonous and perfect.

He told me how unexpected I was. I took it as a compliment.

He said he enjoyed our time together. I agreed.

He asked if I would keep in touch. I promised.

I still chickened out.

Young Selah gave me death stares as only a former goth girl could.

He offered to bring me to the airport. I accepted. His sleek, black BMW cut through the traffic while I sat in the passenger seat and lost my nerve.

Finally, outside departures, he leaned down to give me the double-kiss.

And missed.

His aim was off.

His aim missed the corner he would have hit had he overshot the cheek.

Gerhard Hendriks kissed me. Full on the mouth.

He kissed me softly, lips closed, with faint pressure, but enough I felt it down to my toes. One hand reverently cupped my cheek while the other clasped mine.

Softly, barely more than a breath, he whispered against my ear, "I hope our paths cross again soon."

He walked backward to his car, his eyes still on me. I stood at the curb, mouth open, nodding.

Gerhard wasn't gay.

I was an idiot.

Now I had six hours on my flight to Accra to stew about missed connections.

A six hour flight and six months in Africa to moon over the Dutchman.

I picked up the in-flight magazine and found the map of Africa. Kenya wasn't impossibly far away from Ghana. Using my fingers, I discovered the distance was the same as Portland to New Orleans. Not impossible.

Sighing, I closed the magazine and opened up my laptop. If I couldn't pursue the real Gerhard, I could use him for inspiration for a new novel.

"AKWAABA" SHOUTED THE colorful mural on the arrival building when I stepped off the plane's stairs on the tarmac at Kotoka Airport in Ghana's capital.

Eight o'clock in the evening and warm, humid heat enveloped me. Thankfully July was reportedly one of the cooler months. By cool, temperatures hovered in the eighties between periods of rain and dust. Mixing rain and dust equaled mud. I looked down at my silver sandals and mentally apologized, knowing they wouldn't survive the next six months.

"*Akwaaba,*" the man inside the terminal welcomed me. While he reviewed my vaccinations card, I absentmindedly rubbed my left shoulder where I received seven, or maybe nine, shots for this trip. After verifying I had my Yellow Fever inoculation, he smiled and waved me through to baggage.

Outside customs, chaos ruled when the trickle of passengers met a wave of greeters, family, friends, drivers, children, hucksters and sundry others. I looked for a card with my name amongst the churning sea of people and luggage. After a moment of searching, I spotted a man with a broad face below a high forehead and hair graying at the temples, wearing a colorful shirt and holding a card proclaiming "Dr. Elmore".

I pushed the heavy luggage cart, which held my life for the next six months, toward him through the crowd.

"I'm Dr. Elmore," I explained when I reached him.

A huge smile greeted me. "*Akwaaba!* I'm Kofi, your driver." His enthusiastic handshake matched the wattage of his smile.

"Coffee?" I puzzled out loud.

"*Maa jo.* I am Kofi, like the former UN Director Kofi Anan," he proudly said the name of Ghana's most recognized citizen.

Gerhard had taught me several phrases over dinner last night. *Maa jo* meant good evening.

"*Maa jo,*" I repeated.

After another smile and a brief discussion over who should push the cart, Kofi politely took over and led me into the thick heat of evening in Accra.

"*Eti sen?*" he asked how I was as he drove through thick traffic.

"*Eh ya.*" I hoped it meant I'm fine. I trusted Gerhard to have told me the correct response. For all I knew, I could be saying "monkey sex."

In perfect English, Kofi complimented me. "You speak well."

This made me laugh. "That's about the extent of my language skills."

"It's more than many *Obruni* speak when they arrive. You'll do fine in Ghana, Dr. Elmore."

I beamed over his compliment. "Selah. Please, call me Selah," I corrected him. I could tell I'd become friends with this kind man.

On the short drive to my hotel, modern banks, Western-looking hotels, and gated mansions alternated with cramped adobe and tin roofed buildings. We passed wide tree lined boulevards and dark, narrow dirt streets, which were essentially pathways. Trucks, buses, and passenger vans crammed with people, their roofs piled high with luggage and goods, crawled rather than sped toward the center. At times we merely inched forward through the crowded streets.

"What do you call those?" I gestured out the window, counting no fewer than eight people inside the van stopped next to us.

"Those are *tro-tros,* the most common way to travel for Ghanaians.

Not so good for single *Obruni* women." Kofi's smile left his face.

I heeded his warning. He didn't mean I was spoiled, but my place of privilege as a white Westerner couldn't be ignored. I rolled down my window. Diesel fumes and dust carrying the acrid smell of smoke assaulted my nose, and I coughed.

"You will get used to it, Dr.—Selah. I promise. And when it gets to be too much in Accra, you will visit Cape Coast or Volta for fresh air." He named two of Ghana's most popular tourist destinations.

"I'm here to work, to study at the museum." I needed to qualify my presence, another white face, in this place with a long history of colonial rule, a point of the Atlantic slave triangle.

"And you will do good work, Dr. Selah. I know." His smiling eyes met mine in the rearview mirror. "We are here."

My gaze broke from his to look out the window. At the end of an unpaved road sat a low coffee-colored building surrounded by lush plants.

"Ama's Hotel," he answered my unspoken question.

KOFI HAD BEEN warm and kind, but he was nothing compared to Ama. Everything about her exuded warmth, comfort, love, and home. Upon greeting, she hugged me. Not one of those awkward, stiff hugs between strangers, but a side shoulder hug meant to express her joy at my arrival. Why she would be joyful at the arrival of a tired, slightly smelly—pouting over a man—grown American woman, I didn't question.

The patterned green skirt she wore highlighted the wide expanse of her hips and bottom. With her generous bust and curves, she was Venus in the flesh, adorned by gold bracelets and a rainbow of a scarf wrapped around her head. She asked me questions about everything while she led me from the main building down the open stairs and to a narrow dirt pathway. Somewhere beyond the single story row of rooms, waves crashed against the beach. Once inside, she pointed out the air conditioner—only to be used while I was in the room—the shower, and how to turn on the hot water heater next to it, and a bottle of water next to the sink for teeth brushing. She warned me twice to keep the door closed to avoid both mosquitoes and friendly lizards.

Mosquitoes I could handle. Lizards? Not so much, and certainly not in my room.

With a reminder the kitchen would be closing soon, Ama left me in my quiet, sparse but comfortable space, which would be home for the next two weeks until I moved into university housing or found an apartment. Blue bedspreads with a striped Kente pattern topped the wooden twin beds, and a wood carving of Africa hung on the wall. Otherwise, it appeared identical to any other mid-rate hotel anywhere in the world. Clean, but far from luxurious.

After washing my face, I changed into a maxi skirt. Ghanaian customs around fashion were modest, and I wanted to be respectful, without gratuitous cleavage or thigh exposure in any of my outfits.

The restaurant consisted of colorful cloth-covered tables and heavy wood chairs scattered around a curved veranda open to the air on three sides except the wall which housed the kitchen behind a narrow doorway. Two other white patrons sat at a table with empty plates and bottles of Star beer, but no one else was there besides Ama.

"Come. Sit. Eat," Ama instructed, leading me to a table near the railing. "I only have a little *jollof* and some *kelewele* left. How about a Star beer? Fanta?"

I chuckled at the mention of Fanta, favorite soda of the tropics. I only drank it with any regularity when outside of the US.

"Star please and whatever you have will be fine."

Turned out, *jollof* and *kelewele* were delicious. The spicy rice was the Ghanaian equivalent of Mexican rice, only spicier and richer. *Kelewele* tasted similar to spicy French fries made from plantains—sweet, peppery, and addictive. I'd done my research on Ghana prior to the trip, and anticipated spice and lots of peanut butter, but I hadn't expected to love the food right away.

Soon my table matched the other guests' with plates practically licked clean next to an empty glass and beer bottle.

After charging the meal to my room, I returned to my room to take a shower. Relatively clean, I sat on the bed with a towel around my torso. The hotel had Wi-Fi, slow and spotty, but it worked well enough to check my emails.

Nothing from Gerhard.

I hadn't expecting anything. Of course not.

I looked at my phone, which remained turned off. I'd need to find a SIM card tomorrow to avoid roaming charges.

Ghana might be an emerging country but with Wi-Fi and a cell phone, I wouldn't feel alone for my stay.

Lonely, maybe, but not alone.

THE NEXT MORNING not even the hum of my air conditioner drowned out the crowing rooster. I rolled over and checked my watch. I itched to check my cell phone, but I would have to wait until I exchanged money and bought a SIM card.

My hair stuck out in a wild mess from my late night shower, and I attempted to tame it with a scarf headband.

I needed coffee and breakfast. Hopefully both would be as tasty as my meal last night.

I sat at the same table from last night, thinking of it as mine already. A few people ate and chatted, but the empty tables outnumbered the occupied ones. The view from the railing surprised me, revealing the rolling ocean only yards beyond the last row of rooms. Palms and other tropical plants added green to the grounds around the brown colored buildings.

"Morning. Coffee?" A young woman stood next to my table, startling me from my observations. "There is a breakfast buffet." She gestured over her shoulder to the row of universally popular chafing dishes.

"Good morning. *Maa-che*," I said, practicing my greetings.

"*Maa-che*." She smiled shyly, clearly pleased.

"Coffee, yes. Please." I stood up with my plate to check out the breakfast offerings. A movement beneath the next table caught my eye and I yelped, dropping the plate.

A huge, gray lizard with an ochre-colored head froze near the steps, its beady eyes staring at me. Maybe not huge; it couldn't have been any longer than my forearm, not that I would ever be close enough for an exact measurement. I figured he wouldn't eat me. I racked my brain trying to remember if carnivorous lizards lived in Ghana. Or anywhere. At least it wasn't a python, but I wasn't comforted by that fact. Laughter from the other tables made me turn around.

"You'll get used to them," a blonde woman with a thick German accent said. "They're everywhere. Look, more are over there." She pointed behind me.

I followed her finger to where two additional lizards sunned themselves on the edge of the veranda.

I prayed these weren't the lizards Ama referred to last night. With a deep breath, I turned my back to the reptiles. In spite of my squelched appetite, I approached the buffet. To be polite, I took some of everything to make up for the broken plate. When I bit into the most amazing mango I'd ever eaten, I thought of Gerhard. The pineapple, papaya, and mango tasted better than any fruit I'd tasted at home.

The same thing couldn't be said about the coffee. Unfortunately, it tasted like instant, both bitter and weak. Adding milk didn't help. Nor did adding sugar, something I normally didn't do.

"You'll develop a taste for it, or you'll drink tea or cocoa," Ama said when I frowned at my mug. "May I join you?"

She sat down with a plate of pancakes and a cup of tea.

"Everything else is delicious," I complimented her.

While we chatted, I noticed her accent didn't sound Ghanaian, or much less so than the waitress' or Kofi's.

When I mentioned it, she laughed.

"Oh, I'm not Ghanaian. Not by birth. Ancestry probably, but I grew up in Philly."

My mouth gaped.

"I assumed."

"Well, you caught on quick. Nah, I'm Diaspora. Retired here after teaching for thirty years and opened the hotel to keep myself company. A teacher's pension goes a lot further in Ghana than in the States."

"I can imagine."

"You a teacher?"

"Professor." I explained why I came to Ghana, and we talked about teaching while my coffee grew cold. Surprisingly, it tasted more palatable cold than hot.

Ama filled me in about the typical patrons of the hotel, explaining most tended to be European, African Diaspora like herself, or aide workers of some type. A couple of other academics from the States dined here as well. The occasional entrepreneurial investor types came for drinks and dinner, but typically stayed at Euro-style hotels and newer resorts built for the country's recent fiftieth anniversary of independence. Ama's eclectic guest list suited me perfectly.

She wrote down everything I needed for my morning errands, and offered to call Kofi to drive me. Given everything was located within a short distance, I decided to walk around and learn the city.

Before my errands, I followed the path down a bluff to the beach. Waves roared where they crashed against the brown sand, hinting at a fierce undertow. This section of beach wasn't for lounging and drinking cocktails. Long, narrow fishing boats pulled ashore crowded the sand further down, and two men on horseback rode around a group of thin boys playing soccer in the near distance. The Atlantic stretched out gray and dark beyond the waves, reminding me of the eye color of a certain Dutchman. I shadowed the wet line of sand for a bit, looking for shells or rocks. Sadly, trash, fishing detritus, and plastic outnumbered anything collectible. In spite of its location on the coast, Accra was far from a sleepy beach town, and it showed where the Atlantic met Africa.

Passing official looking government buildings, my walk to the bank lasted only a few minutes. Standing in line to exchange money took over an hour. My newly acquired Ghanaian *cedis* created a colorful rainbow alongside what remained of my Dutch money inside my travel wallet.

First purchase with the *cedis*? A SIM card.

With the card installed, my finger hovered over the screen where my phone told me I had ten new text messages.

I struggled to control my emotions, which teetered on obsession.

What if he hadn't texted?

What if he had?

SIX

No texts from Gerhard.

I sighed, reminding myself it had been less than twenty-four hours since I left Amsterdam.

Then again, we were adults. Adults didn't have to follow the rules of dating, whatever those were nowadays.

I scrunched up my mouth, straightened my shoulders, and gave myself a pep talk. Selah Elmore didn't follow rules. Never had. Why start now?

My text to Gerhard was short:

Arrived. Ama's is all I'd hoped. Mangos are amazing. Thanks for everything.

Short, grateful … what more did it need? I added an "x" and hit send.

Around me, citizens of Accra went about their day. Women wearing colorful wax cloth skirts and dresses walked with babies and toddlers wrapped around their torsos in slings of similar cloth. Some also balanced baskets or large plastic bowls on their heads. Everything from bottles of water to rolls of toilet paper filled the containers. I wondered how far I could walk with a bowl of yams on my skull.

While looking at the fountains in front of Accra's modernist monument to Ghana's first president, I tripped over nothing, confirming I'd never make it as one of those elegant women balancing objects on their heads. Images of finishing school girls with books on their heads and me tripping over my own feet made me laugh.

A young man appeared at my side, dressed in jeans and a T-shirt decorated with an American flag, as I was collecting myself from my near face plant.

"Hello, miss. Are you okay?" Clipped British English mixed with the sing-song rhythm of Ghana's Twi language. He smiled at me.

I smiled back, embarrassed my near tumble had been observed. "I'm fine, really. Thank you."

"Good, good. I am Abraham Lincoln." He extended his hand for the typical Ghanaian handshake.

Laughing, I shook his hand and raised an eyebrow. "You are? The American president? Nice to meet you, I'm Dr. Elmore."

"Yes, I am. He was a good man, I am a good man. You are American, yes, *Mah mee?*

This thin, young man with long limbs, who towered over me, had called me mommy. Or something which sounded similar. Too stunned to speak, I nodded in answer.

"This is good. What is the state capital of Nebraska?"

"What?"

"You can ask me any American state capital and I will answer correctly," he said, proudly.

I grinned. "Nebraska is easy: Lincoln. Same as your name." I doubted his birth-name was Abraham Lincoln, but his charm and enthusiasm led me to follow along. "What is the capital of New Hampshire?"

"Concord. See? I know these things." Another smile.

We walked along the busy road filled with Accra's steady stream of traffic. A couple of stray, brown dogs sniffed in gutters filled with plastic and garbage.

"You need to buy gifts?" Abraham asked me.

I had been distracted by his banter, and had not paid enough attention. We stood in front of a compound of single-story, pale yellow tin-roofed buildings filled with crafts and tourist items. A low sign proclaimed it the "Centre for National Culture," but it resembled an outdoor mall mixed with a flea market.

"You need gifts? I'll show you the best shops. My brother has a drum store. My auntie sells beads."

Abraham Lincoln was not merely another friendly Ghanaian; he was a shopper's Sherpa. My research told me about the young men who guided tourists to their family's shops, bypassing competitors' booths.

"Ah, no shopping today, Abraham Lincoln. I will be in Accra for many months."

He hid his disappointment with a tiny smile. "You will remember me? Ask for Abraham Lincoln when you return for shopping. I will find you the best deals."

I nodded and promised I would. From the corner of my eye, I spied fresh coconuts for sale. The young man running the stand held a short machete in one hand and hacked into a green fruit to open it before inserting a plastic bendy straw. The contrast between the ancient knife and modern straw fascinated me, reminding me I wasn't even on the same continent as Kansas.

I offered to buy Abraham a fresh coconut.

"Coke?" he counter-offered.

After handing him a cold glass bottle Coke, with a green coconut in hand, I strolled down the High Street to Ama's.

So far, day one in Ghana had been a success.

DESPITE NEVER LEAVING the city, a fine layer of dust and dirt coated my skin when I walked down the terracotta-colored road to Ama's. I needed a shower or a hose down. The second was a better description for my shower when I turned on the water but forgot to start the water heater first. Luckily, the cold water refreshed me after the heat of wandering the streets. I looked up as the water slowly heated and screamed.

A tiny lizard perched upside down on the ceiling in the corner of the small bathroom. Its body measured no longer than one of my fingers. Size didn't matter. Its mere presence inside a closed room with a very naked me made my heart stop.

Keeping one eye on the gecko, or whatever it was, I turned off the water and grabbed a towel. I slowly backed out of the room in case it decided to leap down and attack me. I didn't exhale until I closed the bathroom door. Hopefully it would find its own way back outside.

The lizard fright and adrenaline rush, along with the typical exhaustion which followed a first day in a new, unfamiliar place, crashed over me. Wrapped only in a bath towel, I lay on the bed for a quick nap, hummed to sleep by the air conditioning.

I awoke several hours later, dimmer light peeking through my drapes. Because the sun set around six year round in Ghana, it wasn't yet time for dinner. Close to the equator, twelve hours of daylight were a given no matter the season.

Before getting dressed, I inspected the bathroom for reptiles and thankfully saw none.

Envious of the colorful skirts and dresses I'd seen on the women earlier, I put on a blue and white striped skirt and jade green shirt to have a bite and maybe a drink at the restaurant.

I took a seat at "my" table with my laptop and notebook. The same young woman from breakfast greeted me and handed me a menu. I found out her name was Sarah, something I overlooked asking earlier.

Before ordering, I confirmed the tonic was cold. Nothing worse than a warm gin and tonic without ice. Some of the European-style hotels might have had filtered ice, but it wasn't worth taking the chance. My stomach would have preferred drinking tonic with its anti-malarial quinine to the weekly pills I had inside my bag. Either would be preferable to malaria itself. The writer in me could romanticize the tropical disease, but it could be brutal. I double-checked that my purse contained mosquito spray.

The message light on my phone blinked in the darkness of my bag. With the distraction of my near face-plant, meeting a dead president, and close encounter of the scaly kind, I'd forgotten I'd turned it on.

My stomach fluttered when I opened my inbox.

Akwaaba. Glad you made it. Amsterdam misses you.

I smiled and reread the short message. He hadn't given me much to analyze. Sipping my gin and tonic, I plotted my response.

"Mind if I join you?" Ama stood next to my table, holding a glass bottle of Coke.

"Please. I have a million questions for you."

"We might need snacks for all those questions." She called Sarah over and asked for some *kelewele*, my new favorite food. "The way you grinned at your phone I wasn't sure if you wanted company. Husband? Boyfriend?"

My smile faltered. Gerhard was neither. I wasn't interested in the former, and the latter was impossible given our geographic issues. "Neither."

"Lover? No one smiles that way about a friend or family member." Ama's eyes twinkled as she sipped her drink.

"Unfortunately, no. The potential is there, but geographically it would be impossible."

"You won't be here forever. Who's to say what's possible? When I was your age, I never imagined I'd be sitting on this side of the Atlantic waiting for the afternoon rain."

At her mention of rain, I noticed the hazy blue sky had become gray.

"Does it rain here every day?" I asked when the first drops created dark circles on the dirt pathway.

"In July? No, not like the monsoon rains of May and June that feel like you're showering outside wearing clothes."

"Sounds fun. Is it bad that whenever I think of rain here, I think of Toto?"

"The dog from the *Wizard of Oz*?"

I laughed. "No, the band."

"Oh!" Her own laughter joined mine. "Wrong Toto."

"Although the analogy works, too. I don't think lizards show up at breakfast in Kansas."

"The lizards are harmless. However, that Toto song is an ear-worm. And probably the reason generations of Americans think of Africa as a country, not a continent."

We fell into a discussion of Toto's *Africa* lyrics. The rain ended around the same time we reached our conclusion about the words; they didn't make sense, but were definitely, without a doubt, about longing for love, as most songs were.

Tables filled with patrons, bottles, glasses, and plates of food while the sky darkened with evening. No sunset for my second night in Ghana. I joined Ama's group, which consisted of Ursula, the German woman from breakfast; the Americans, Nadine and Nathan, professors of anthropology and sociology, respectively; a gorgeous, dark, bearded Italian named Vincenzo on his way to see the elephants in Mole; and his scowling, thin wife Marta. She was probably lovely and didn't appreciate my flirting. I stopped once Ama politely pointed out their marital status, but her scowling didn't.

The night wound down after plates of fish with a mysterious, but delicious, sauce had been consumed. Ama explained some of the unfamiliar names like *omo tuo*, *fufu*, and *banku*, while Nathan joked about the famous *shi-to* pepper sauce giving the "shit-o's" if eaten too much.

I didn't think about my phone or text messages until I returned to my quiet room close to eleven. There wasn't a great signal, but I hit send on another text to Gerhard:

Fufu, banku, I miss you too.

I giggled at my lame attempt at rhyming.

A reply pinged almost immediately.

Do you? This might make it worse.

Attached was picture of a very large windmill towering behind a very handsome Gerhard. I smiled at his gorgeous grin.

I responded: *Impressive.*

My phone chimed.

I laughed. Ursula glanced over her shoulder at me, raising her eyebrow.

"Ignore me." I held up my phone.

Chuckling, and maybe blushing a little at the thought of monkey sex with Gerhard, I typed my response before putting my phone away.

Never the former and only the latter with the right man.

My Fanmilk frozen brain made me bold. Thoughts of monkey sex with Gerhard made me horny. Damn. I left Dutch BOB at Ama's.

Good to know.

We drove over the Volta River and into the hills of the east, heading for the Hohoe region. Signs giving kilometers to Ho and Hohoe informed us we were getting closer to the monkey sanctuary.

Upon arrival at Tafi Atome, Kofi parked near the guest house in the village. I bounced out of the van, succumbing to my monkey excitement.

We were surrounded by the cinnamon-colored earth I had expected to find in Ghana. The dusty, unpaved road led into the forest beyond a small cluster of buildings, a pastel painted school house, open stall shops, and the guest house with a dozen brightly painted huts serving as rooms.

Inside the lobby/gift store/sanctuary entrance, I bought a room temperature orange Fanta and a large bottle of water. After collecting the keys for our rooms, Ezekiel, the man behind the counter, told us we should wait until later in the afternoon for the monkeys. With a promise of meeting up at the entrance, I wandered over to my room in a red painted hut with a tin roof. A simple double bed and a night table holding a single lamp were the only furniture inside. No air-conditioner, but mosquito netting hung above the bed, screens covered the windows, and hopefully there would be a cross-breeze with the shutters open to enhance the small ceiling fan.

I glanced at my phone again. No signal. I turned it off to save the battery.

Accra was a capital city full of modern growing pains, like never-ending construction and traffic. Now more than ever, I felt I was in Africa. The air smelled of rich earth, wood smoke, and something spicy, and I was about to hand-feed monkeys.

We met at the office and followed our guide, Kwami, to the edge of the forest where a group of children played on the dirt. Boys kicked around a soccer ball with their bare or sandal covered feet while girls chased each other in a game of tag. Goats milled about, and a scrawny kitten attempted to climb inside an aluminum bowl.

Upon seeing us, the children ran over, calling out "hello" and "candy." Sensing something maternal about Nadine, they surrounded her first while I stood to the side. Adorable faces, scuffed with dirt, above mismatched, motley-clothed, thin bodies smiled up at Nadine. Despite my feelings about children, my heart clenched over these sweet beings. I reached for my supply of pencils inside my purse to give to them.

"Thank you, auntie," said a wisp of a voice belonging to a girl with huge brown eyes. Her head reached as high as my hip.

"You're welcome." I smiled down at her.

Kwami said something to the kids, making them laugh and scatter.

"What did you say?" Nathan asked.

"I said you came to visit monkeys, not silly children." He handed us each a bunch of miniature bananas to feed the primates.

Chatter in the branches above alerted us to the arrival of the Mona monkeys. Suddenly, there appeared two, then three, then a dozen black, gray, and brown monkeys in the trees around us. Kwami demonstrated how to hold the banana. A monkey clambered down the tree and jumped on his arm to carefully open the banana and eat it, while calmly sitting on his forearm.

I clapped my hands together in pure joy.

Carefully, I squatted down and held out a banana, holding my breath. A small monkey dashed over and ripped the banana from my hand before scampering across the dirt and into the tree. Startled, I fell back on my heels and sat heavily on the ground, laughing.

Kwami laughed and helped me up, instructing me to tighten my grip. Sure enough, the second monkey acted less wham-bam-thank-you-ma'am and sat on my arm, politely eating bites from the banana. Her bright, deep amber eyes focused on mine for a second.

There were firsts you remembered your entire life:

First kiss.

First love.

First sex.

I would never forget my first Mona monkey.

I named her Mona Lisa. I felt certain we shared something special, and she would always remember me, too.

AFTER MONA LISA and I shared our moment, the group followed a path through the sanctuary's forest. New monkeys approached for bananas and to chatter at us from the trees.

Not a single piece of feces was flung.

No monkey sex was observed.

Under strings of round lights at the village's one restaurant, we shared stories about our travel adventures over dinner. Ursula had us in tears with her story of boxing a kangaroo that tried to steal her backpack in Queensland. Nadine warned us about the side effects a dip in the Dead Sea could have on a woman's tender bits. Nathan reminisced about tacos al pastor he found near a bus station in the Yucatan. We bonded over our adventures well into the evening.

Far from the light pollution of Accra, our flashlights lit a narrow path through the inky night down the road to the guest house; the sky too hazy for starlight.

Not until I tucked myself under the mosquito net did I think about Gerhard and how well he would have fit into our international group.

The next morning, I reluctantly admitted I wasn't as much of a world traveler as I pretended. After a night of sweating under the netting and thinking malaria-carrying mosquitoes had become trapped inside with me, I confessed to the group I needed air-conditioning and a proper toilet that didn't require a walk through the deepest, darkest night   with only my flashlight lighting the way. Ursula agreed with me, saying she longed for a toilet where you could flush the paper instead of putting it in a little trash bin. We acknowledged Western plumbing had spoiled us.

Unshowered, covered with a thick layer of red dust and happier because of monkey love, we piled into Kofi's van. I napped for a short while until we stopped for Nadine to buy Kente cloth from a simple wooden stand along the road. If Tafi Atome was a village, this cluster of huts with thatched roofs, round, plain adobe walls, and chickens scratching the barren dirt was an outpost. Young men with bare feet worked looms, creating long strips of geometric patterned cloth at amazing speed. I handed out hard candy to the children, who once again surrounded us, wide smiles and big eyes happy to see *Obruni*. Each of us bought something from the stand; a few *cedis* went far in a village with physical evidence of real poverty around us.

Reality of this subsistence living left us quiet when we climbed into the van. There by the grace of God we went, blessed by our birthright as Westerners. I turned in my seat to watch the village shrink behind us. A pack of children chased our retreating van down the road for a bit, arms waving, smiles big, and silly antics abounding. I waved at them, helpless to fight my tears or grin.

Nadine patted my arm and handed me a tissue. "They'll break your heart and make you believe in God all with a single look."

Smiling, I sniffled. "I don't even like kids." I laughed. "Damn them!"

With a sympathetic look and a shake of her head, she turned around, chuckling at my outburst.

On the return to Accra, Kofi blasted the Sunday soccer game on the radio. My understanding of the game began and ended with the universal "goooallll" shouted by the announcer. If Kofi repeated it, we cheered along for his team scoring, bonding over the commonality of us versus them.

tonics. They could have been in any bar where businessmen gathered after work. Already the men sounded foreign to me after my weekend with the monkeys. My mind drifted with memories of big brown eyes and elfin bodies in the Kente village.

A cough from the group of men brought me out of my reminiscing. I met a pair of hazel eyes. Apparently, I'd been staring at their table.

"Care to join us?" a deep voice asked. It belonged to a pudgy man with glasses and dark hair. The sleeves of his pale yellow button-down were rolled up to his elbows.

"Sure." I shrugged and walked over.

"You want something to drink?" Not Gerhard asked.

"I'll have a Star, thank you." I looked around the table. Expensive watches subtly displayed each man's wealth. The majority of left hands bore wedding rings, except Not Gerhard.

"American?" Pudgy asked.

"Yes, from Portland. Oregon," I volunteered.

"New York," Pudgy said. "But the rest of these guys are from the Netherlands."

My ears perked up.

"What brings you to Accra?" My interest was piqued.

"We came for a conference on sustainability in micro-lending next week. Doing some sight-seeing before it begins." Pudgy acted as the mouthpiece for the group.

"Sounds fascinating." It didn't.

"And you? Wait—" He interrupted himself. "—Let me guess."

This should be amusing. I caught Not Gerhard's expression and subtle frown.

"You're here to work on an orphanage. Or a school." Pudgy's eyes roamed my chest as if my cleavage held the answers. Perhaps the size and scope of my breasts would provide support to his assumption.

"Medical clinic," said a man with dark hair and a wrinkled blue shirt. The third man at their table agreed.

"And you?" I asked Not Gerhard.

He tapped his index finger on his chin and studied my face. After a moment, he spoke, "Organizing women to form a co-operative." He paused. "Selling beads or some sort of craft."

"Interesting," I said. "You're all wrong."

"Missionary?" Pudgy guessed again.

Missionary? As if! "Academic."

"I was close! I said school!" he whined like a child.

"Close, but I'm not a volunteer. I don't even like children." Or adults who sound like them, I wanted to add but didn't.

I explained what brought me to Accra, making it less salacious than I typically would have. Pudgy, despite his wedding ring, stared at my chest too often. The Pudgys of the world were one of the reasons I distrusted marriage.

With his constant chatter, he also made it impossible to chat up Not Gerhard. Luckily, Ama rescued me when she asked me to join her for dinner. I said farewell to the group, making eye contact with Matt aka Not Gerhard. I didn't bother remembering Pudgy's name.

REBECCA'S STALL IN Makola market contained floor to ceiling stacks of neatly folded Dutch wax cloth. Wild patterns featured every imaginable color. Possibilities overwhelmed me. I wanted everything. Ama and Rebecca pulled bolts of fabric and piled them on a narrow table in the center of her open air stall. Rebecca measured my waist and hips, complimenting me on my abundant curves. I loved her.

After selecting fabric for four skirts, we said good-bye with a promise to return a couple days later to pick up my purchases.

Makola churned with vendors and shoppers—the Ghanaian equivalent of Whole Foods on the Wednesday prior to Thanksgiving.

Ama led me through the food section of the market. At Makola, the familiar and bizarre mixed together under a high roof blocking the hot sun. Giant aluminum bowls held gallons of fresh ground peanut butter. Chilies from tiny to enormous filled baskets set on the floor and tables. Pyramids of living snails the size of geoducks sat next to ordinary tomatoes and eggplants. Tailless beaver-looking animals called grass-cutters sat inside cages near chickens. Ama explained they weren't for pets.

My senses went into overdrive from the smells and sights, as well as the crowd of shoppers and vendors. Women shouted conversations to each other across aisles, laughing at inside jokes. At the edges of the market, *tro-tro* and taxi drivers jostled and argued over customers and parking spaces.

Ama pulled me by the arm into the shade on the other side of the road and handed me a bag of filtered water. "You're looking a little peaked."

I gulped some water. "Thanks. Wow. The market was overwhelming." I exhaled and fanned myself with my hand. A pair of stray dogs sniffed around a stack of crates in the sun at the market's edge.

"Makola always is. You'll get used to it."

I'd heard 'you'll get used to it' countless times since arriving. "Not sure about that. I might have to live off of chicken and rice at your place."

"There are modern markets in Accra. You'll be fine. Or you can stay with me."

I blinked at her while I sipped water. "I can't. I'd love to, but my budget doesn't allow for months of hotel stay."

"No, not at the hotel. I have a little house. You could rent a room. You had planned to rent a place, right? Rent from me. I'll accept whatever you were planning to pay."

I couldn't believe my luck. "Are you serious?" I asked, needing confirmation I wasn't hallucinating from my near panic attack.

"Sure. Don't take this the wrong way, but I'd worry about you staying at some random apartment on your own."

I shot her a dirty look, my hackles rising. "I'm fine on my own. I've always been on my own, since school. And I've been fine, thank you."

"I'm sure you've done just *fine* on your own, but one thing you'll learn, is no one is alone. You need community to survive. For Ghanaians, it's their family and tribe. For us *Obruni*, we have to make our own tribe."

The little village of Kente weavers. The communal table at Ama's.

"Did you imply it takes a village?" I asked, my tone laced with sarcasm.

"Aha!" She gave me an indulgent look and patted my arm. "You're beginning to understand."

We walked in the direction of High Street and the hotel. I noted a bookstore I would revisit later. Ahead stood a polished new building with the letters *TNG* on the side.

"I didn't know TNG had an office in Accra," I said, more to myself than to Ama.

"TNG? Oh, yes. Of course. They do a lot of good work. I've known several of their employees over the years. Good people who want the best future for Ghana."

"They're sponsoring the sculpture exhibit I'm researching."

"Next time some of the TNG people visit the bar, I'll introduce you. In fact, the group you chatted with last night? Some of them work for TNG I think."

Not Gerhard came to mind. I wondered if the real one had hung out at Ama's. "My Dutch friend Gerhard said he had an assignment here three years ago. Sound familiar?"

Ama wrinkled her forehead. "No Gerhards. Sorry."

"No worries. It's a big city." Another missed connection.

"Is this the man who had you smiling like a school girl last week?"

I nodded.

"Do you miss him?"

"I do. It's silly. We only knew each other a few days, but thanks to cell phones, we've been texting."

"I'll repeat what I said the other day, you never know what the future holds."

"I'm worried you might break out singing a Doris Day song," I teased.

"I think you might have heat stroke. You've stopped making sense." She winked at me.

Later in the afternoon, Ama showed me her small house near the hotel. "My" room had pale mauve floor tiles, a full size bed, thick wood blinds, its own air conditioner, and a ceiling fan. A private, modern bathroom sealed the deal. The modern kitchen and living room overlooked a paved courtyard with a gazebo Ama called a sun hut. Situated between the museum and the hotel, it was perfect.

"Good?" Ama asked.

"More than good."

"We'll move your things tomorrow."

I had the feeling once Ama had decided I would live with her, I didn't stand a chance to say no.

Not quite old enough to be my mother, she acted maternal nonetheless.

"I haven't heard you mention a Mr. Ama. Do you have kids?" I asked on the short trip to the hotel.

"I have two sons. One is an engineer in California; the other one is married and works for a software company in Massachusetts. No husband, though. Divorced many years ago. Why do you ask?"

"You're very maternal," I confessed.

"I've been a mother hen my whole life. I bossed around my younger siblings, acting like a little mother. I have the mothering gene in spades."

I laughed at her obvious statement. "I hadn't noticed."

She grinned at me. "I'm mothering you, aren't I? I do that with guests I like. I take them under my wing."

"What about me said I needed your help?"

Studying me, she tilted her head. "I said this earlier at the market, but behind your fierce independence you wear as armor, I sensed a little loneliness."

My eyes widened.

"Can I ask a personal question?"

I nodded.

"Have you ever been married?"

I shook my head.

"Didn't think so. Not that there's anything wrong with that, but in Ghana it's odd for a healthy, smart woman not to be married. Or have kids. Family is everything here."

"I have friends, close friends. And a consuming job." My voice sounded as defensive as I felt.

She nodded, but didn't speak, letting my lame defense hang in the air between us.

"I never wanted either," I said. "I don't need them to feel complete. I think it's bullshit a woman is only complete if she's bound to a man and bears children."

"You sound like women from my generation who burned their bras and slept around because they took the pill."

"Doesn't sound too bad to me."

"Yes, but eventually your boobs sag and you end up with an STD. Or HIV."

We walked in silence for a few minutes. In Africa, the specter of AIDS wasn't an abstract concept like it was at home, where the medicinal combo to keep people alive and symptom-free was easily attained. Orphanages here were filled with the youngest victims of a generation affected by the disease.

"Okay, I'm not saying you have sexually transmitted diseases," Ama spoke first.

"Thanks. For the record, I'm safe and sane when it comes to my lovers. The early nineties were scary times to be exploring my sexuality."

"What were we talking about before I got all heavy?" Her typical boisterous personality dimmed.

"My unmarried and childless existence."

"Ah, yes."

"The procreating ship has sailed, so if you need to nag me about something, you'll have to focus on the unmarried part."

Her smile returned, and her eyes sparked with mischief.

"I see that look in your eye. No set-ups!" Truth be told, I loved a good set-up, playing the role of the setter-upper, not the setter-upee.

She attempted to look innocent. "I would never play matchmaker."

I laughed. "Lies! Not an hour ago you offered to introduce me to your friends from TNG!"

"Oh. Right." She joined my laughter. "I'd never set you up with random men. Only serious candidates." She paused. "Too bad Kai isn't in town. He might be able to handle you."

Laughing and teasing each other, we walked back to the hotel. On Monday, I had my first appointment at the museum. My life in Ghana was settling into place.

MUSEUM DUST HAD its own particular, unique scent. It smelled old and vaguely clinical. My cotton gloves, worn to protect objects from the oils on my hands, showed the gray dust as if I had done a cleaning inspection.

Emmanuela, my contact at the museum, had given me a short tour before leading me into the windowless storage areas and archives where I would spend most of my days. The rooms had minimal climate control, and were definitely not up to the standards of museums at home. Utilitarian shelving units held row upon row of figural sculptures—the focus of my research.

We chatted while she showed me the collection, including a recent donation, which needed to be catalogued. Emmanuela also taught at the local university. She invited me to attend one of her lectures and perhaps teach a class or two. Her offer was flattering, and I readily accepted it. It would be interesting to sit in on classes.

I left several hours later. Checking my phone, I walked down the wide tree-lined boulevard toward the water. This section of Accra displayed its British colonial history with large white mansions behind gated walls. A new five-star Euro hotel rose above the older mansions, outshining the contemporary exterior of the National Theater. Adobe huts with thatched roofs and big eyes in thin faces felt worlds away instead of kilometers. I sighed at the contrast.

I texted Gerhard a recent fact I'd learned.

Dutch chocolate is a lie. It's really Ghanaian chocolate.

How I never put that together before surprised me. Cocoa plants didn't grow in Holland.

A few minutes later my phone pinged.

Brilliant deduction, Sherlock.

Our conversations had reached the comfortable, snarky phase.

Another message appeared.

Dutch Wax cloth isn't Dutch either.

I laughed.

All lies. Next thing you'll tell me your name isn't Gerhard and Anita isn't really your sister. LOL

I held the phone, waiting for a quick response, but didn't receive one. He must have had to run off. I checked my watch. Giving up, I turned off my phone to save the battery and stuffed it inside my bag.

Before returning to the house, I stopped at Ama's for lunch, reclaiming my favorite table. I glanced around, hoping to spy Ursula's familiar blonde hair or the nearly identical short, gray, curly hair of Nadine and Nathan, but was disappointed not to find them. The only familiar face belonged to Sarah who brought over my favorite chicken stew. I missed the familiarity of my new friends.

Using the hotel's Wi-Fi, I checked my email on my phone. Nothing from Gerhard, but I had new emails from my friends Quinn and Maggie with a subject line of "Love Missionary Style". The email made me laugh in the way only old friends could. Now feeling lonely both for friends old and new, I decided on a post-lunch nap. When in doubt, nap. New motto.

EIGHT

MY DAYS FELL into a routine: breakfast with Ama, the museum for a few hours, lunch at the hotel, afternoon back at the museum, dinner at the hotel, and home to bed. The sun setting at six meant nights stretched long and dark far earlier in July than at home. I heeded Kofi's advice and rarely went out after dark on my own, either going to the hotel or home for dinner.

In between activities, there were infrequent texts with Gerhard. It had been almost a week since his odd response to my joke about everything being a lie. He told me if I knew the truth, he'd have to kill me. Given what little I knew about him, maybe he was a secret agent or spy.

Today I wore one of my new maxi skirts from Rebecca. Blue, green, and red colored the pattern of scissors cutting tiny pieces of paper. I instantly loved the fabric when Rebecca showed it to me, exclaiming it reminded me of rock, paper, scissors. Looking down, I smiled at the randomness.

Ama's friend Kai would arrive tonight, and she'd organized a welcome dinner at the restaurant for all of us to meet him. She promised me it wasn't a set-up, but it smelled like one, walked like one, and quacked like one.

To distract myself, I spent an hour at the bookstore near Makola market, wasting time between work and cocktails at Ama's. Isaac, who ran the shop, knew me by name and I often chatted with him more than I looked at books. Similar to my friend Abraham Lincoln at the craft center, his knowledge of American history and politics impressed me. He often proudly reminded me how Obama was half African, not caring he was Kenyan and not Ghanaian.

When I arrived at Ama's, I spotted Ursula at my favorite table. After sitting down, I glanced around the space, not seeing Ama or any other familiar faces. My own gin and tonic joined hers while we chatted and caught up about Ursula's work with a women's bead cooperative.

While it grew darker, Nadine and Nathan joined us, adding additional glasses to the cluster on the table. I peered around at the other tables and spied Not Gerhard sitting with another group, engaged in deep conversation with Pudgy. Catching his eye, I raised my glass in greeting. He smiled and mirrored me with his own glass.

"Kai's plane is delayed," Ama said, sitting down at our table. "Since he won't be arriving until nine, it'll be too late once he clears immigration and customs. Can we reconvene tomorrow night for dinner?"

I nodded along with the others and exhaled loudly in a sigh.

Ama looked at me from the corner of her eye. "It's not a set-up, Selah."

Ursula jumped into the conversation. "Set-up? Oh, who are you setting Selah up with?" Her eyes wandered over to the frat club table.

"No one is setting me up with anyone. I'm too old and too set in my ways."

Ursula laughed. "Hardly. I'm ten years older than you and a widow. If you don't want the set-up, I'll take it." She looked at Ama, who subtly shook her head. With her thick blonde shoulder length hair, Ursula looked more like a lioness than cougar.

"I don't know why no one believes me when I say I'm not setting Selah up with Kai." Ama held a straight face for a couple of beats before smiling. "Fine. I enjoy putting interesting people together. Look at this group. Do you think you randomly found each other?"

Nathan coughed. "Now that you mention it."

Ama straightened her back. "I have a knack for making connections. Set-ups, matchmaking, call it what you want."

I laughed and sipped my near empty drink. "Quack, quack," I said softly to myself.

Nadine caught my eye and smiled. "Well, this talk certainly makes me look forward to dinner tomorrow night more than ever."

"You're all meddling meddlers," I growled. "I'm perfectly capable of finding a man. If *and* when I want one."

"Oh, we believe you. You've had the eye of that man across the restaurant most of the evening," Nathan said.

The other three women at our table turn to look at Not Gerhard.

"Subtle, very subtle," I groaned.

"He's coming over," Nadine happily informed me.

"Great," I said.

"What's great?" Not Gerhard asked.

I looked up and smiled at him. "I was saying how great Ama was for bringing me another drink." I shot Ama a pointed look. "How are you, Matt?"

I introduced him to the rest of the gang, who warmly engaged with him. More than once, I caught Ursula leaning over to check out Matt's backside.

Basic information exchanged, Matt got to the point. "I wanted to ask Selah if she would join me tomorrow afternoon at a contemporary art gallery. I thought maybe she could explain the art to me." He rubbed the nape of his neck. "You're all invited, of course."

Ama set down my full glass. "That sounds perfect for Selah. Unfortunately, I have to work." She stared at the others at the table, who suddenly had afternoon plans.

After Nathan's cough, I realized I hadn't responded. "Sure. Of course. When?"

We arranged to meet at the gallery before he said goodnight and left.

"Well, look at that. Not a set-up at all and Selah has a date."

I huffed. "Hold on, it's not a date. We're meeting there, and for some reason he thinks I'm an expert on contemporary art."

"He's very handsome," Ursula said, a twinkle in her eye.

"He is," Nadine concurred. Even Nathan had nice things to say.

I wanted to explain he ran a sad, distant second place to Gerhard, but it would open a whole can of sardines that I didn't need opening. Real Gerhard hadn't texted me all day. I sighed. Not Gerhard would have to do for now, however long that now might be.

"He's here for a week," I said.

"Even better. No threat of long-term commitment or being tied down. What kind of set-up would it be for a week?"

"I'd let him tie me down," Ursula spoke quietly.

My mouth gaped, as did the others'.

Kinky German.

"What?" she asked. "There's nothing wrong with a little light bondage if it's consensual."

Ama tapped her fingers on the table, clearly embarrassed by Ursula's confession. "Okay then." She cleared her throat. "Let's eat."

THE NEXT AFTERNOON I arrived twenty minutes early to meet Matt. Sitting along the beach, the pink building housing the gallery perched next to the busy Tema Road. Kofi dropped me off, but I asked him not to wait.

I walked behind the building to the beach. Western-style beach resorts with scenic palm trees surrounding pools populated the eastern side of Accra. The sand looked much cleaner on this beach, and in the distance awnings and loungers at the resorts created bright spots of color. Sitting on a lounge chair by the pool for a day or weekend would be a nice break.

I made a mental note to look into a weekend at the beach. A trip to Cape Coast topped my list of mini-trips, but Labadi Beach was closer.

Inside the lobby, I didn't spot Matt. The main galleries filled the upper floors, and I headed there, thinking I'd missed him when I walked to the beach.

I scanned the top floor galleries, but no Matt. Once I found him, we could return and take our time while I confessed I knew nothing about contemporary Ghanaian art.

The second floor held smaller rooms, each dedicated to a single artist, but no Matt.

I entered the stairs to return to the main floor to wait for him in the lobby, feeling ridiculous about not exchanging numbers last night.

I rounded the last flight of stairs and spotted Matt standing near the front of the lobby, the bright light from outside throwing him into silhouette. The distance and light made him look less Not Gerhard than ever. I couldn't even see the hook in his nose.

My cell phone chirped with a text from Gerhard:

What are you wearing?

Cheeky Dutchman.

Watching while Matt typed away on his cell phone for another moment, I sighed, promising myself to let Gerhard go. Matt was here now. He was handsome in an Almost Gerhard way and most importantly, interested. I responded to Gerhard's text.

Too bad you're not here to find out.

Stepping out of the pool of sunlight at the front doors, Matt walked toward me, the sun creating a halo behind his blond hair.

I smiled and waved, resolved. Matt was Matt.

And he wasn't the man walking straight toward me.

NINE

NOT NOT GERHARD stood in the lobby of the art center.

My brain sputtered in its attempt to resolve what was happening.

Gerhard, my Gerhard, stood looking at me where he'd stopped about ten feet away, a safe distance from my brain exploding.

My brow furrowed, my eyes squinted, and my mouth could have caught fish.

"What the hell?" I wasn't certain if I'd spoken aloud. I looked around the empty space for guilty parties. Or cameras. Surely, someone was filming me as a practical joke.

Gerhard, or maybe his evil, or not evil, twin, slowly approached me. "Selah?"

As if my identity was the one in question.

Greeted with my stunned silence, he tried again. "Selah? Hello?" He waved his hands in front of my face in a kind of wax-on, wax-off manner.

I stood, frozen.

Gerhard.

Not Not Gerhard.

Gerhard.

His laughter broke through my brain's attempt to rationalize this.

I squinted at him. Maybe I had heat stroke. Or was dehydrated. Clearly, I was hallucinating from not having enough to drink today. I attempted to remember the last liquid I'd consumed. It had been hours. That explained it. When had I last eaten? A mango at breakfast? Some plantain chips?

Maybe I fell down the last flight of stairs and hit my head.

I needed a cigarette. Why did I quit?

"Selah?" Concern tinged his voice.

My mind had snapped.

Poor Matt probably thought I'd lost it as I stood and gaped at him like a mad woman. He was right to be worried. I needed to find Kofi to take me home. Damn it, Kofi had dropped me off and left. Who made that decision? Right. Me.

The man slowly reached out to touch my shoulder.

"Hey," he said, softly, calmly.

"Hi," I said.

"Thank God. I thought you were in shock."

"I think I am. I might be dehydrated, and I only ate a mango this morning. Maybe we should reschedule. I need to lie down somewhere dark."

He chuckled. "Reschedule what?"

I didn't dare look straight at Matt. Instead, I stared across the lobby at a large, colorful fish sculpture on the wall. "Our tour of the gallery today. I'm not feeling well."

"Selah?" another voice called from a few feet away.

Great. My hallucination had doubled the number of imaginary Gerhards. I hoped at least one man stood in front of me or I was talking to myself.

"Selah?" the first Gerhard asked.

I focused my eyes. Two men stood there. One wore khakis and a pink Oxford. My eyes traveled up his chest to a handsome face, with hazel eyes and a hooked nose.

"Hi, Matt," I said, relieved.

My eyes snuck a glance at the other man, who also wore khakis, but with a white shirt casually untucked and slightly wrinkled. Gerhard wouldn't wear a wrinkled shirt. If he was a hallucination, my brain would imagine him in a suit. I let my gaze move to his face, a familiar face with a slight layer of scruff. And eyes the color of the North Sea.

I OPENED MY eyes, finding myself on the bottom step. I didn't recall sitting down.

Matt knelt in front of me, concern furrowing his brow.

"Hi, there you are." He sighed with relief. "You fainted."

"I did? I think I was hallucinating or seeing double. Or something. Everything sounded tinny and I felt hot."

"You did." He chuckled. "Your friend went to find you something cold to drink."

"My friend?"

"The man you were talking to when I arrived."

"You saw him?"

Matt stared at me. "Yes, of course."

I blinked and took a deep breath.

"Did you catch his name?"

"There wasn't time between the awkward staring and the fainting. He's your friend, isn't he?" His voice changed from worried to defensive.

"I'm not sure."

"He wasn't threatening you, was he?"

"No, not threatening."

The sound of footsteps on the tile echoed across the lobby. Both Matt and I turned our heads.

A smiling Gerhard held up an orange Fanta.

"You scared me." He handed me the cold bottle.

"I scared you?" I scoffed.

"Didn't you receive my text?"

I furrowed my brow. "I didn't."

"Hmmm." He rubbed his thumb across his bottom lip. "I sent you a cryptic text rife with clues earlier today."

I continued to stare at him.

"The one about the elephant not needing luggage? Because it has a trunk?"

"That was your way of saying you were coming to Ghana? Could you be more cryptic?" One of us was out of our gourds, and it might not have been me. I remembered Matt, who had moved to stand on the stair above me.

"I guess I should introduce you two." I flailed my hand between them. "Matt, Gerhard. Gerhard, Matt."

Awkward settled over our little threesome after they shook hands. From Gerhard's sour expression, I guessed he and Not Gerhard were having a staring contest. Maybe they were trying to figure out if they were twins separated at birth.

Matt must have lost because he cleared his throat and said, "Let's reschedule for tomorrow, Selah. I think you're right; you should probably lie down."

I twisted my neck to look up at him. "Okay. If you're sure."

His eyes still on Gerhard, he agreed.

I sipped my Fanta and waited for them to pay attention to me.

Gerhard looked down at me, smiling. "Let's get you to Ama's."

"I'm heading the same way. You can catch a ride with me," Matt offered.

"My driver, Kofi, is outside." Gerhard reached for my elbow.

"Kofi? Ama's Kofi?" I asked.

"Yes, one and the same. He drove me."

"Oh. Okay."

"Are you agreeing to come with me?" Gerhard asked, a smile twitching at the corners of his mouth.

"Well, Kofi is my ride, too." Nothing about this made any sense.

I faced Matt. "I'm sorry. Rain check?" My brain stretched to form coherent sentences.

"Of course. I might wander around for a bit since I'm already here," Matt said, the fight gone from his posture.

I apologized again and walked outside with Gerhard.

Kofi gave me a Cheshire grin from his spot standing next to the car. "Wonderful, you found Dr. Selah."

I stared at Gerhard. "Did you come looking for me? How did you know where to look?"

He grinned and pointed at Kofi. "I have connections."

I sat in the back of the car, still feeling dazed.

Gerhard chatted with Kofi, while keeping his body turned toward me, his eyes wandering my face.

"Are you a tiny bit happy to see me?" he asked softly when there was a break in his conversation with Kofi.

I turned to look at him, really look at him. He appeared to be the same man I met in Amsterdam, but there was something different about him.

"Give me several hours and a stiff drink or two to overcome over my shock," I replied, a smile tugging at my mouth.

"You got it." He reached over and touched my hand.

Instead of taking me to the house, Kofi drove us to the hotel, which was fine because I wasn't kidding about needing a drink. Rarely in my life had I been stunned speechless. Or fainted.

Gerhard rested his hand on my shoulder when we entered the open lobby at Ama's. His touch felt familiar, but was probably a safety precaution should I decide to face plant or swoon again.

Ama stood at the front desk facing away from us, but turned at the sound of our footsteps. "Hello! There you are!" Her face split into a huge grin as she scurried around the desk to embrace Gerhard.

I had to half hop to the side to avoid being knocked over by her enthusiastic greeting.

After a moment filled with laughter and back-pats, she turned to me. I received a half hug as she steered us to the veranda. With a squeeze to my shoulder and a backward glance at Gerhard, she asked, "Where did you find Kai?"

"Who?"

TEN

"Who who?" Ama asked.

"You sound like an owl," I said. "You said Kai, and I said who?"

"I heard your who. That's why I asked who. What do you mean who?" She steered me to the long table while alternating between staring at me and behind my shoulder where I assumed Gerhard followed us.

"You said something about me meeting Kai. Or finding him." I scratched my cheek and touched my forehead. Maybe I was having a reaction to my anti-malarial drugs. I'd heard they could cause psychotic dreams. Maybe this was a psychotic episode. Nothing made sense.

Gerhard coughed from behind us.

Ama turned and asked him, "Do you know what's wrong with her? She's not making sense and looks flushed."

"She fainted at the art gallery. I think she needs to lie down. Or eat. Probably both," Gerhard answered.

I slumped in a chair and watched the two of them stare at me. Ama rested the back of her hand on my forehead. I swatted it away. "I'm not sick. I don't think. Maybe. I think I'm having a psychotic dream from the malaria meds. Only I'm not asleep."

"You fainted, sweetie. Did you eat today?" she asked, motioning for Sarah.

I repeated the list of foods I'd consumed for the day. Ama tsked her disapproval.

After sipping some cold water, I exhaled, feeling more myself. I looked over at Gerhard, still needing confirmation he sat at the same table, at Ama's, in Ghana, with me.

"What are you doing here?" I asked him.

His eyes crinkled charmingly in the corners when he smiled. Charming eye crinkles. "You can see me? I'm not an apparition?"

"So you do know Kai?" Ama asked, glancing between the two of us.

"Who's Kai?" I repeated, staring at Gerhard.

"Here we go again. What do you mean who is Kai? Kai's sitting in front of you."

I raised an eyebrow while I continued to stare at Gerhard, waiting for him to disagree with her. Instead, he nodded and pointed at himself.

"I don't know any Kais. I know a Gerhard."

"Who's Gerhard?" Ama asked, confusion coloring her voice and making her sound exasperated.

"I am," Gerhard replied.

"I thought your name was Kai." Her brows furrowed and she crossed her arms.

Mirroring her, I crossed my arms. "Now do you understand my confusion, Ama?"

"Son, you have some explaining to do," she stated, using her mom voice.

While his gaze flicked between the two of us with our arms crossed, Gerhard stroked the scruff on his cheek, letting us stew for a minute.

"So who are you?" I asked.

"Both?"

"Both question mark?" I echoed his question.

"Both. Kai's a nickname for Gerhard. No one really calls me Gerhard since my father shares the same name."

"Well, that sorts it out, doesn't it?" Ama laughed. "Kai is Gerhard and

Gerhard is Kai, and somehow you two know each other. Want to fill me in how?" She looked at me.

"Gerhard is the man I met in Amsterdam. Who was introduced to me as Gerhard, who let me call him Gerhard and never once corrected me." I tightened my grip on my biceps while I tried to wrap my mind around the double names.

"Why would you do that?" Ama asked. "You've always been Kai."

"What she said," I added.

He held up his hands, palms facing us. "Anita started it. She met Selah at JFK and told her to look up Gerhard Hendriks when she arrived in Amsterdam."

"Maybe she meant your father?" I snarked.

"Doubtful. They never got along."

"Anita?" Ama asked.

"His sister," I answered.

Ama looked at me from the corner of her eye, then stared at Gerhard-Kai with her brows lowered. I glanced between the two of them while they held some sort of silent conversation.

Kai broke the staring contest and coughed.

"So, Kai, if Kai really is your name, why are you in Ghana?"

Kai, not Gerhard. This would take some adjustment, but it was a much sexier name.

Kai, oh Kai.

Yep, Kai worked.

Too bad my confusion and vague anger crowded out my excitement that he was sitting here with me.

"I, uh—" He stumbled over his words and paused. "I may have rearranged some projects and adjusted my travel schedule." He sounded unsure, not the confident Gerhard I knew. Maybe he acted different without the suit and tie. "I'm in Accra for the conference on micro-financing. And maybe more." He gave a quick glance in my direction before his eyes focused on his hands in his lap.

"Wait, you're here for how long?"

"This week. Maybe longer if projects can be reassigned."

Ama clapped her hands. "That's the best news! Don't you think, Selah?"

I blinked and sipped my water. Who was this Kai man who switched plans to be in Ghana and why? Nothing about him being here made sense.

My eye caught Gerhard's. Excitement, hope, and nervousness competed in his expression, but the steadiness of his gaze unnerved me.

"Selah?" His lips curled up into a faint smile.

"What?"

"Ama asked you if you thought my arrival was the best news."

"Oh, right." I finished my water.

"So?"

"I'm thinking. It's a lot to think about. I'm mourning my dear friend Gerhard." I frowned. "I don't know this Kai guy."

"You rhymed," Kai Not Gerhard said.

"Well, this tricycle should really be a bicycle," Ama said, gathering her skirt and standing. "I have hotel business of some sort to do somewhere else. Dinner at seven." She patted my shoulder and ruffled Kai's hair when she walked past us.

I looked at my watch. His welcome dinner was scheduled for three hours later. Three hours to digest my afternoon of Kai Not Gerhard and Matt Not Gerhard.

"Ugh." I rested my forehead on the table.

"Feeling dizzy again?" He dipped his head to see my face.

"No, not really. Unless feeling like an asshole is the same feeling."

"Why are you an asshole?" Amusement tickled his words.

"Did I really faint when I saw you at the gallery?" I rolled my neck to the side to look at him with one eye. One eyeful of Kai was all I could handle at the moment.

"You did," he said, unleashing the full Gerhard smile. "I've never had a woman pass out upon seeing me."

Embarrassment flooded my body. "Don't let it go to your head. I had low blood sugar. I blame the anti-malarial meds."

He frowned. "I'm sorry you're sick from them."

Damn his concern.

"Thanks. I'm glad you aren't a psychotic episode." I half-smiled.

"Me too. Although, I'm pleased your mind would choose to hallucinate about me."

"Pretty confident, aren't you?"

He shrugged.

I noticed his arms were tanner. "Did you really visit Kenya, or was that a ruse?"

"Ruse?"

"Like the whole 'Call me Gerhard' thing in Amsterdam."

"I never told you to call me Gerhard. You did that on your own."

"You let me."

"I kind of liked it."

"You did like it."

"I did."

"Why would Anita tell me your name is Gerhard if everyone calls you Kai?"

"I asked her. She said it was because I would know it really was her who told you to contact me."

"Like a code?"

"Like a code."

"You have so many women hitting on you by saying they met your sister, you need a code?"

"You're the only one Anita has done this with."

"Really?"

"Really."

"What's so special about me?"

He stared at me for a moment. "You're different."

Not beautiful or special or celestial. Different.

"Thanks. I think." I furrowed my forehead.

"It's a compliment. You're different in the best of ways. Smart, clever, witty, and independent."

Not pretty or charming or ethereal.

"Your sister has never set you up? Ever?"

He rubbed the back of his neck, running his hand up through his hair, causing it to stick out with the humidity. I could feel the heat causing my own skin to dampen.

"No, never."

Something lurked in the depths of his deep blue eyes, but I'd had enough revelations from him for one afternoon.

"I think I need to lie down." I stood up from the table.

"I'll walk you to your room," he offered, standing as well. When I rolled my eyes at him, he continued, "I don't want you overcome and fainting again before you get there."

"I don't have a room here. I'm renting one in Ama's house."

"Oh." Without his typical confident swagger, his shoulders dropped.

"Are you staying here?"

"No, I'm at the hotel where the conference will be held, the Ambassador, over on Barnes road."

"I know it. I walk by it on my way to the museum."

"Could anyone miss it? It's enormous. So, if you aren't staying here, where were you planning to lie down?"

"That's a good question. I guess I'll have Kofi take me to the house if he's still around." Expecting to see him magically appear, I glanced around the space. He didn't.

"I'll go with you. He can drop me off at my hotel or I could wait at Ama's."

Blinking at him, I tilted my head. The day had rendered me stupid. That was the only logical answer.

"You could. I don't really need supervision."

"I know, but for some reason I'm afraid to let you out of my sight. You might disappear."

"Or reveal my name is really Cindy, and I'm not even a professor."

He laughed. "This will take a lot more time to get over, won't it?"

"It throws off everything. I thought I knew you, or at least was beginning to get to know you. Now, you're this whole other person. You dress differently." I let my gaze wander down his wrinkled shirt and khakis to his sneakers. "You have a different name. I'm beginning to suspect you aren't really a banker and maybe have dozens of secrets yet to be revealed."

He gave me a little grin, his eyes searching my face. "I may be a spy and have a closet full of skeletons, but I'm still the same man you met in Amsterdam."

I met his eyes.

"I can prove it."

"How?" I asked, my voice breathy.

He stepped closer, close enough for me to inhale his spicy scent now mixed with sweat—not stinky sweat—good, man smelling, pheromone laden, salty sweat.

"This," he said, leaning down.

He cupped my face with both hands before his lips met mine—soft, smooth, firm. The same sensation from when he kissed me before slid down my body, settling between my thighs. I closed my eyes and kissed him back in case he evaporated into my memory. When I opened my mouth, he deepened our kiss, moving one hand to my hip, pulling me against him. His other hand curled around my jaw, his fingers entwined through my hair while he proved his existence with his lips, tongue and teeth, hands, torso, and hips.

I moaned, and he smiled against my mouth. This type of kiss led to more. More required privacy, not a veranda restaurant in Ghana, a country that frowned on PDA, and this kiss was capital D display.

We broke apart, breathing heavy.

"Um, I don't think Ama would appreciate us making out in her restaurant," I said, catching my breath.

"She'd kill me." He grinned, his own chest moving rapidly with his breath.

I affected him, too. This fact delighted me.

"Your place or mine?" he joked.

Tempting.

I gasped, pretending to be offended.

"I'm kidding!" He wrapped his arm around my shoulders. "We've only just met. I'm Kai, by the way." He stopped and faced me, sticking out his hand to shake.

I laughed. "Hi, Kai. I'm Selah. But you can call me Dr. Elmore."

We shook hands and snapped our fingers as we pulled apart.

"Aha!" I shouted at our success.

He laughed at me. "I see you've learned the Ghanaian handshake. Kofi must have taught you."

"I've been practicing with him, but could never achieve a nice loud snap. How'd you guess?"

"Who do you think I learned it from?" He winked and grabbed my hand, pulling me outside to find Kofi.

I NEVER DID lie down and rest. Instead, Gerhard, Kai, and I sat in the sun hut at Ama's house and talked for hours. I meant the two of us, not some other random man named Gerhard. Or Kai. It would take time to adjust to the new name. We chatted and held hands. His touch tethered me to the moment. I needed to prove he was real with constant contact.

"You're tanner."

"I flew to Kenya for a couple of days. I tan easily I guess." He shrugged.

"That seems out of the way."

"I needed to set-up the project and find someone to potentially take it over for me. You know, since I stalked you to Ghana instead." His eyes met mine and twinkled.

"Did you really change everything to come hang out with me?"

"Crazy, right?" His hand went to his hair and rubbed the crown of his head, causing strands to stand up in every direction. I liked this new unbuttoned, disheveled man.

I'd like to unbutton and dishevel him.

I definitely felt better.

"A little. I mean, we only met and had dinner a few times. Who does that?"

He watched me carefully, playing with my fingers for a moment. "I do. I'm the kind of crazy man who meets a woman and trails after her to another continent."

"Is this something you've done before?"

"I've never followed anyone to Africa. This is all new for me."

Who was this man? My heart flip-flopped in my chest. His word flattered me, but they also made me want to bolt. Maybe he was right to think I posed a flight risk.

"In my defense, I'd been asked to speak at the conference prior to meeting you. Months ago."

"So you're here for the week?"

"The week. A month. Maybe more."

A month? More?

"Yes, a month. At the least. If I can find the support, maybe three."

I hadn't realized I'd spoken out loud. Typically, I kept my mental babbling internal.

"What are you thinking? Other than I'm a crazy fool."

"Why didn't you tell me you'd be in Ghana when I was here?"

"Ah, right. That." He picked at a string on the inseam of his pants. "I find it difficult to trust people when I first meet them. They hear my name or TNG and have preconceived notions about me." He stared pointedly at me.

"Hey now. Your name meant nothing to me. I only recognized TNG from the exhibit. Should I search for you online?" The thought had frequently crossed my mind. Only before today, I'd have been searching for the wrong man.

"You might have hit me up for additional grant money. Or to fund your own perverse naked project."

I arched an eyebrow at him. "Perverse?"

"You're missing my point. I didn't want us to be about business. My life is all about business now."

"And escaping from women who stalk you, hoping to get into your bed," I teased.

It was his turn to quirk an eyebrow at me.

"I didn't stalk you. You stalked me." I didn't correct the second part of the statement.

"Yes, but you made all sorts of assumptions about me."

This was true. "No, I didn't." I looked out into the sunlit garden.

"Then why aren't you looking at me?"

"I thought I saw a lizard over there."

He stared where I pointed. There wasn't a lizard. Damn beasts. They always appeared out of nowhere, why couldn't one have shown up on command?

"Okay, fine. I assumed things about you because you were Mr. Suit and named Gerhard. Most of them were good things, though."

"What kind of things?"

"You were successful and smart, and from an exceptional gene pool that bred strong, tall, beautiful, athletic people who might one day lead a race of super humans," I babbled.

"Beautiful? Shouldn't that be handsome?" His smile revealed a dimple in his right cheek.

How had I missed his dimple? Had I forgotten the dimple? Dutch dimples. I was doomed.

"Fine. Handsome."

"I think you're beautiful."

There it was. The word every woman wanted to hear.

"Go on."

He wrapped a thin strand of my hair around his fingers and tugged me closer. "I think you're beautiful, and I've been thinking about kissing you for weeks."

I gazed into his eyes, which were close enough to be slightly out of focus. His dark lashes framed his deep blue eyes, which had a ring of silver near the pupil. Tiny freckles dappled his nose. He released the strands of hair from his fingers to cup my jaw.

Instead of kissing my lips, he leaned in and kissed first one cheek, then the other with agonizingly slow movements. Our breaths mingled, but he didn't kiss my mouth. He moved closer to my ear, his breath tickling my neck, torturing me, building up my desire to crash my mouth to his.

"Kiss me, then." My voice trembled.

"I am kissing you." He emphasized his words by pressing his lips against my forehead.

I groaned and shifted to meet his eyes again. Merriment and lust danced behind those dark lashes.

Fuck this.

I reached up to his neck, clutched his hair, and pulled his mouth to mine. He laughed before returning my kiss.

Our inappropriate for public kiss of earlier had nothing on this one. In the privacy of the screened sun hut, I unleashed my pent-up frustration. I moaned like a porn queen, grateful Ama wasn't home.

His hands left my face, skimming down over my breasts, then settling on my hips, encouraging me to move closer to him. I obliged by straddling his thighs.

Bless long, full skirts.

Settling me on his lap, he took over, controlling the kiss and letting his hands roam my body. I gently pulled at his hair, cupped his face, and dragged my fingers along his scruff before venturing further south to explore his wide shoulders and biceps through the thin linen of his shirt. His body was El Dorado, and I sought his hidden treasure.

Full body contact in humid afternoon air created stickiness and wetness, which had nothing to do with arousal. I could feel sweat glistening on my neck and chest, pooling between my breasts, but didn't want to stop kissing. Who needed air?

Kai's broke the kiss as he worked his way down my neck, kissing and licking a path to my collarbone. "Mmm, salty," he said.

I froze. We were making out like teenagers, and I was sweating like the proverbial whore in church. Sweat plus arousal equaled a sweaty pussy. Swussy. *Sexy? Not sexy.*

"Sorry. It's hot."

North Sea blue flashed at me. "Why are you apologizing?"

"For being sweaty."

"It's Ghana. Everyone's sweaty. Here, lick me." He offered up his neck.

"Seriously?"

"Come on, you know you want to."

"Are we doing body shots? Is this spring break?"

He laughed, then licked the corner of his mouth. "I love the way you taste."

I blinked and my Kegel muscles involuntarily tightened at his words. This man could be my undoing.

I licked him—of course I licked him—on that magical place right below his ear where the corner of his strong jaw jutted out. I could cut steak with his jaw. Maybe I'd try later. For now, I traced my nose along his scruff, inhaling his good sweaty, man smell. When I reached the spot of soft skin below his ear, I darted my tongue out to taste him. He tasted salty, too. I wanted to lick him all over his body, starting at his ear and working my way down, much further down. He could be my personal salt lick.

Kai moaned and rolled his neck further to the side to increase my access. He obviously enjoyed it. I took his lobe between my teeth and lightly bit down. His hands tightened at my waist. I exhaled warm air near his ear as he rocked his hips against me.

Kai was hard. Ger hard. I snickered.

"What?" His eyes slowly opened and met mine.

No way would I tell him what made me laugh.

"Nothing. I giggle when I get excited."

His side-long look told me he didn't believe me. With a quickness that startled me, he tickled my sides.

Growing up with two brothers, I assumed I'd lost the receptors for tickling ages ago. Instead, I was more sensitive than typical people who hadn't grown up being tortured by teasing siblings.

"Ack! Stop!" I laughed, trying to catch my breath while I squirmed and wriggled on his lap, attempting to block his hands with my arms tucked tight to my sides. "Enough!"

His laughter joined mine.

"Not sexy," I squealed. Squealing wasn't sexy either.

"Tell me."

"Never." I hopped off his lap, out of breath, my sides aching.

He crossed his arms and glared at me. "Laughing at me isn't good for my delicate male ego."

I let my gaze drop to where what had brushed against my thighs stood evident by the tenting of his pants.

"Appears to me your ego is in fine shape." I raised an eyebrow and stared at him.

He didn't move to adjust himself or hide it. "I'm a healthy man."

"That you are. That you are indeed." I found myself staring at the top of his thighs. I thought I saw his peen twitch.

Doomed.

ELEVEN

APPARENTLY, EVEN AS adults it was possible to spend hours making out and not realize it. Kai and I arrived late for dinner that night, much to Ama's and Ursula's delight when they saw my flushed face and kiss swollen lips. Internally, I groaned, knowing no matter how old I was, or how old they were, they would still tease me about it when Kai was out of earshot. I owed Maggie an apology for my meddling last summer. Meddling was endlessly fun and better than being the center of attention when it came to potential romance.

Romance? We had a week. Maybe more. A month.

A week was enough. A month would be plenty. Kai and I could have a lot of sex in a month.

I crossed and uncrossed my legs thinking about it. He sat next to me at the table, and his hand wandered underneath the cloth to find my thigh. Warmth at the point of contact infiltrated the thin cotton of my skirt to heat my skin. His occasional squeeze didn't help the gathering heat elsewhere.

The day's temperatures had lowered and a breeze blew off of the ocean, but I still flushed. I sipped from my glass of beer, hoping to quench the flames, knowing they had nothing to do with the temperature or thirst.

Kai coughed, drawing my attention to him. "Selah? Ursula asked if you would like to join them this week in the Volta?"

I blinked at him, then met Ursula's eyes. Her wink told me she had no expectation of me joining them.

Meddling meddlers.

"I …" I met Kai's interested expression. "I think I'll have to pass."

His hand squeezed my thigh before finding my own and intertwining our fingers.

"Thought so, but wanted to ask to make sure. I wouldn't want to leave you behind, all alone," Ursula said.

Boy, she laid it on thick.

"She won't be alone," Kai stated with his charming smile. "I'll keep her company."

Ama, Nadine, and Ursula sighed in unison.

Damn lethal Dutch charms.

Despite Ama kindly informing us she went to bed early, what a heavy sleeper she was, and how she wouldn't wait up for me, I decided there was no way I would bring Kai to her house.

Instead, I grabbed an overnight bag while Kai and Kofi chatted in the driveway, waiting for me.

We had a week. Maybe a month. I wouldn't waste time thinking about what everything meant or the future. We had now.

Carpe vir! Seize the man!

SOME PEOPLE MIGHT think sleeping with, and by sleeping I mean fucking, a man they'd recently met made a woman a slut.

I disagreed.

Two consenting adults, who both agreed to engage in sex with each other with no emotional strings attached and a mutual understanding—combined with sexual chemistry, respect, and a desire to pleasure each other—were about the healthiest kind of people there could be.

Being a woman not in my twenties, or even thirties, unmarried, never married, no kids, lacking the mothering gene, far from a size two, meant people saw me as a spinster, a charity case to be pitied, or worse, a pariah out to steal the good, married men.

In my book, there was nothing wrong about spinsters in the true definition. Or a slut, if she acted safe and healthy.

I wouldn't go quietly into middle age.

No way.

I was healthy and safe. I knew what got me off and how. And I had a very hot, very turned on man—younger man I might add—who wanted me in the most carnal way.

I would be a fool to keep my knees together for propriety.

However, I wasn't prepared for Kofi's frown when he dropped us off at The Ambassador.

"You are a lady, Dr. Selah," he reminded me, his expression serious.

I gave him a small, confused smile. "Thank you."

In the lobby, I asked Kai what Kofi meant.

"He doesn't approve of you spending the night with me. That sort of thing isn't done in Ghana by proper ladies."

"He literally frowned upon me when I got out of the car," I said.

"Better than the look I received. I'll explain things to him tomorrow."

"What sort of things? I'm pretty sure he knows about the birds & the bees. He has five kids."

Kai laughed. "No, I'll explain about us. Set him straight."

"About? Will you tell him you're not stealing my virtue?"

Kai's face grew solemn. "I didn't know you weren't a virgin."

I choked on my own spit, my cough echoed across the marble floor and high ceilings of the grand lobby. Once I caught my breath, I gave Kai a side-long look. "My virtue is none of your business."

He clutched his heart and acted offended. "I'm devastated."

"Listen, the HMS Virginity sailed from San Francisco a long time ago. You were probably a toddler then."

"Ouch." He frowned, and his eye crinkles disappeared. "I'm not much younger than you. Age is relative."

"Sure, easy for you to say."

"Call me a whippersnapper, and I'm calling this whole thing off." He continued to flirt when we entered the plush elevator, but as soon as the doors closed, he cornered me. "I hope you have the stamina to keep up with me."

Where he pinned me with his hips, I could feel his hardness. He loomed over me, dominating in the most delightful way.

"I'm closer to my sexual peak than you are to yours. I hope you can handle me," I whispered. Further words fell away when his lips crashed into mine.

Apparently, somewhere between the lobby and the elevator, we had lost all pretense about where this was heading, which was fine by me. I didn't mind direct. In spite of my wavering and chickening out in Amsterdam, I was still myself. I didn't need wooing and proclamations to seduce me into bed.

The ping announcing our arrival on his floor broke us apart, barely. He turned and backed me down the hall, his hands guiding me while his lips occupied themselves on my neck. I hit the wall near his door when he released me to find his key card.

Speaking of beds, holy luxurious king-sized bed with a million thread count sheets. If my twin beds at Ama's could be any mid-rate hotel, this room earned its five stars. Polished dark woods, masculine grays, and crisp whites decorated the mini-suite with a sitting area on one side, and the aforementioned bed peeking out behind a column of a wall holding a flat screen TV.

TV. I hadn't watched any since I left home. Suddenly, I missed my reality shows and the twenty-four-hour news cycle. I walked over to it and lovingly stroked its black surface.

"Did you caress the television?" Kai asked, standing behind me.

I turned to face him. "Maybe." I looked around the space. "Was the elevator some sort of portal?"

"What do you mean?"

"This hotel belongs in New York. Or Vegas. Or Shanghai. It feels too grand, too fancy, too pretentious to exist in the land of Mona Lisa monkeys."

"Do I even want to know about these Mona Lisa monkeys?"

"Long story."

"Another time, then." He glanced around the space. "It is kind of pretentious. Especially for people here to discuss loans for small businesses which could run for a month with the cost of a single night."

"I'm trying not to judge."

"Too late?"

"Too late. I don't understand the whole money entitlement thing."

He shrugged and looked slightly uncomfortable. "Another good reason you didn't know who I was when we met."

"Are you an entitled bastard?" Images of him in his custom suits came to mind.

"Let's say I came from privilege and have been trying to make up for it ever since."

"Sounds noble and humble."

"Better than entitled bastard?"

"Much."

"Some people might say I'm still a bastard." He stalked closer to me, a lion trapping his prey.

"Who?" I whispered, my pulse thrumming in my ears.

He tipped his head and stared at me. "Why do I have the feeling you prefer the bad boys?" His eyes sparkled in the dim light from the room's low table lamps. He ran his thumb over his bottom lip.

"Who doesn't?" My voice trembled, betraying my excitement. Bad boys were my weakness. His suits and clean cut looks threw me off, but the look in his eye, and this new, dominating energy, had nothing to do with good deeds.

My back hit the wall, and I angled my face to meet his eyes, now hooded and heavy with lust. He dragged his thumb along my jaw. When it neared my lips, I grasped his thumb, sucking the tip into my warm mouth.

Making eye contact, the spark from a few moments earlier morphed into flames.

I nipped the fleshy pad of his thumb, dragging my bottom teeth across the underside, giving him a taste of things to come. The thought of coming made me tighten my thighs together, seeking relief from the building ache.

"Selah," he whispered, his voice husky.

I waited for him to continue, but instead he pulled his hand away from my mouth and replaced his thumb with his tongue. I much preferred the latter. His hands roamed down my body. One hand squeezed my breast while the other skimmed over my hip before resting on the curve of my ass. From the way his hands moved, it seemed he couldn't decide if he was a boob or ass man. I had plenty of both for him to choose from.

Our height difference meant he had to contort himself to kiss me anywhere south of my neck. I put us both out of our misery when I escaped the cage of his arms and led him into the bedroom. At the edge of the bed, he surprised me by spinning me around to face him. I fell backward into the soft bedding, whiteness enveloping me.

"You look like a hot house flower in a field of snow." His gaze scanned me from head to toe. He bent down and slowly removed my shoes, skimming his hands up my calves and under the long wrap skirt. His touch alternated between nothing to a scrape of his short nails.

I squirmed and moaned, and he hadn't even reached my thighs yet.

He kicked off his own shoes, and then undid the buttons of his shirt. I leaned up on my elbows to watch.

Locking eyes with me, he took his time. My impatience got the better of me, and I leaned forward to finish the job, shoving his shirt off his broad shoulders. I took a moment to take in everything from his tanned skin and compact cluster of hair between his defined pecs. A slightly darker trail of hair started at his navel and ran south into his still buttoned pants. He was fit—swimmer or rower fit—all broad muscles at the top and narrowing down to his hips.

fingers under the lace. I could feel the vibrations against my skin when he stifled a chuckle against my breast.

Game on, Dutch boy.

I sought out his hardness and realized he still wore his pants. After unbuckling his belt and undoing the zipper, I found what I wanted; its hard length and heat making it impossible to miss.

"Your pants."

He raised his face from my cleavage. "What about them?"

"Off." I tugged at them. "Now."

"So demanding. I'm not used to being bossed around this much."

I glared at him. "Now."

He laughed and stood, dropping both his trousers and his boxers. His beautiful cock stood at attention, gently bobbing as he stepped closer to the bed.

Yes, beautiful. Some are.

His cough drew my attention north of his cock for a brief moment. I licked my lips and smirked.

This would be fun.

Dressed, Kai was beyond merely handsome, but naked he was magnificent, with sculpted hard lines and angles. And the V. His body should have been memorialized in marble.

After rolling on my stomach, I motioned him closer, grabbing his hip and pulling him the final inches to me where I could trace my tongue along the paths set by my fingers. Perfection.

He moaned and tangled his hands through my hair, less pushing or guiding, more to balance himself while I dragged my lips across the line of dark hair near his navel to the other hip. I was teasing him and loving it. His fingers tightened around a few strands of hair, the pain causing me to look up at him.

"It isn't nice to tease." His voice sounded stern, commanding.

"Yes, Sir," I answered, licking my lips and then licking him. "Better?" I asked.

He only nodded.

From this angle, I could support myself with one arm, leaving my other hand to wander his body. When I scraped my nails along his hips, he squirmed, and I made a note.

My current position also allowed me to take him fully in my mouth, which I did repeatedly, gently scraping my teeth along his flesh when I retreated.

Soon he was panting and gently thrusting his hips, restraining himself, or trying to. I cupped his balls, gently squeezing before slowly tracing a finger behind them.

"Stop," he muttered and touched my cheek.

I opened my eyes, peering up to see the strain on his face. With a final swirl of my tongue, I released him but held onto the base with my hand.

"Stop?" I asked.

"Yes, I'm close, and I don't want to finish in your mouth the first time."

With a devilish grin, I asked, "Would you prefer my hand?"

He growled and managed to fling me down on the bed before I realized he'd moved.

"Your mouth is very smart."

"Is that a compliment on my oral skills?"

"No."

I frowned.

"No, not that you shouldn't be complimented. You should. It was perfect, but you always have a comeback or remark. You can never be serious." He crawled over me until our faces were inches apart, his voice and expression were serious.

"I take sex very seriously. Blow jobs especially."

"See?"

"I'm serious."

"You're teasing again."

I grinned. "Maybe."

He kissed me and shut me up with his tongue. I didn't complain. I loved his tongue. Secretly, I was relieved he'd stopped me. Oral was a means to an end, not the full act. I didn't love oysters, either, because they reminded me of semen, and I preferred to swallow neither.

Kai's hands reacquainted themselves with my boobs. One hand slid around and cupped my ass, rolling my hips closer to his. I still wore my underwear, and that was wrong. I reached down to shimmy out of it and Kai stopped me. His own hands tugged down the lace, leaving me bare for him.

"Let's see if you enjoy being teased."

Turns out, I did enjoy it. Teased, licked, lapped, and whatever he did with his scruff. Scruffed?

Kai had skills.

I gave up trying to figure out his technique downtown and went along for the ride.

"Unf."

"Ooh."

"Right ..."

"...there."

"Yes."

"Damn."

"Yes."

I hoped the walls of his room were as thick as the plush carpet, because I was loud. Kai's hair stood on end from where I clutched it. I nearly squashed him with my thighs as I transformed into a shuddering, clenching, panting ball of ecstasy on the bed.

He kissed my inner thigh and dragged his scruff across my skin again one last time, then sat on his haunches and smiled down at me. He swiped his thumb across his lips and sucked the tip.

I lay there, helpless against his mojo.

And we hadn't even fucked yet. As evident by his still turgid cock.

I giggled over the word turgid.

"Something funny?"

I rolled my eyes. "I think I've orgasmed myself silly."

"Is that possible?"

"Apparently so."

He smiled at me and stroked himself. I stared. It was a sight to behold.

"Perhaps we should stop."

"Are you kidding me? Let's go for stupid."

I reached for his cock; he reached for a condom. I thought about commenting on his preparedness and assumptions. Instead, I quietly observed him, trying to will condoms to be sexy. He leaned over me, bracing his weight on his elbows while I guided him, releasing him when his tip brushed against me.

We moaned in unison when he stretched and filled me.

Damn.

Kai rocked and my hips rose to meet his. I kept my eyes open to watch his face change with each movement. I was close when he rolled us over for me to straddle him, his thumb on my clit, pushing me closer to the edge. His fingers pinched a nipple. His tongue peeked out as he lifted his mouth to my breast and licked.

Game over.

I spiraled and fell, losing myself in the pleasure of another orgasm.

And he was still hard.

I loved younger men.

He flipped us again and took over, thrusting and seeking his own pleasure. His brow furrowed with concentration. An expression, which could be pleasure or pain, or both, took over his beautiful features. His rhythm staggered, and with a final thrust, he stilled.

Even his come face was beautiful, like one of Michelangelo's tortured slaves.

We lay on our backs horizontally across the bed, and I brushed a damp lock of hair from his forehead. He caught my hand and kissed my palm.

He opened his eyes to look at me. "You're incredible, Selah."

"Likewise." My smile was lazy and sated. "We should do that again."

"Right now?" He laughed. "I'm not eighteen."

"Lord, no." I sighed. "I don't even know my last name right now."

With a smirk, he said, "Mission accomplished. You're not only silly, but stupid."

I laughed. "Congratulations."

"What's my prize?" He stood up and headed to the bathroom.

"We get to do it again?"

The water in the shower drowned out the sound of his laughter.

Mmm, shower sex. My body responded. I wondered how long until he would be ready to claim his prize.

TWELVE

I WASN'T SURE if his stamina was due to his super-human genes or the copious amounts of dairy I imagined he ate growing up, but Kai had the recovery period of a race horse. Assuming race horses had quick recovery times.

With its ultra-hot water and amazing pressure I could stay in his shower forever. The hot naked guy added to my bliss.

After the shower, we collapsed into bed for a few hours, until Gerhard brushing against my ass woke me up again. By Gerhard, I meant his penis, not the man. Gerhard was too perfect a name not to use. I would never tell Kai I named his penis. *Who does that?* Teenage girls in Judy Blume books and weirdos. Obviously, I was neither.

Round three ended with my shoulders hanging off the bed and an inability to remember the day of the week.

"Coffee."

"What?" he mumbled from his position with his face in the pillows.

"Coffee. I need real coffee." I lifted my head.

"Cappuccino?" he asked, his voice muffled by the down.

"You have cappuccinos?" Rolling myself as gracefully as possible, I twisted my body to lie next to him on the pillows.

He faced me and nodded. "Room service?"

I sighed. "Even if this is some alternative reality, I'm saying yes and drinking all of the cappuccinos I can until I wake up and realize it was a dream."

He pinched my arm.

"Ouch!" I rubbed the spot and batted his pinching fingers away from me. "Why did you pinch me?"

"To prove you're awake." He grinned and jumped off the bed before I could retaliate. Grabbing a fresh pair of boxers from a drawer, he put them on, and sauntered into the living area while I enjoyed ogling his ass. "Do you want breakfast?"

Of course I did. I had a week. I wanted whatever he would give me.

If said giving included cappuccinos and croissants, even better. Neither were the best I'd ever had, but they beat the watery instant coffee at Ama's. Wealth and privilege had their bonuses.

I wasn't expected at the museum until the next day, so we spent the morning on the couch watching TV. I wrapped a thick white hotel robe around myself, and after some pestering, Kai wore one too. We resembled marshmallow-people hybrids. Decidedly unsexy, but somehow he overcame his marshmallow-ness to still be handsome. I wish the same could be said for me.

"Pool?"

I looked at him from the corner of my eye. "What about it?"

"We should go downstairs and sit by the pool."

Naked and sexual with Kai was one thing, but would I parade myself around in a bathing suit in front of him? I mulled it over for a minute until I realized my one and only swimsuit sat safely tucked away at Ama's.

"No suit. Do they frown on skinny dipping?"

He shook his head and smiled. "I'm one-hundred-percent certain they don't approve of skinny dipping."

"Well, if we aren't having sex in the pool, then I guess I'll be happy to sit on a lounger and watch you swim."

He choked on his cappuccino, causing a cloud of foam to break free and land on his hand.

"Was that an option?"

"Obviously not here." I stared at him, willing my face to remain serious.

"Someday we'll travel somewhere with a pool where such things are encouraged."

"Ew, can you imagine the chlorine needed to swim safely in that pool?" I shuddered.

"I meant a private pool. Or a lake."

"Lake?" I screeched. "With fish? No way."

"You're making it difficult to fulfill the fantasy."

"You want to fulfill my fantasies?"

Meeting my eyes, he nodded. "Of course."

I stared at him for a beat or two. "Who are you?"

"Didn't we clear that up yesterday?"

"We cleared up the name, but really, who are you?"

"I can't tell if you want me to answer you literally or if you're being funny."

"It's kind of rhetorical."

"Why?"

"I've never met anyone like you."

"Is that good?"

He sat at the far end of the sofa and I briefly studied his face before nodding. "It's good. Disconcerting, but good."

"Let's quit while I'm ahead. You get dressed and I'll grab my trunks for the pool."

Outside, sunshine blazed down, but a light breeze blew fronds of palm trees surrounding the pool area. I sat under an umbrella on a chaise lounge watching Kai swim laps.

Everything went into slow motion when he exited the pool. His blond hair darkened by water made his eyes more striking against his tan skin. Not that I stared at his eyes. I was too busy envying every water droplet racing over the muscles of his chest and abs, drawing my eyes further down his body to where his swim trunks clung to his thighs and Gerhard.

Droplets of cool water sprinkled my bare legs. Looking up, I met a smiling Kai with his hand still near his hair where he had shook the water onto my skin.

"Hey now!" I scooted out of the way.

"You looked lost in a daydream."

"Kind of. Did you swim competitively?"

"How did you guess?"

"Besides your classic swimmer's body?"

He smirked at me. "I did. I swam on the Harvard team. Long distance."

"Mmm."

"You approve?"

"I do."

"I didn't figure you for the type who dated us jocks in school." He reached over me for a towel, deliberately dripping water on me again before wrapping white terry cloth around his hips. From the clear outline visible beneath the thick pool towel, it looked like the water wasn't cold enough to cause shrinkage.

"Oh, never. We didn't even have football at my college. But I've grown up and matured. Become more open-minded."

"What were you like when you were younger?" His aviators blocked his eyes, but his body language showed his interest.

"Angry. Goth. Black spiky hair. I wanted to rebel against everything."

A smile tugged at the corner of his mouth. "Sounds like someone else I know."

"Really?"

He nodded and sat on the lounger next to mine. "Why so angry and rebellious?"

"Probably because I had a completely normal and uneventful childhood. Parents are still happily married. My brothers and I got along, besides the normal teasing. I did well enough in school to be bored. Classic American middle-class life."

"Where did you grow up?"

"California."

"Los Angeles?"

"No, nothing as glamorous as that. A suburb near San Francisco. Close enough to go into the city and see the hippies and punk rockers, but far enough away that the mall was the main social hangout."

"We didn't have malls in Amsterdam."

"I imagine not."

"And you? You didn't want the happy life in the suburbs?"

I observed him while I figured out how honest to be. I'd had various parts of his body inside of me, but emotional honesty existed outside my comfort zone.

"I didn't. I never wanted the husband, or the kids, or the dog, parakeet, turtle, guinea pig…" I let my list and sentence fade away while I studied him for a reaction. "I know it's odd, and most people, mostly women, think it's a lie, but I didn't."

"Didn't past tense?"

"Don't. Present tense. Did part is a done deal at this point."

He arched an eyebrow.

I waved my hand in a circle over my torso. "Older woman. Like the HMS Virginity, that ship's sailed, too."

"Oh."

In the silence that fell between us, I waited for him to speak.

"Wow, that became heavy quickly," I said after an awkward moment.

"No, don't worry. You were being honest."

"And you probably didn't expect to have this conversation today."

He reached over and entwined our fingers. "I didn't expect you to spend the night with me last night either. Everything with you is unexpected."

"Unexpected in a good way?"

"Unexpected in the best way—like a surprise you never dreamed of, but the best surprise you've ever had."

If we weren't sitting by the pool, I'd have kissed him then and there. Instead, I led him up to his room to have my evil way with him.

THE NEXT NIGHT Kai took me out to one of the beach resorts in Labadi to see a band he first heard three years ago. I hadn't been out at night since my arrival, unless I counted dinners at Ama's. Tonight felt wild and adventurous, and very much like a real date.

Kofi drove us out to the beach. His warm smile had returned, and he shook Kai's hand enthusiastically when he dropped us off at the club.

"Everything sorted with him?" I asked Kai after Kofi drove away.

"I think so. We chatted waiting for you to come downstairs."

"Want to clue me in on what you said?"

"Nope. Some conversations should remain between men."

"That sounds sexist."

"I knew you would think that. Typically, Ghanaians are traditional people with set roles."

"I'm beginning to understand, but my inner feminist struggles with it."

"I think you struggle with set roles and expectations in general."

I blinked at him. "You figured that out quickly."

He laughed and took my hand, leading me down a plant-lined path, following the sound of music. "I figured it out in Amsterdam. You love to label and catalog things, but you don't like the same done to you."

I started to protest, but realized he was right.

"Your lack of arguing tells me I'm correct."

I huffed. "Fine. You're right."

He smirked down at me.

"Don't become smug, okay?"

"Okay." He kissed my knuckles and released my hand, placing his palm on my shoulder blade to guide me. It was old fashioned and probably chauvinistic, but only in the best way.

Beats of reggae music greeted us when we reached a large patio, which served as restaurant and club.

Leaning down to speak close to my ear, Kai whispered, "Dance with me."

Normally, I didn't dance. At least not in public anymore. "Sure."

He led me onto the small dance floor, already filled with couples dancing.

He spun me around and then placed his hand on my hip, drawing me closer. I let him lead. Not surprising, Kai could dance. We alternated between swaying and turns. With each spin, my full skirt swirled around my calves in a sea of yellows and blues. The warm, salty breeze, and slow, steady beats of the drums lulled me into a haze. We could be in any tropical place in the world, another couple in paradise.

The music changed to an up-tempo beat, and I laughed while I tried to keep up with Kai. When I stumbled over my feet, I laughed harder until I had to stop to catch my breath. Taking pity on me, he led me to a table and ordered beers and water.

"Where did you learn to dance like that?" I asked, sipping my water.

"School, I guess. My father insisted on formal dance lessons—such as the Fox Trot and waltzes. My act of rebellion was to learn how to breakdance."

I snorted. "You can breakdance?"

He nodded. "Not well, and not anymore. There was an unfortunate incident involving The Worm." He shuddered and laughed at himself.

I could only imagine what sort of thing a boy could injure doing The Worm. Poor Gerhard.

"You're very good."

"At breakdancing?"

"No, at dancing."

"This surprises you?" He smirked.

"It does, but I should give up and accept you will probably never not surprise me. Or not be good at something."

His dimple appeared when he leaned over to kiss my cheek.

"Surrender," he whispered.

I met his eyes and slowly nodded.

I had no immunity to his charms, my defenses were failing, but could I give up control?

LATER IN THE week, during dinner at Ama's, Kai announced he'd be staying in Ghana for the next three months. The regular gang had returned from Volta and was joined by a few of the guys from the TNG group, including Matt, aka Not Gerhard. Kai's announcement earned him a hug from Ama and cheers from everyone else. After her hug, Ama whispered something in his ear and patted his face twice—an odd, motherly gesture for the happy moment.

My heart raced at the idea of spending three months with Kai—under him or over him. Three months wasn't a rendezvous. It was something more. A fling? An affair? Something not quite a relationship because relationships didn't have set end-dates.

Kai's arm around my shoulder defined me as his the whole evening. It either marked his territory or he had a compulsive need to touch me. While I preferred the latter, I suspected the former. His whispered "surrender" from early in the week had confirmed his need to possess.

Matt and I chatted for a few minutes about our missed trip to the art gallery. He promised to take me up on my offer if he returned to Accra while Kai grumbled next to me. When I turned to stare at him, Kai asked Nathan something across the table, refusing to meet my gaze. Kai's fingers tapped on my shoulder. Instead of feeling endearing, it annoyed me. I wasn't a toy to be fought over or a tree to be marked.

Boys.

I excused myself, letting Kai's arm fall to the back of my chair.

Standing at the bathroom sink, I splashed water on my face. My head spun, not from the gin and tonic or beer, but from the man sitting out there who'd showed up a few days ago and invaded my world. Now instead of a week-long sex-a-thon, he'd be around for half of my stay. He'd already possessed my body, bringing me pleasure I hadn't experienced in years. I craved his touch, but at what cost?

Surrender. His voice echoed inside my thoughts.

To what?

Someone knocked on the door.

"Occupied," I said.

"Selah?" Kai's voice sounded through the thick wood.

What the—

"Kai?"

"Are you okay?"

I opened the door to find him leaning against the frame, a shy smile on his face.

"I'm fine."

"Are you sure? You left abruptly and have been gone a while."

"No, I'm fine. Doing the usual." I gestured at the toilet and sink.

"You're not mad?"

Was I mad?

"Why?"

"I acted a little caveman with Matt."

I crossed my arms. "You think?"

He nodded. "I know I did. Something about him making a date with you set me off. I should apologize."

"You don't owe me an apology." I uncrossed my arms. "You don't owe me anything."

He frowned. "I do. It was rude. You're a grown woman who doesn't need a jerk like me claiming you like a piece of meat."

I sighed. "Thank you." Smiling, I admitted, "I kind of enjoyed it. Until you growled at poor Matt."

"I didn't growl at him."

"You did. And I might have bruises on my shoulder from your fingers."

"You do?" He looked chagrined.

"I'm kidding, but you have quite the grip." I rubbed my shoulder.

"I'm sorry." He swept his hand through the stray bit of hair that flopped on his forehead. "Let me make it up to you."

I raised my eyebrow, all sorts of dirty thoughts dancing through my mind. "How?"

"Come away with me for the weekend. I'll get a car, and we'll visit Cape Coast."

"Really?"

"Yes, we'll spend some time together."

"Haven't we done that already?"

"I mean outside of the bedroom. There won't be elephants, but we can explore the castles and the park."

"You're planning a romantic getaway to the slave castles? Sounds grim."

"Okay, not the most lighthearted place, but let's go on an adventure."

I couldn't resist him. "Let's go."

"We'll leave this weekend. I promise, no caveman."

"Drats. I was hoping you'd pull my hair at least."

His charming charmer smile returned. "That I can do."

ABOUT AN HOUR west of Accra, Kai cleared his throat, his focus leaving the road when he turned to look at me from behind his sunglasses.

"I need to be honest with you about something."

"And you waited until I was your captive passenger to do it?"

"I didn't want you fainting."

"I don't faint. The shock was your fault."

"Okay, I don't want you to run away."

"Are you kidnapping me?"

"This isn't a kidnapping."

I tugged at my seatbelt as if it were a restraint and stared at him. The gesture meant to show I didn't feel worried, but with each caveat, I became more unsettled.

"You're beginning to freak me out." I rested my back against the door of his older model Range Rover.

"I know. I'm sorry. Okay, maybe I worried you'd be mad or make a scene."

I crossed my arms. "Spit it out, Kai."

"About Anita …"

"What about her?" My skin prickled.

"She's not my sister."

My mouth gaped. "She said Gerhard, you, Kai, is … are her brother."

"Right. That's not true." He tapped his fingers on the steering wheel.

"Like how you're not really Gerhard, Anita isn't really your sister?"

Who knew the Dutch were wily and duplicitous? Not all Dutch, maybe only this Dutchman. I'm sure the rest of the citizens of The Netherlands were lovely, honest, forthright people.

"Exactly."

I knew before he said it.

"She's my ex-wife."

THIRTEEN

STUNNED, I SAT in silence with my mouth open, looking neither beautiful nor smart.

"Anita is your wife?"

"Ex-wife." He stared at me. "Ex."

Who were these super human, beautiful weirdos lying about their names and relations?

"Just to clarify, she's never been your sister?"

He laughed. "No, never. Wife only. Now ex-wife."

"How ex?"

"What do you mean?"

"How long have you been divorced?"

He glanced at the road, then back at me. "Four years, almost five."

I silently did the math …

"We divorced when I was thirty."

Thirty and divorced? "When did you get married?"

"Too young."

I stared at him. "Fourteen? How young are we talking?"

"Twenty-two, the summer after I graduated Harvard."

"That is young."

He faced the road again when a truck moved into our lane.

"Why didn't you tell me when we met?"

He frowned and looked over his shoulder to steer around the truck. "I don't really know. Anita set it up by saying she was my sister, and because I figured we'd never see each other again, why contradict her."

"But …"

"But …" He paused. "I like you …" Another pause. "Enough to stalk you to Ghana."

"Stalked me to Ghana, had your way with me for a week, and still didn't tell me the truth."

"Remember when I told you some people think I'm a bastard?" He ran his hand over his neck.

"I do."

"Well, it's a pretty big club."

"Club? Of ex-wives?"

"No, the Kai is a bastard club. Besides my father and sometimes Anita being members, there are probably others. I haven't always been the best man."

"Or comfortable with the truth."

"That too." He smiled shyly. "But I want to be truthful with you."

"Why?"

"Because I like you." He reached out to touch my leg. I didn't move away. I had nowhere to move with my back against the door.

I stared out at the green rolling hills to the right. The occasional tin roof of a home or chop joint broke up the lush foliage. While I observed the scenery, I digested Kai's revelation. Alongside the shoulder of the road, black plastic bags littered the ground, a reminder of the crap we leave in our wake—sometimes literal, but mostly figurative crap.

"Why did you call Anita your sister?"

"I didn't."

Revisiting our conversations, I tried to recall him ever saying his sister and couldn't.

"Do you even have a sister?"

He shook his head.

"When I texted you saying I met your sister in JFK and calling you

Gerhard, did you think I was crazy?"

He nodded. "A little. Like I said, I immediately texted Anita to find out what was up."

"The code?"

"Right. We agreed you might think that it was weird my ex-wife was setting you up with me."

I pinched my thumb and forefinger together. "A little."

"We're not one of those divorced couples who hate each other."

"Apparently not. Unless setting you up with me was some sort of attempt at revenge."

"Never. Anita is more of a sister to me, now."

"You could be related. You're both overly tall and blond, like giant Dutch Barbie and Ken."

He chuckled. "Gee, thanks." He glanced over at me again. "Are you mad?"

I took a deep breath and exhaled. "Honestly? A little. I'm confused more than anything."

"A little I can work with."

"First the name thing, now this."

"We can blame Anita for both."

I gave him a side-long look. "I'm sure it's fine to throw your ex under the bus, but you never set me straight before. Why now?"

"Ama."

"Ama? What does she have to do with all this?"

"At dinner the other night, when I announced I would be staying, she gave me the scary Ama speech."

"After she hugged you?"

"And slapped my face? Yeah, then."

"What did she say?" I chuckled thinking of Ama taking on Kai, all six foot something of him.

"She told me to do right by you and stop with the games."

"She knows about Anita?"

He nodded.

"Yet she never told me either." I frowned. Ama and I needed to have a little chat when we returned to Accra.

"I asked her not to. When I arrived, you told her my sister Anita introduced us, and when I didn't correct you, she suspected something."

"Why the sneakiness?"

"You've said several times you aren't the marrying kind, and you don't have the mothering gene."

"And you are."

"I was. Divorced, remember? I haven't rushed to remarry."

"I still don't understand." I shrugged.

"I didn't mean to deceive you. I had no idea what to expect from you, from this trip. I don't believe our pasts define us. You know me as the man I am now. Why complicate things with my history?"

"That makes sense. I guess."

"I'm sure you have a few secrets and interesting stories in your past."

I blinked at him. If he only knew.

"Now that I'll be staying for a few months, it changes things."

"It does?" I stared at him.

"For me it does. This isn't only about sex. I didn't come to Ghana to get laid. It's never been about the sex." He paused. "At least not for me."

I let his words settle inside my brain, allowing them to dissolve against my skin. "What is *this*?"

"Dating?" he asked.

"Dating." The word hung between us. "Okay."

"You're not mad?" He sounded relieved.

"I wouldn't go that far. You're like one of those Russian dolls."

"How so?"

"You keep revealing new layers, new secrets."

"Isn't that the joy of dating? Getting to know someone?"

"I thought the joy of dating was having sex on a regular basis."

"Maybe you weren't doing it right." His smug grin returned.

"Watch it, cocky. I'm still mad at you."

"Let me make it up to you when we arrive at the hotel." His hand moved up my thigh, leaving a trail of heat behind it.

Sex was easy. The everything else, when it came to Kai, made my head hurt. At home I avoided complications and history, never sticking around long enough to have to deal with someone else's baggage, let alone my own.

KAI PULLED OFF the main road and parked along a dirt shoulder, promising food and an amazing view for lunch. I hoped the view came with booze. After his revelation, I needed a cocktail. And a cigarette. I clawed inside my purse for my gum, ruing the stupid idea of quitting smoking.

The restaurant sat perched on a low bluff overlooking a narrow cove where waves crashed against dark rocks. Beyond the shade of the thatched umbrella above our table, the sun beat down, water sprayed from each large wave cresting the rocks, and unseen birds squawked in the nearby palm trees.

A thousand thoughts flickered and fought for attention.

Ex-wife.

He ordered grilled fish and beers for us while I stared out at the ocean.

Kai had been married.

Of course a man like Kai would have been married. He probably wanted to be married again.

Our beers arrived and I sipped mine, still silent and stewing. The calming effects of nicotine from the gum slipped into my bloodstream.

Barely visible through the hazy air, an enormous white structure loomed above the water in the distance.

I gestured to the ghost building. "Is that Elmina Castle?" It did resemble a castle with its parapets and towers. However, beneath its whitewashed exterior lurked the ghosts of slavery's horrible history.

Kai turned and squinted into the sun. "It is. Built by the Portuguese, but occupied by the Dutch for over two hundred years when this area was called the Gold Coast."

Two hundred years of slave trade. Thinking about the enormity hurt my heart, yet looking around, life went on along the coast. Fishing boats bobbed in the water and crowded the shore; resorts lined the beach. Modern life surrounded the vestiges of past atrocities. Death, love, horror, sickness, birth, and happiness coexisted in this place as they did everywhere.

"Strange to think about the horrors of history while sitting in the sun, eating and drinking." He frowned, his forehead furrowed.

"History is odd that way." I gazed at the crashing waves.

"Odd how?"

"Buildings and places hold memories. We imbue them with human emotion and memory. A rock, a field, a building become vessels for our memories. The rock on a battlefield is no more special than a rock on a beach. It's easier to hold onto something in the past when you can still see, taste, or smell the memories."

He stared at me for a beat or two.

I continued, "The need for memorials, to mark, to say 'this happened' or 'this person lived' is as old as humans. We celebrate our triumphs and mourn our defeats and failures with physical reminders."

"That's true on personal levels."

"Very much. It's universal, from a ring to demonstrate your love to arches celebrating the dead no one living can remember."

"The history still exists in stories and books, even if the physical evidence disappears," he argued.

"True, but memories fade. We need tangible reminders—places to visit, to touch—in order to feel."

"The same could be said for love."

"Not a believer in absence making the heart grow fonder?" I asked.

121

"No, not really." He lifted his sunglasses. "I think love can die from neglect. Not think, know."

"Speaking from experience?"

"I don't know how much you want, or need, to know about my past, about my life with Anita, or about my mistakes." He waited for me to nod, then continued, "The short version? I've grown up a lot in the last five years." He laughed. "That's an understatement. In my teens and early twenties, I believed I could do no wrong. Anything I wanted, I had. Anyone I wanted, I had."

That I could believe.

"I split my time between Europe and America, acting spoiled on two continents."

"How many continents have you visited?"

"Six. You?"

"Five. I'm interrupting. Sorry, continue."

"No, it's okay. I love that you enjoy traveling." He met my eyes. "Sure you want to hear this?"

I motioned for him to continue; he'd piqued my interest. I wanted to learn about Anita, and what went wrong.

"Anita's parents were friends with mine, but we didn't see each other often. I attended boarding school in the States."

Boarding school? Holy rich boy.

"One summer during college while I was home for a month, Anita and I met again at a party. Turned out, she'd been going to Brown."

Damn super humans with their super human smarts.

"We started dating. Everyone approved."

"Approved?"

"Her parents, my parents."

"Ah. The golden couple."

I thought of my friends Ben and Jo. Despite fooling around with me freshman year, Ben was destined to marry someone like Jo. They were the perfect couple with the perfect life and perfect kids.

Kids.

Suddenly something Anita had said at JFK flashed in my mind.

A teen daughter.

"You have a daughter."

FOURTEEN

KAI NEARLY CHOKED on his beer. "Anita told you about Cibele?"

"She told me she had a daughter, but not her name. I'm guessing that means you're Cibele's father?"

He gave me a tiny smile. "It does."

I nodded, my ears ringing. My brain swam with beer, nicotine, and revelations.

Not only was Kai the marrying type, he was the daddy type.

Kai was a DILF.

Or in my case, a DIF.

I didn't do kids. For the most part, they didn't like me and I didn't like them, especially the little ones. And babies? No way. Too much screaming and shit. Literal shit. Too many babies born the last two decades. When my friends had outgrown their baby-making phase, the gays started adopting. Or breeding. My best friend Quinn and his husband had a baby. Or surrogated a baby. I didn't know the lingo. Lizzy had joined our motley family of friends and brought along non-stop regurgitation and pooping. And cuteness, I reluctantly admitted. She'd be much better in a few years. Or decades.

A teen daughter.

Kai had a daughter.

"You have a daughter."

He nodded. "You said that already."

"I'm in shock. Be nice."

"I'm sorry. I've fucked this up with my lack of honesty when we met in Amsterdam."

"Do you normally talk about your ex-wife and daughter when you first meet a woman?"

He shook his head and chuckled. "No, but then again, I'm not normally introduced as a brother. This whole meeting has been ..."

"Unexpected?" I used his description of me.

"To say the least."

I turned away to find our waitress. Once I caught her eye, I made the international hand gestures for another round of large beers. After I resettled into my chair, I found Kai regarding me with wariness, his thumb rubbing the scruff on his chin.

"What?"

"Nothing."

"So tell me about your daughter."

He continued to scan my face.

"Or not."

Our beers and food arrived, disrupting the staring contest taking place at our table.

"Anita got pregnant senior year at Brown."

"Planned or unplanned?"

"Unplanned. I didn't handle it well at first."

"Bastard behavior?"

"Pretty much. I got drunk the following weekend and mourned my life."

"You thought your life was over? At twenty-one?"

"Having a baby wasn't our plan—at all."

"Ever?"

"We had a great relationship, but the distance and our ambitions didn't lend themselves to the idea of marriage and a young family."

I understood completely. Earning my doctorate held priority over other aspects of my life for a decade.

"But you did get married? What changed your mind?"

"I did the right thing. When we told our parents Anita was pregnant, we received pressure to marry. I realized I was acting like a spoiled child, thinking only of myself. But I loved her."

"Who? Anita or the baby?"

"Both. Cibele owned me from the moment her little heartbeat appeared on the monitor."

My own heart skipped from the love in his voice. Something deep inside of me flickered.

He continued. "Even with the blessings of our parents and a lavish wedding, I didn't feel ready. Twenty-two, newly married, and a father while working on my MBA created one cranky jerk."

"Yikes."

"Yikes is right. Anita is a saint. She postponed grad school while I finished, then agreed to move home for me to work with my father."

"Sounds very traditional." I didn't hide my disdain for the word.

Kai frowned and tapped his fingers on the table. "We were young. All I focused on was ambition and making my own money before I hit thirty."

"Then what happened?"

"I hit thirty. And the shit hit the fan. I had achieved everything I wanted professionally. I made more money than I could spend in a lifetime; I had the office and the title; and I also had the ego."

"Sounds charming."

"Anita agreed."

"And your father?"

"His disdain came later."

Another Russian doll to be opened another time.

"And when the shit hit the fan?"

"I woke up and realized I didn't like myself. Or even recognize who I had become. I had everything I thought I wanted and realized it didn't make me happy. My marriage had faded from lovers into roommates without me realizing it. Anita wanted more for herself. She deserved more."

"Good for her."

"Good for all of us. Anita is happy and that makes me happy. She loves Chicago and what she does. Cibele is happy."

"And you? Are you happy?"

His fingers stilled. "Getting there."

"Do you visit Chicago often?"

"A couple of times a year. Cibele joins me on my trips sometimes and visits our families in Amsterdam." He frowned. "It's never enough time."

My heart softened at his obvious love for his daughter. I recognized yet another side to Kai. "I can tell how much you love her."

"She's my heart."

I hated to admit to myself, but there was something sexy about the love he had for his daughter. Not in a creepy way. Maybe the shock hadn't worn off, or the beer had gone to my head, but I did something I never do when people started talking about their kids. I asked to see a picture.

Kai took out his phone and tapped the screen. His wallpaper displayed a young girl with stormy sea-colored eyes and lavender streaking her blonde hair. Her black Cure T-shirt caught my eye.

Be still my Robert Smith loving heart, Cibele was a twenty-first century goth girl.

"The purple is new." He chuckled. "My parents were not amused, but I love it." His voice was filled with pride.

"I love that band." I pointed at her T-shirt. "I remember my first concert."

"You'll be her idol."

His words implied I'd meet her someday. The idea sent cold waves of fear crashing against my legs, hinting at an undercurrent that could pull me under. Whatever warm feelings I'd had about Kai's daughter minutes ago washed away. After a month of knowing each other—a month which included a handful of days together and a week of sex—this was too much, too soon.

"Selah?" His voice snuck through the cold fog in my brain. Warm fingers intertwined with my own.

"Sorry. Lost myself in memories of boys with black hair and red lips," I fibbed.

"As you do." His voice teased.

"Thanks for sharing about her."

"Thanks for listening."

The moment settled between awkward and polite. I poked at my fish; its dead fish eye stared up at me. My appetite disappeared. "Maybe we should drive to the hotel."

He eyed me warily. "You okay?"

"Sure. Digesting."

"But you hardly ate anything."

"Figuratively digesting."

"Ah."

"Ah." I covered my plate with my napkin. My stomach sank, not from the food, but from realization. Despite telling myself Kai wasn't my type, it was me who wasn't his. Nothing about me said golden or perfect. If anything, at best, I could have been Rizzo to someone's Sandy. Spotlights and leading men were out of my reach.

"Shall we?" He stood and extended his hand.

Resolving myself, I met his eyes. We had now. A couple of months at best. *Carpe diem.*

He laced his fingers with mine before bringing my hand to his mouth, kissing the skin, then gently biting it, sending shivers down my body.

OUR HOTEL ROOM overlooked a pool and grassy area. Surf crashed beyond the white painted trunks of swaying palm trees. Although we were a few miles closer to Elmina, the castle couldn't be seen from our resort. Still, its history shadowed my mood. Or perhaps it was the conversation at lunch. After arriving, I'd feigned sleepiness from lunch and a desire to nap. Kai took his laptop and sat on our balcony, giving me the space I needed but hadn't asked for.

I couldn't turn off my brain enough to rest.

Kai had a daughter. An ex-wife. A daughter.

Last year I'd ended a relationship when the man wanted me to meet his children. It hadn't been right to move forward when I never wanted to be a mother, let alone a step-monster. I rolled onto my side, staring through the screen at Kai's long, lean body sitting in a chair only feet away from the bed. His tan, athletic legs were propped up on the railing. The bright sunlight highlighted the fine blond hairs on his arms and legs. I had a strong urge to run my nose along his limbs, feeling that hair against my skin, knowing he'd smell of sun and spice.

Groaning, I rolled to the other side, my back to the golden boy.

What about him turned me into an uncertain, insecure ball of girly doubt?

Ugh, I sounded like Maggie last summer when Gil reentered her life.

My hand punched the pillow on Kai's side a few times, before grabbing it and putting it over my face.

"Are you attempting to suffocate yourself?" His voice sounded muffled through the pillow.

"Maybe," I mumbled into the fabric.

"I can't hear you." He lifted the pillow away.

When I sat up and tried to grab it, we ended up tugging at it for a minute in some sort of lame pillow fight. I huffed and let him win.

"I think that might have been my first pillow fight." He grinned at me.

"You call that a pillow fight?" I reached over and swiped his other pillow, whacking him on the shoulder.

He didn't duck. After a handful of seconds standing there with his mouth gaping open and the pillow hanging limply by his side, he responded with a full swing, aiming for my head.

Falling backward on the bed, it was my turn to be shocked.

No way would he get away with that. I knelt and let him have it, ducking from his attacks. Soon both of us were laughing and breathless. I collapsed against the mattress, keeping the pillow over my face for protection. When the blows ceased, I peeked up at him from under the corner of the pillowcase. He stood over me, a broad grin on his gorgeous face. Hair tousled, his laughter shaking his chest, he was glorious, irresistible.

Damn him.

"Come here." I summoned him with my finger.

The bed bounced where he landed next to me. "That was fun."

"I can think of more fun we can have on this bed." I tugged him closer by his shirt.

"Oh really?" he asked. "What did you have in mind?" A long leg moved across mine, pinning me down.

"Something involving less clothing."

"I approve of that more than being whacked with a foam pillow." His eyes sparkled as he shifted over me. Grabbing my hands, he pulled them above my head, holding both in one of his while his hips anchored me. "Now that I have you where I want you, will you tell me what's happening inside that big, beautiful brain of yours?"

I lost myself in the deep blue of his eyes for a moment. "Nothing."

He raised an eyebrow and squinted down at me. "Nothing is the wrong answer."

I closed my eyes to his intense gaze.

"Hey, no hiding." He released my hands to tap my forehead.

"I'm not hiding." I opened one eye. A single eyeful of Kai was enough. "Talking wasn't what I had in mind when I said more fun than a pillow fight, just saying."

"I figured." He rolled his hips into mine, showing me he had more on his mind than talking.

My eyes fluttered closed at the contact while heat gathered in my center. "You can't expect me to concentrate on thinking when you have me pinned to the bed."

"Should I get up?"

"No!" I shouted.

He chuckled as he gently bit the skin at the corner of my jaw.

"Let's make a deal. Less talking now, more talking later." With both eyes open, I attempted to assure him I meant it.

"Deal, but I won't forget." His steely gaze held the resolution of his promise.

"Deal. Now make me forget my name." I pulled his face down to mine.

His lips paused a breath away, and he whispered, "My pleasure."

Our lips pressed together; tongues explored while our hands roamed. I nipped his bottom lip, pulling it into my mouth and sucking. He expressed his approval by moaning and thrusting his hips, rubbing my clit with the seam of his shorts through the thin cotton of my skirt. Besides fucking Kai, my next favorite thing was making out with him like teenagers. Only we never stopped with the dry humping.

I raised my hips, encouraging him to roll over, but instead of following my silent command he pulled my hands above my head again.

"I'm in charge now." He lifted his eyes to meet mine. "Hold on."

My eyes widened with excitement, and I obediently wrapped my hands around the wood slats of the bed.

"Good girl. I've decided you think too much."

"What's your solution for that?"

"I'll do the thinking for the both of us." He knelt and unbuttoned his shirt. The white fabric slowly parted to expose his chest, the ripple of abs below his pecs, and finally, the thin trail of hair leading to Gerhard.

"Eyes up here, sweetheart."

I flicked my gaze to his, then focused it to his hands where he undid his belt. When they paused, I lifted my eyes again. "What?"

"You weren't following instructions."

"But that's my favorite part. It's like Christmas and unwrapping the best present."

Shaking his head, he licked the corner of his lips. "What should I do with you?"

"You could always gag me," I suggested.

"I could, but I enjoy your mouth too much." He stretched down to kiss me, but pulled away before I could extend the kiss further.

I pouted. Clearly, I didn't like giving up control.

He kissed me again and swirled his tongue with mine. He whispered, "Play along and I'll give you everything you crave. Stay still."

I nodded and tightened my grip on the bed. Now completely naked, he spread my legs. An impulse to squirm bubbled up inside me. I wondered if he'd spank me as punishment. Warmth turned to heat.

He stripped me of my clothing, and I lay splayed in front of him, my hands resting above me. While he observed me, I studied his body, memorizing every line and curve. Lost in the sight of him, I squeaked when he pulled my legs down to the edge. He knelt on the floor and rested his hands on my open thighs.

"Beautiful," he whispered from between my hip bones.

Closing my eyes, I sighed with pleasure while he kissed an arc from one thigh to the other. It tickled and teased, driving me to beg.

"Please."

I needed more stimulation. My fingers played with my nipples, tugging and pinching as my hands cupped my breasts. Soon his fingers entered me—first two, then three—turning and curving to hit a place inside of me that made my spine arch. My feet sought traction, needing to tense and brace as pleasure took over while he sucked, licked, and kissed my clitoris.

"Fuck," I said when he curled his fingers and stilled his tongue, pressing down right on the spot, sending me over the edge. He held my legs open when I tried to close them to release some of the pain, which followed such intense pleasure.

While I rode out the waves of my orgasm, he kept his fingers inside, but eased away from my oversensitive clit.

I was legless with bliss.

"Well, that worked." He smiled smugly from between my thighs.

"You're a snake charmer, Hendriks."

"More like a pussy charmer. I'm not done with you yet. Roll over."

His voice held a stern edge when he stood.

I complied, moving to the center of the bed.

"Up on your knees."

I braced my weight on my forearms and curved my ass up seductively.

He slapped me on one cheek, and then the other. A warm tingle replaced the initial sting.

"I love your curves," he said.

I turned to peek at him. His eyes were focused where his hand caressed the swell of my bottom. He stepped over to his luggage for a condom before returning to the bed.

"Head forward."

I liked his bossiness.

I faced forward and waited for his weight to dip the mattress behind me.

The hairs on his legs I'd admired earlier tickled my thighs when he settled himself behind me. I inhaled and held my breath, waiting for the moment he entered me, slowly exhaling when he did.

I tilted forward when he thrust behind me, finally giving into gravity and letting my chest hit the bed. It changed the angle, allowing him to be even deeper when he rocked.

This wasn't slow lovemaking. This was passion unleashed as he pummeled my body with his.

Groaning, Kai pulled out. He flipped me over and entered me again.

Our gazes locked, our breaths mingled. Fighting the temptation to close them and break our connection, I kept my eyes open.

I loved it.

This moment.

This connection between us.

Nothing else existed while we came together over and over again.

Finally, he closed his eyes and arched his neck. A low, guttural groan escaped his lips when he shuddered and stilled. He flopped next to me, pulling me close with one hand while the other removed the condom.

Blissed out and genuinely sleepy, I sighed, resting my cheek on his chest. "I like it when you're bossy."

"No, you don't." He kissed the crown of my head.

I giggled. "I did enjoy it. Even the missionary position at the end."

"You don't always have to be in control, love."

"Mmm hmm."

His chest shook with his amusement. "Trust me."

I stretched backward to gaze into his eyes.

"I know I've given you little reason to with all the revelations, but now you know my secrets."

"All of them?" I raised an eyebrow.

"The biggest ones. The most important parts of me you didn't know." His earnest tone emphasized his words.

"I like knowing your big parts." My nails scraped through the hair below his belly button.

He tightened his abs at my touch. "Not only about sex and body parts, Selah."

I did know, and what I knew scared me.

FIFTEEN

EVERYTHING WAS HOPELESS, pointless, and futile. Okay, the last two meant the same thing, but when Kai and I visited Elmina "castle" prior to returning to Accra, both applied to my emotions. Despite my intellectualizing of places not holding memory, the dark, dank spaces inside Elmina affected me more than I anticipated.

History was messy, ugly, angry, and violent. Rarely was it as pretty as depicted by the paintings hanging in museums.

I cried at the stories told by our guide.

Horror could occupy space, haunting it.

I never wanted to return.

I gasped for air and turned my face to the strong sunlight when we exited the door. Sitting on a bench facing away from the building, I focused on the living taking place around me. To my left, a pair of goats nibbled green grass on the lawn, ignoring the "keep off the grass" sign. A young woman sold trinkets on a small piece of cloth set on the ground at her feet, and two men chatted next to a large tour bus while several children wearing blue school uniforms played tag in its shade.

Kai handed me a bottle of water.

I chugged the warm liquid, and then exhaled. "Thank you."

"It's a powerful place."

I nodded in response.

We sat for a moment without speaking. My usual defenses of snark and humor failed me. I had no words.

He broke through my silence. "You okay?"

I shook my head. "I … I wasn't expecting to have such a strong reaction." I gulped water. "Makes our conversation yesterday an exercise in intellectual masturbation—all my theorizing about place and object."

With a chuckle, he put his arm around my shoulders. "Life does go on, history forgotten." He squinted toward the long fishing boats crowding the water. "Forgotten and repeated."

"What do you mean?"

"Slavery isn't a thing of the past in Ghana. Or anywhere in the world."

I stared at him.

"See the boats?" he asked. "Many of those boys and young men working on them are contemporary slaves or work for little pay. Parents sell their children to the fishermen, who make promises of school and a better life. Instead, they spend their lives on boats, detangling nets and living in fear of beatings."

The boats rocked on the water, their colorful green nets dotted with brightly painted buoys. Small boys scampered around several of them.

"Are you serious?" I asked, unable to comprehend how right under my nose slavery existed in the shadow of a monument of the slave trade.

"One hundred percent," he said, his voice serious.

"How do you know about this?"

"It's my work."

"I thought you were a wealthy banker, suit wearing super power, captain of industry, master of the universe type."

He rubbed his hands up over his jaw and scruff. "I was."

"But not anymore?"

Frowning, his mouth formed a tight line. "Not anymore. I told you yesterday, I've been working to change over the last five years. This is part of it."

I shifted my body to see his face clearly. "What does that mean?"

"Instead of making money for the sake of having money, I focus on using it to do better in the world."

"A modern day Robin Hood?"

He smiled and grabbed my hand. "Kind of. Except the part about robbing the rich. I don't rob them. I convince them to do the right thing, not only for themselves, but for everyone."

"How do you do that?" I asked, stopping myself from imagining Kai's long legs encased by green tights. He'd look hot, and ridiculous, but still sexy.

"Remember the conference last week?"

"On micro-finance?"

"That one. I started TNG's program, along with our Fair Trade policy. We're focused on divesting from companies who have slavery in their supply chains."

"Forgive my ignorance, but does that apply to a lot of companies?"

He laughed, its sound hollow. "You have no idea."

"That bad?"

"Worse."

"This is your life's work?"

"It is now."

"You mentioned pissing off your father. Does this have something to do with it?"

"You caught that?" He exhaled and rolled his neck. "Gerhard was not exactly amused with my decision."

His father, not his penis, I reminded myself.

"Why not?"

"For one, it made him uncomfortable. My life crisis made him examine his own life. At the beginning, I acted pretty self-righteous."

"Drank all the Kool-Aid?"

"Not sure what that means."

"Converts who go full tilt boogie on whatever new dogma they discover."

"Ah, then yes. There may have been an unfortunate vegetarian and hemp phase."

I couldn't help myself; I laughed, loud and inappropriate for the setting. "Did you grow your hair out?"

He brushed his hand over his hair while his lips curved upward. "I did. Even spent three months living at an ashram in India."

"You didn't!" I hit his shoulder with my hand, causing him to tip away from me.

"I did the whole vow of silence thing." He pretended to zip his lips closed.

I covered my mouth with my hand to stifle my laughter. "You are so not a suit wearing Gerhard!"

"I've been trying to tell you this."

"I didn't believe you."

"Evidently."

"But in Amsterdam you wore those suits."

"I had meetings which required suits. I kept some vestiges of my old life."

"You look killer in a suit."

"Now you're sad I'm not a banker?"

In the sunlight, I studied the miniature freckles across his nose and the crinkles from smiling in the corner of his eyes. Banker, do-gooder, it didn't matter. "Not at all. As long as you still occasionally wear a suit."

"Why do I have the feeling you have a thing for costumes?"

"Like Halloween?" I asked innocently.

He stared into my eyes. "Like role-play."

"How did we switch from talking about slavery to role play?" I deflected.

"I have no idea." He cocked his eyebrow at me. "Nice avoidance there."

"I don't think it's appropriate to have that conversation here." I gestured behind us.

"You're probably right."

Kai may have pulled all of his skeletons out of the closet, but I wasn't ready to reveal mine. And certainly not my pirate fetish.

He really would look hot wearing tights.

"Thanks for bringing me here."

"You're welcome."

"And talking me down off the ledge after."

"Anytime."

I faced the white-washed building, saying a quick prayer for the lives changed forever by its existence, including my own.

On the road to Accra, I said, "Now tell me about long-haired, yoga doing, bendy, silent Kai."

AFTER THE EMOTIONAL weekend of facing both Kai's past and Ghana's history, I needed some Selah time. Kai informed me he had to visit the Volta region for meetings for the week. He sweetly asked me to join him, but I declined with a promise to make it up to him when he returned. I spent my days at the museum, working my way through a collection of bronzes Emmanuela pulled for me. In the evenings, I sat inside the sun hut and read before dinner.

Ama checked on me my second evening alone.

"Careful of the mosquitoes, dear girl," she said entering the sun hut. "You might not hear them coming over your ear buds."

I muted the music on my laptop. "I'm taking my meds."

She gave me a motherly look, which basically equaled a frown and sad eyes. "You take care of yourself perfectly fine on your own, but sometimes you have to let others pick up the heavier burdens."

"You didn't come outside to remind me to put on bug spray, did you?" I eyed her with caution.

"Of course, but life isn't one thing and not others." She sat across from me on the long bench.

"No, it's never that simple."

"How are things with Kai?"

"Here we go …"

"You're surprised I'm asking?"

"I'm shocked it took you two days."

Her laughter filled the enclosed area. "I was respecting your need for space."

"You and Kai share boundary issues. He's texted me several times both yesterday and today. I like my alone time and space."

"And Kai likes you," she said, smiling. "And he knows what he wants."

"It's the man who's the issue."

"Don't you like him?"

"I do."

"Hmmm …"

Closing my laptop, I waited for her to continue. She stared into the dark garden for a few moments.

"I'm trying to figure out what the issue is. Give me a clue," she said.

"Besides the lying, and the wife? And the daughter?"

"He told me yesterday he'd come clean with you. Finally."

"He did. Kind of. He told me about Anita and when I met her she mentioned having a daughter."

"And having an ex-wife and child is a deal breaker?"

"They have been in the past."

"Selah, honey, do you really want to be with a man with no past? Not sure there are very many virgins in your age group."

I chortled.

"Right, you'd eat a virgin alive."

"I can't imagine starting from scratch."

"Perhaps a lapsed priest?"

"Probably a virgin."

"True. You could find a nice missionary, one who could be easily tempted into corruption and lust."

I giggled at her suggestion. "That's all kinds of wrong, Ama."

"I'm highlighting your options for a man without baggage."

"I get it."

"Don't let Kai's past define him. He works hard, loves his daughter, and is easy on the eyes." She fanned herself with her hands. "Plus, he's demonstrated he can commit long term. Sounds like a catch to me."

"And the lying?"

"Did he lie, or omit?"

"Aren't they the same thing?" I asked, incredulous.

"Not at all. Have you told him about your lovers and fear of commitment? Or those smutty pirate books you write?" She gave me a pointed look.

I rolled my eyes. "No, but—"

"But nothing. Men become stupid when they fall in love. Boys tease; men do stupid things."

Men weren't the only ones who did stupid things.

"You're not defined by the stupid things you've done, or not done. Don't apply rules and expectations to that wonderful man you won't follow yourself." With a pat to my leg, she stood up and straightened her skirt.

"Gotcha." I pouted.

"Don't stay out here, sulking and getting bit by mosquitoes," she called out, walking to the house.

A telltale buzz near my ear reminded me I hadn't put on bug spray. I tracked the flying insect buzzing around me until it landed on my leg, where I promptly killed it. Ama was right about the nasty little buggers. She was probably right about the other things, too.

I sent Kai a quick email asking about his plans for the rest of the week.

My inbox burst with unanswered messages from Maggie and Quinn. I opened the oldest one and found a picture of Maggie, Gil, Quinn, and Ryan with Lizzy, smiles wide, and in Lizzy's case, drooly. Despite my dislike of babies, I smiled. The joy evident on my friends' faces superseded my cynicism. Lizzy's fat cheeks and dimpled arms reminded me of the little faces in the Kente village. Her life was blessed from birth in ways she would not understand for a long time. If ever.

OVER A BOX of dusty sculptures on the following Monday, I shared my thoughts with Emmanuela about the weekend visit to Cape Coast. Surprisingly, she'd never visited either Elmina or the Cape Coast castle.

"Why do I need to visit a place to know its history?" she asked. "History is carried in the minds and souls of people."

Her words echoed my own thoughts before I stood on old stones in sunless rooms and let my imagination run wild. Not my memories, but the thoughts and ideas my mind conjured up about experiences I never had.

I touched the miniature sculpture in my glove-covered hand, running my finger over her curves and pointed breasts. Picking up my notebook, I wrote down the catalogue number and set aside the sculpture to be photographed.

"Dr. Elmore?"

"Yes?"

"What is it about these sculptures that speaks to you?" She frowned, looking down at an Akuaba fertility figure I'd set aside earlier.

"Humans have the same genitals and secondary sexual characteristics no matter where on the planet we live, yet each culture depicts them differently. Or fetishizes them different, I should say." I pointed at another fertility doll. "This is for fertility, right?"

She nodded.

"Yet what's the biggest thing on the figure?"

"Her head."

"Shouldn't it be her breasts or hips, the typical symbols for female fertility?"

She shrugged.

"Her head resembles the round moon, another representation of fertility, but I'd prefer to think her big brain is the focus."

"And this interests you?" Doubt and confusion tinted her question.

"It does, very much."

"But many of them look silly." She held up a male figure with a long penis pointing vertically down.

"Exactly the same as real humans," I said with a straight face. I held up another fertility doll with a large, round bottom and pointed at my own hips. "See? Even in something fairly abstract, we can find ourselves."

She giggled. "Are your students very interested in your classes?"

"I think most take it to look at naked bodies. A few are serious about studying art, but not many."

"Most people do not realize the importance of museums." She gestured around our cramped workspace, lit from older lamps and a single dusty window high in the wall. "The same as the castles, they're important for our history."

"Even if no one visits them?"

"Yes. We know they exist and the objects exist. That's enough to remind us of our history. We don't need to live in the past to remember."

EMMANUELA'S WORDS ECHOED through my mind while I walked down the road to Kai's hotel. He'd returned earlier in the afternoon and invited me for drinks.

I sat in the shade by the pool, sipping an icy cold orange Fanta with real ice cubes. Entitlement had its perks. A warm hand lifted my hair from my neck and lips brushed the exposed skin. I jumped even though I'd know his touch anywhere.

"Did you think your waiter was acting fresh?" His voice sounded light, jovial.

"The waiter smells of musk and peanut butter." I leaned up to kiss his cheek, but he moved to kiss my lips instead. A week apart had only deepened my hunger for him. Apparently, the same was true for him.

Kai glanced around the patio. "Should I order a drink?"

"Unless you want to skip the drink and go directly upstairs?"

The words had barely left my lips when he tossed too many *cedis* on the table and grabbed my hand, lifting me out of my chair.

Alone in the elevator, he pressed against me, kissing me breathless. His spicy scent invaded my senses. When I reached for him through his pants, he arched his erection into my hand.

"God, I've missed you," I whispered into his neck, nuzzling the curve where it became his shoulder, the place where his pheromones were strongest. "You were wrong, you know."

He buried his nose in my hair. "About what this time?"

"About absence."

Leaning away, he stared down into in my eyes. "It took only a week?"

"A week was enough."

Once in his room, I knelt at his feet, tugging at his belt and unzipping his fly. I hungered for the feel of him, the taste of him on my tongue. He stroked my hair and tucked a strand behind my ear. Lust and passion reflected back at me. I pushed his boxers down over his hips, exposing all of him.

Kneeling allowed my hands to be free to roam and explore his skin. One hand snaked around to squeeze his ass. He moaned and tightened his muscles. My other hand encased his cock at the base, stroking in rhythm with my mouth. I explored him with a single, slick finger, finding the hidden place to drive him wild. Instantly, his fingers tightened in my hair, making me hum at discovering another way I could excite him.

It didn't take much before he warned me, "I'm close."

Heady with the power of pleasuring him, I continued, rather than pulling away, until he stilled and exploded down my throat.

His shuddering breath and unsteadiness on his feet made me smile.

"Where did you learn to do that?" he asked.

"I have secrets of my own." I stood and headed to the bathroom to clean up. I didn't mention Quinn told me about prostates years ago during one of his "how to please a man" speeches over cocktails—emphasis on cock.

He kicked off his pants and boxers, then trailed behind me wearing only his shirt, which he unbuttoned along the way.

"What kind of secrets?" he asked, starting the shower while I washed my hands.

I smirked. "Girl secrets."

"I've told you mine." He pretended to pout while his hands reached for the zipper on my dress.

"And I've shown you mine. Or one of them."

After removing my dress, he slapped my ass. "What are we going to do with you?"

"Have sex with me in the shower?"

"I meant in general."

I laughed and stepped into his oversized shower, away from his swatting palm.

"I have ways of making you share." He towered over me, trapping me against the cool tiles.

"Oh, I'm counting on it." I kissed him, knowing soon it would be my turn to reveal my skeletons.

SIXTEEN

KAI MOVED OUT of his hotel into a rented house shortly after our return. Located inside a gated community, the nondescript house could have existed in Florida, or any other suburban sprawl with a warm climate. Houses of variations on a theme lined a newly paved street, alternating between one and two stories, each with a gated, short driveway and yard. By standards at home, some of the homes even qualified as McMansions. TNG owned the house and provided it for employees during their tenure in Ghana. It would be home for Kai for the next two months.

I kept my room at Ama's in name only, slowly filling a drawer or two in the bedroom at Kai's and keeping a second set of bathroom supplies under the sink. However, my need for alone time hadn't disappeared. When Kai traveled to Volta or other areas of Ghana, I slept in my little room and had dinner at Ama's.

Everything fell into a happy routine.

Until Kai took me to visit the Ga coffin makers in Teshie.

A stranger date never happened.

Unless a dating site for single morticians existed. Even then, would they bring a date to the office, so to speak?

I balked when he told me his plans.

"This is the worst idea for a date. Ever."

"Is it a date?" He grinned at me from behind the wheel of his Rover.

"You asked me to join you, it's a date."

"Excellent point." After parking on the shoulder, he pointed at a row of carnival animals and decorations lined up along the railing of a second story veranda. Past the cheetah, monkey, elephant, and lion, I spotted a shoe.

Shoe?

Carnival shoe?

"Is that a shoe?"

"Yes, it's a shoe."

"Wait! Are those the coffins?"

He grinned. "They are indeed. Come on."

I scrambled out of the car and followed him up the steep wooden steps to the veranda. At the top, rows of fantastical sculptures, I mean coffins, filled the open space. Airplanes, Star beer bottles, peppers, and even a cell phone—each colorful creation designed to hold a body.

"What the actual hell?"

"Not hell, heaven, *Mah mee*," a young man said from his chair in the corner. "These are the best coffins for the best kind of people."

He reminded me of my friend Abraham Lincoln. I blushed, embarrassed he'd heard me.

Kai greeted him with an expert handshake, snap and all. "My friend has never seen these types of coffins," he explained.

Our young guide, Kojo, described how the Ga tribe used these fantasy coffins to represent an aspect of a person's life, believing they helped transport the spirit to the afterlife.

"If you had to choose one coffin, which would you pick?" Kai asked.

"Are we buying my coffin today?" I looked at him from the corner of my eye while Kojo revealed a hot pink satin lining inside of a chicken. "Cause that's really morbid."

"Not if you believe in the afterlife."

"I'm not sure if I do." Talk of death and afterlife sent a shiver down my spine, like someone walking over my grave. I knocked on the wood top of a pepper casket for luck. "What would you chose? Perhaps the black dress shoe?"

"It can also be a vice or a passion, not someone's profession." He opened a beer bottle and slipped inside.

The image of him inside a coffin, even a ridiculous one, sent another cold chill down my spine. If you could taunt the universe, lying down in a coffin had to be one of the biggest no-nos.

"Get out," I whispered down at him.

Opening one eye, he peered up at me, arms crossed in Dracula pose. "I want to suck your blood."

"Stop. Please. Get out," I begged.

Seeing my discomfort, he hopped out of the bottle faster than a genie, engulfing me in his arms and pressing my cheek to his chest.

"Oh, sweetheart. It's silly. It's only fun." He hugged me tighter.

My breath caught in my throat, causing me to hiccup. "I know."

Warm hands rubbed along my back while I composed myself. "I didn't mean to upset you. For the record, I'd never be buried in a beer bottle. Hideous really."

I hit his chest with my fists while he shook with laughter. "I hate you."

"No you don't. If you did, you'd be fine with burying me in a coffin in the shape of a tilapia."

"True. Although, I think a rooster might be more appropriate." I stepped away from his embrace.

The question in his eyes meant he'd missed my joke.

"Because you're cocky."

He grinned, puffing out his chest. "Yes, and for good reason." He rubbed his thumb along his lower lip.

Cursed Dutch charms.

To make up for my panic attack, I bought a model of a pepper coffin for my kitchen. Kai tipped Kojo a few *cedis* when we left.

In the car, he turned to me before he started the engine. "What happened back there?"

My cheeks heated with a blush. "Same thing that seems to happen whenever we take one of your adventures. I got overwhelmed."

"That was it? Are you planning to faint again?"

"I only fainted once."

"True, but you acted woozy after Elmina. I didn't figure you for the fainting damsel in distress type." Beneath the teasing ran an undercurrent of concern.

"Me? Damsel in distress?" I scoffed. I might have snorted for emphasis.

"Maybe you don't see yourself clearly. You obviously need a man to come to your rescue."

Now he was really pushing my buttons. I couldn't decide if I wanted to slap him or kiss him. Or both.

"Maybe you aren't good for me if these things only happen when you're around." Crossing my arms, I stared at him.

The eye crinkles appeared and his lips twitched, fighting a smile.

"Fine," I huffed. "Want to know what happened? You climbed into a coffin and pretended to be dead."

"A beer bottle coffin."

"Still. You can't taunt death that way."

"I wasn't taunting death. Provoking death is doing something dangerous, like skydiving or climbing Everest."

I glowered at him.

"Wait, you're superstitious!" he announced as if he'd guessed the right answer in a pub quiz.

"Am not."

"You are. You, Selah, believe in juju, spirits, and black magic."

"I believe you put something out there and the Universe listens. Even when you're joking."

"Did you have a Ouija board when you were a kid?"

I did, but wouldn't admit it.

"You did. Let me guess, tarot cards in college?"

Damn him. I nodded.

"Aha, you were one of those girls."

"What kind of girls?"

"The ones who flirted with the occult enough to scare themselves and give their black clothing, Goth, club kid vibe some authenticity."

"I was never a club kid."

"But the rest is true. I should have known when you said you hung out in San Francisco."

"Way to stereotype a city."

He started the car. "I have the perfect solution for any bad juju I created with the coffins."

"Where are you taking me now? A graveyard?"

"No, we're going to Kofi's house."

A SHORT DRIVE later, we arrived in a smaller village outside Accra's ring road. Kai stopped to buy a bottle of schnapps at a tiny shop. Outside the store, he phoned Kofi and spoke briefly in a mix of Twi and English.

Kofi's sedan sat parked in the driveway of a yellow stucco house with a mango tree out front. After Kofi and his wife greeted us with handshakes and big smiles, Kai presented the bottle of schnapps. Grace invited us to sit at a table in the shade of the tree, then headed inside. She returned with an older man, who held onto her arm while she slowly walked him over to the table. I couldn't tell his age, but his hair was nearly completely white and his eyes milky in a way that suggested cataracts. His wide smile revealed several missing teeth, but the gaps didn't detract from the joy on his face.

Kofi introduced us to his father-in-law, Solomon, an elder in their village. Even without traditional dress, Solomon created a demand for respect in his colorful short sleeve shirt and faded blue pants, loosely held up by a thin belt.

"*Maa ha. Eti sen?*" Solomon greeted first Kai and then me.

"*Eh ya*," we said at the same moment.

Holding my hand he asked, "*Ye fro wo sen?*"

"Dr. Selah Elmore." I smiled at him and was rewarded by a pat on the arm with his boney hand.

He asked Kai something I didn't understand, which made Kai laugh. "No, not married." Both men looked at me. The older man frowned and Kai's eyes crinkled before he winked.

Winking Dutch. Fuck me.

Please.

Grace brought out a tray with small glasses and a bottle of water.

I leaned over to Kai. "What's happening?"

"I told Kofi you hadn't witnessed a libation ceremony yet. Thought you might enjoy seeing another side of how Ghanaians acknowledge death."

I raised my eyebrows at him. "This isn't a social call?"

"Oh, it is, but one with some ancestors invited to join us," he whispered.

I concentrated my attention on Solomon and Kofi, who explained we'd brought the schnapps as a gift to the family. Solomon held up the schnapps with its elaborate label and bowed his head to give thanks, then opened the jade colored cardboard.

What followed surprised me with its simplistic ritual, seemingly ordinary and extraordinary at the same time. Not unlike giving thanks at a meal, we focused our attention on Solomon, who said a prayer, pouring a meager amount of schnapps into one of the glasses. He lifted it up to the sky and spoke quietly.

Kai leaned over and explained while Solomon acknowledged the spirits of his ancestors, all of our ancestors, inviting them to join us. "He first praises God and the ancient gods of Africa."

Solomon touched the glass to his lips, and then poured liquid on the ground three times ahead of swallowing some.

"And finally the earth, honoring those who have come before us," Kai continued. "Giving blessings to their memories, and in return, asking

151

for their blessings and protection."

Solomon then passed the glass to Kofi, who poured another shot of schnapps into it. Kofi repeated the process, quietly speaking when liquid hit dirt.

Kai would be next, and then me. "What do I say?" I asked, nervous but mesmerized.

"Acknowledge, bless, and ask for blessings." He touched my arm. "Speak to your ancestors as you would a good friend."

If the friend were Quinn, we'd be thinking old school about homies and forties. I wondered about the origins and correlations between the two. I would have to mention it to Quinn and find out if he agreed.

Kai handed me the glass. I'd zoned out and had no idea what he spoke during his turn.

"*Me daa see.*" I thanked him, then took the glass and exhaled to focus my brain away from rappers and gangsters. Clearing my mind, I remembered my grandparents and then Lizzy, picturing her smiling face while laughing at my brain's weird ability to jump from serious to trivial and back. While the dirt darkened with schnapps, I asked for strength and clarity. Finally, I sipped from the communal glass.

Ghanaian schnapps tasted of gin and strong moonshine, not the peach schnapps of my teen years. And it was warm. I forced myself to swallow, knowing spitting out a libation would be frowned upon by not only those present, but by generations of ancestors. My throat tightened, but I managed to swallow it.

After I passed the glass to Grace, Kai poured me a glass of water, which I gratefully accepted. "Thank you," I mouthed.

He rubbed my shoulder, watching me from the corner of his eye.

When Grace finished, Solomon sat down and the conversation turned to my visit, Kai's work, and how the local football teams were playing. I listened mostly, my mind still processing the libation. A handful of chickens scratched at the packed dirt, and a rooster crowed from somewhere behind the house.

Two of Kofi and Grace's younger children arrived home from high school, their yellow and brown uniforms rumpled from their long day. The sun lowered in the sky, and Kofi invited us to stay for dinner. I offered to help and accepted the task of setting the table with Ruth, the youngest daughter. The simple meal of groundnut soup and fufu tasted delicious despite my dislike of peanut butter. Kai laughed at my expression when Kofi translated Solomon's stories of pythons swallowing men whole, complete with instructions for us to sleep with one leg bent if we slept outdoors. I assured everyone it wouldn't be an issue for me.

Standing in the dark outside of the house, we said our lingering goodbyes. Typical of leaving a gathering of family, our farewells circled around to conversation several times prior to sticking. Grace and I hugged, promising to see each other soon. I surreptitiously wiped my tears, suddenly homesick for my parents.

Kai held my hand on the drive to his house. "What did you think?"

"Still one of the strangest dates I've ever had, but it was a lovely day."

"Forgive me for the coffin trick?"

I paused for a moment. "I do, but if you die, I'm not pouring the good stuff on the ground for you. You'll have beer and like it."

He smiled, but didn't turn to look directly at me. "If?"

When, not if. Every one of us would die eventually, but live on in the memories of those who loved us. "Fine, when. Or if you die before me."

"Probably not likely, given you're so much older than me." His reflexes were faster than mine when I reached across to pinch his arm. The car swerved into the other lane while he evaded my fingers. "Hey! Don't distract me." He laughed, but I stopped my assault.

I'd get him back later.

SEVENTEEN

"HAPPY BIRTHDAY, SELAH!" a chorus of voices cheered when I walked into Ama's. Candles and paper flowers decorated our table.

I gaped at Kai, who shrugged, and then at Ama, who grinned.

"How did you know about my birthday?" I asked.

"You gave me your passport to copy when you first arrived in July. I wrote the date on my master calendar."

"Sneaky," I whispered when she hugged me.

"She did the same thing to me in June," Ursula stated, handing me a present wrapped in wax cloth.

"My birthday isn't until November," Kai volunteered. "The fifteenth if anyone cares." He cleared his throat and stared at me.

"Duly noted," I said, walking over to him, letting him fold me into his arms.

"Already on the calendar." Ama grinned.

Kai's fingers drew patterns on my shoulder during dinner while Ursula charmed him, inviting him to visit her project and bring me along. After two full months in Ghana, our motley group had become a family. I counted my blessings. I would miss them after this ended. Nathan and Nadine planned to fly home in early November, avoiding the Saharan Harmattan winds and holidays that typically played havoc with flights.

I couldn't begin to imagine saying good-bye to Ama.

Or Kai.

We had another month together before the "now what" conversation. He'd hinted at returning or extending his stay. Each time, I nodded and responded positively, but vaguely. Eventually we'd find ourselves on the opposite sides of the planet.

"Why the sad face?" Ama asked me.

"Nothing. Birthdays always make me feel a little maudlin." Her question triggered other emotions, and I wiped away the sting of gathering tears from the corners of my eyes.

Kai's arm tightened around my shoulder. "I was kidding about the age thing," he said softly, his dimple deepening with his smile.

"It's not the growing older part. It's silly, really. I've always disliked my birthdays, and the markings of passing time—another semester, another year, another decade."

"It goes by fast," Nathan agreed.

"Too fast," Ursula added.

"There's never enough." Nadine shook her head.

Ama raised her glass and said, "To making the most of the time we have now."

I met Kai's beautiful, fathomless blue eyes and repeated the words. He clinked his glass with mine, and softly kissed my lips.

"What are you planning to do with your final month?" Nathan asked Kai.

I wrapped my hand around his hand where it rested on my shoulder.

"I'll be wrapping up the Volta project. After, I hope to take Selah north to visit the elephants."

I turned to him in surprise. We'd joked about seeing the elephants, but had never made set plans.

"When?"

"Early November. I'll finish my project in October, and then we can take a week, do a mini-safari. For your birthday present," he said, smiling at me.

I sat up straighter and twisted to face him. "Really?" I grinned at him.

He grinned back. "Really. We'll fly to Tamale, then drive to Mole from there. Unless you're jonesing for the two day drive and stop in Kumasi."

"Maybe on the way home?"

"Anything you wish." He kissed my palm.

Ama and Ursula sighed loudly.

"Damn, you two make me want to take a lover," Ursula said, fanning herself.

"Me too." Ama lifted her glass to her forehead and rolled its damp surface across her skin.

"Stop." I laughed.

"I was serious. Kai, do you have a brother?" Ursula asked. "Or a divorced father?"

Kai snorted. "Sorry on both accounts. Although, you could do better than Gerhard. My mother is a saint."

"Darn it. I'll just have to amuse myself with one of Selah's books. I mean, Suzette's."

I choked a little on my water. Kai rubbed my shoulder while I stared across the table at Ursula.

"Who's Suzette?" he asked.

The table stilled, conversation ceased and gestures froze, identical to a game of Freeze Tag. Ama opened her mouth to speak, but I raised my hand first.

"I am."

"Wait, your name isn't Selah?" Kai crossed his arms and raised an eyebrow. "After all of the trouble you gave me over my name?"

I scrunched up my face and tucked a loose strand of hair behind my ear. "Yes, my name is Selah. Suzette's my pen name."

"Pen name?"

"She's Suzette Marquis!" Nadine exclaimed, evidently unable to contain herself.

Kai looked at her blankly. "Am I supposed to know who that is?"

"Not unless you read romance books, especially the steamy ones," Ursula said.

"Is that something you do?" Nathan asked. "Read steamy bodice rippers?" His voice held a level of disdain most men had for the genre, not realizing how vastly improved their sex lives were because of their wives reading habits.

"No." Kai studied me. "You write smutty books?" His eyes twinkled with amusement.

I nodded. "It's one of the things I do—besides being a tenured professor and respected researcher."

"Not only are they smut, but they're about pirates!"

I shot Nadine a look. "Since when are you my biggest fan and promoter?" I asked her.

"I downloaded them to my Kindle." She smiled happily at me.

"Them?" Kai laughed. "How many pirate smut books have you written?"

"First, they're romance, maybe erotica. Second, four are currently published."

"How many aren't published?"

"More." I sipped my beer.

"Nadine, can I borrow your Kindle?" Kai asked.

"Of course."

I rolled my eyes.

Kai leaned over and brushed his lips against my ear. "I can't wait to get you alone, my little secret keeper."

A frisson of excitement sped down my spine, igniting a lust centered between my legs. Damn him and his ways of turning me on with a look or a couple of words.

I whispered, "Bring it. I need to do some research for my new book."

His eyes widened, and he gave me his slow, one-sided smile, which brought out his dimple.

I hadn't written more than chapter notes since he arrived in Accra, the longest dry spell since I began writing novels. He'd been distracting.

However, that didn't mean I hadn't stored away little moments and gestures as research for my next project. My little notebook had become half travel journal, half Nordic pirate smut—a delightful combination.

ONCE WE RETURNED to his house, Kai told me to wait in the living room. Muffled sounds of rummaging and cursing like he'd stubbed his toe filtered out through the closed bedroom door,

"Everything okay in there?" I called from where I perched on the arm of the sofa.

"Fine!" he replied, followed by a heavy thud, which could have been either a drawer hitting the floor or a man falling down.

"Are you sure?"

"Yes!" His voice strained to sound cheerful.

What the hell was the crazy Dutchman doing?

After what I perceived to be hours, but according to the wall clock in the kitchen was less than twenty minutes, all noises and cursing ceased.

"Hello?" I worried he'd knocked himself out with whatever he was doing. Standing, I moved to walk down the hall if he didn't respond.

"Are you sitting down?"

I sat down heavily in the nearest chair. "Yes."

"Close your eyes."

"I hate surprises," I shouted. "Unless you brought me a Mona monkey!" Honestly, I'd kill him if he bought me a monkey, but the idea sounded cute in the moment.

"No monkey. Damn it!"

"Then stay in there."

"Did you close your eyes?"

I hadn't. "Yes."

"Close your eyes and put your hands over them."

Huffing, I closed them and covered my face with my palms. Secretly,

I loved it when he became bossy. "Ready."

The bedroom door creaked opened and the sound of feet on tile echoed down the hall. Even with my hands over my eyes, I peeked, trying to discover his surprise. I caught a glimpse of bare feet standing in front of me. His hands touched my hair when he wound the silk of one of my scarves around my head, over my hands.

"Keep your eyes closed and move your hands."

"You're blindfolding me?" I settled my hands in my lap.

"Of course. Otherwise you'll try to peek."

The scarf blocked out the light. However, if I tipped my face backward, I could peer underneath it. My narrow view held only bare feet and rolled up khakis. Kai gently pressed down on my head. "Stop peeking."

I sighed. "This is the big surprise? You're blindfolding me?"

"It's the beginning. Now stand up and follow me into the bedroom." His hand pulled me up and held mine as he led me down the dark hall. The lights must have been off, because despite my best efforts, I saw nothing through the scarf. He let go of my hand and rested his on my shoulders. "What's the worst thing you can be on a pirate ship?"

Pirate ship? What the ...

"Answer me." He tilted my chin up with his fingers.

"Um ... a thief?" I guessed.

"Close, but no."

"A spy?"

"And what do spies do?"

Ah ...

"Lead double lives," I whispered.

"They do. They lie and keep secrets, too."

I nodded.

"And should be punished."

Aha. I licked the corner of my upper lip. "How should they be punished?"

"You tell me, since you're the expert on pirates, Suzette." He stood closer; his heat radiated off him.

"Well …" I paused to inhale his scent. "They could be flogged. Or forced to walk the plank."

"Seems reasonable to me."

"Do you have a plank inside the bedroom?" I asked.

"No, no plank."

Beneath the scarf, my eyes opened and widened. My breath hitched. I reached out my hands to touch his chest, wondering if he was shirtless.

Before I could make contact, Kai chuckled and grabbed my hands, holding both by the wrist with one of his. "No touching."

I stuck out my bottom lip. "Yes, sir."

"Sir?"

"Captain?"

"Better."

He led me over to the bed and gently pushed me down on the mattress. "Now keep your eyes closed until I tell you."

"Or you'll punish me?" My voice dripped with lust.

His hand slapped my hip. "No talking."

He adjusted me on the bed until my head nestled in the pillows and my arms stretched out to the bedposts where he bound them with scarves. He'd evidently raided my stash.

Once he bound me, he slowly removed the scarf from my eyes.

"Open," he commanded.

I blinked in the low light of the room, slowly focusing on the candles on the dresser and nightstand while my vision adjusted. With one foot resting on the end of the bed in a pose befitting Fabio, my Nordic pirate come to life stood, staring at me. Without a belt his pants hung low on his hips, revealing the V and his treasure trail. As I suspected, he was shirtless. What I didn't expect was the scarf around his hair. Or the eyeliner.

Holy swashbuckler come to life.

I noted every detail about my Nordic pirate, then tossed back my head and laughed, cackled really.

With my hands bound, I couldn't wipe the tears that streamed from my eyes and dampened my hairline. I laughed until my sides hurt. Unable to breathe, the sound of a slowly dying whistle of a tea kettle escaped my lips. When I finally quieted I observed Kai, who kept his pose but laughed along with me.

"Arrgh." He crawled up the bed and over me. "You're the worst pirate wench ever."

I grinned at him. "Are you wearing eyeliner?"

He closed his eyes, revealing his handiwork. "I am."

"Nice scarf."

He removed it with an elegant flourish. "Thank you. I didn't have a lot of time."

"If you had more preparation, what would you've done?"

"Found a parrot at least. Maybe a hook."

My laughter bubbled up again, but stilled in my throat. With the eyeliner darkening his eyes, he looked less like a pirate and more like every Goth and punk rock boy who broke my heart in high school.

"Wow, we've come a long way from the Gerhard I met in Amsterdam." I opened my legs to accommodate his hips, encouraging him to lean into me.

He complied and settled himself, gently rocking into me. The hint of friction made me squirm.

"We have, Suzette."

I rolled my eyes in an attempt to look innocent. "Right. That."

He moved the collar of my dress and nuzzled into my hairline. "That." He nipped the tender skin where shoulder met neck.

"Not something you bring up in regular company, really."

"No, not in polite company." He scraped his teeth along my collarbone, causing me to tighten my legs around his hips.

"It never came up."

"Pirates rarely do." His hand moved to cup my breast, seeking and pinching my nipple. "There was one conversation when we discussed role play."

I moaned when his hand skimmed down my side, and his fingers pressed into my hip, driving me insane.

"Right," I whispered while he undid the top button of my dress. "Well, that conversation was …"

His warm breath caressed the skin of my exposed breast.

"… about Robin Hood."

He rolled to his side to allow his hand room to wander under my skirt. "And?"

I panted and squirmed. "Two very unrelated subjects."

"Are they?" he asked, biting down on the peak of my nipple.

I closed my eyes. "They are."

The last buttons of my dress popped off when he pulled it open. "Oops."

I opened one eye.

"You're not sorry."

"Not at all." His gaze centered on my lace panties. "These we'll save." He tugged them down and off.

"There's something you forgot."

He sat on his knees. "Have I? Pray tell what would that be?"

"You haven't kissed me yet."

His mouth curled up into smirk. "Impatient?"

"Just stating a fact. Pirate books have a lot of kissing."

"Do they?" He supported his weight on his hands in a plank over me, but far enough above, even stretching my neck I couldn't kiss him.

I nodded. "And pillaging."

"Mmm." He skimmed his nose along my jaw, the scruff on his cheek scraping after it. "Pillaging is my favorite part."

"Will there be pillaging now?"

"Maybe," he whispered, and nipped my earlobe.

"Soon?"

A low chuckle rumbled his chest. "I'm having too much fun torturing my prisoner."

I sighed when he lowered his pelvis briefly to mine, only to groan when he pushed off the bed and stood up.

"Where are you going?" I asked.

"To find a gag. You talk too much for a spy."

My mouth dropped open, but quickly I shut it.

Smiling, he shook his head and undid his fly. "I have other plans for your mouth."

My expansive pirate vocabulary for scabbards and timbers danced through my mind while he stripped. Maybe it was the eyeliner, or the candlelight, but he'd never been more handsome. How did this man end up in my life, and how did I end up in his bed?

I didn't have time to dwell when he knelt above me, straddling my chest. With my hands bound, I had only my mouth to pleasure him. I looked up at him, trusting him.

"Now what were you saying about my mouth?" I batted my lashes and licked my lips, then extended my tongue to lick him.

He groaned and leaned down to kiss me deeply, bracing himself against the headboard. Our current position allowed him complete control of the pace and depth. Normally, I hated giving up control of any kind. Yet I trusted him. He wouldn't hurt me.

If anyone would do the hurting, it would be me.

"I love your mouth." He groaned in pleasure. Sliding away from my lips, he reached into the nightstand drawer for a foil packet. A tug on both knots released my arms. With a kiss to each wrist, he made sure I was okay. While he rubbed my skin, he kissed me deeply. Our kiss was sloppy, wet, and perfect. I tangled my hands into his hair and pulled him closer to me, using the momentum to roll us over. My hips lined up with his and my thighs straddled him.

"The thing you should know about my pirates." I held his hands down on the mattress. "The captain is a woman. She's the one in charge and giving orders." I rolled my hips, feeling his erection glide against my slickness.

Kai smiled. "Why doesn't that surprise me?" He thrust against me, the tip of him rubbing my clitoris.

I released his hands and lifted up, guiding him into me.

"It shouldn't." I rocked above him.

His hands came up to my breasts, supporting them while rubbing his thumbs over my nipples.

Closing my eyes, I let myself find my rhythm that would bring me to the edge. I guided one of his hands to where we joined. He pressed a finger against my clit, knowing what I needed.

I slowed and found the angle where he hit my g-spot with each thrust. Hovering in the place between pleasure and orgasm, I opened my eyes, finding his gaze locked on my face. The passion in his eyes pushed me over the edge. With each wave of bliss, I fell for the beautiful, disheveled man beneath me again and again.

Kai grabbed my hips, continuing our rhythm. "Can you go for another?" He reached between us, seeking to extend my gratification.

I could have another. Double Dutch became my new favorite thing.

EIGHTEEN

THE HEADLIGHTS OF the Rover created a narrow path of light along the evening road while we drove in silence. Outside of Accra, few lights brightened the dark night. Even little towns like Somanya settled into almost complete darkness at night, lit only with the occasional bright bulb in a chop bar or roadside business. I leaned against the doorframe and looked up at the stars, letting my hair whip around my face with the warm air while we drove to Accra from a week spent along the Volta River, feeling a million miles from the pollution and noise of the capital. Conversations and events from the weekend clogged my thoughts.

While Kai met with Chinese managers of a local textile factory further north near the dam, I sat in the shade by our resort's pool next to the river and wrote. His stunt on my birthday inspired my writing again. I squirmed on my lounge chair, recalling how he bound me with my own scarves.

Across the pool a loud commotion broke out near the restaurant. Raised voices in English carried over to the pool area. I shaded my eyes with my hand. A large, white man, his face red with anger, stood with a piece of paper clenched in his hand, shouting at the waiter, Simon.

"You stupid, ignorant boy," the American raged at the waiter, who was decades past being a boy.

The waiter wasn't yelling or even raising his voice when he responded.

Whatever had been spoken further inflamed the screaming American. He stepped closer and jammed his finger into Simon's chest. Expletives and spit spewed from the older man's mouth.

What could be so terrible he'd react that way?

I stood and adjusted my caftan, intending to interrupt the verbal barrage.

"No, miss. Do not go over there," Afua, one of the managers, cautioned me. "That man is nasty and will say terrible things to you, too."

My American woman sensibilities told me to jump in and stop what I was witnessing. Afua, as a Ghanaian, on the other hand, let men be men, fighting their own battles. I gaped at both the ugly man and Afua, my gaze bounced between them as if watching a tennis match.

"But ... he shouldn't speak to Simon, or anyone, that way."

"Yes, miss. He is a bad man, but he has nothing to do with us. There is nothing we can do."

I pushed my sunglasses up into my hair. "Nothing?"

She frowned and continued, "No. He will leave and be the same elsewhere. Maybe in his country this is normal."

I studied her face, not understanding how or why she could remain disengaged. The shouting ended with the man throwing *cedis* on the table and floor, then stomping away. When he passed the pool, he made eye contact with me. "No one in this damn country has a brain. It was better when Europeans ran this Godforsaken continent, then things got done and you didn't have to deal with the natives."

I blinked, stunned he'd addressed me as if I'd agree and support him. I opened my mouth to speak, but Afua cut me off with a hand on my arm. She frowned again and subtly shook her head to stop me. Out of respect, I didn't speak my mind to him. In the end, she was right. He'd be an asshole no matter what I said. I turned away, not acknowledging his words with a response.

When I told Kai the story later at dinner, he listened with a sad expression, letting me vent on and on about the rude American.

"I'm sorry you're upset." He rubbed his thumb across the back of my hand where it sat on the table between us.

"Upset? Try infuriated."

"Why?"

"Because he was horribly insulting to Simon and Afua."

"Do you think he's the first foreigner to say those things to them?"

"No," I said, defeated. "I wanted to slap him."

He grinned at me. "I would've enjoyed witnessing that. I'm sure you can hold your own in brawls and bar fights."

"And with ugly *Obruni*."

"Ah, yes. *Obruni* can be an insult, as well as a general name for foreigners."

"I figured." I scrunched my mouth to the side.

He sighed. "Today was an ugly day all around. I hit a wall at the factory—the Great Wall of China. The Chinese completely shut down talks with our group. Very frustrating." His fist slammed down on the table, jostling the flatware and glasses.

I'd never seen Kai frustrated or angry.

"I'm tired of people exploiting others."

"Do you think I'm an ugly *Obruni*?"

"I think you're beautiful." He stilled. "Why would you ask?"

"I've been here for months, but haven't given back or volunteered with orphans or AIDs patients, or even made a donation. Aren't those expected? All I've done is eat and shop, and be a tourist."

Kai sat back in his chair and contemplated me. "Are you feeling guilty?"

"I wasn't. But after witnessing and overhearing that asshole today, I've spent the afternoon wondering if I should be doing more."

"More of what?"

"More 'good work'. Helping people, like the missionaries."

"Missionary work? You?" He smirked. "Saving souls?"

I gave him a sidelong glance. "Given I can't save even myself, no."

"It's an easy hole to be sucked into, deciding everyone here needs to be saved. From what, it depends. Save their souls, save their lives, save their forests, monkeys, rivers … you get the point."

"You forgot the children."

"Ah, yes. Save them most of all."

"Building schools is a noble thing. I could do that."

"Can you use a hammer? Or make adobe blocks?"

Shaking my head, I whispered, "No." I sighed. "I'm hopeless."

"If you're wanting to do something charitable, do it. Don't do it out of some misplaced white, European guilt."

"Like what you do?" My realizations from the afternoon made me feel prickly and defensive.

"You think my motivation is white, European guilt?" he scoffed and crossed his arms, resting his elbows on the table.

"Didn't you call yourself Robin Hood?"

"I think that was you."

"Right, yet you're working for the better good, freeing slaves, or whatever it is you do, out of a sense of honor."

"And you think my work has to do with lingering Dutch heritage in Africa?" His voice lowered and held an edge.

"Maybe."

"You know nothing. I do what I do because it needs to be done."

"It's a big assumption on your part."

"Is it?"

"Afua told me not to confront the American because nothing I said would change him. Made me think really, nothing we do will change anyone or anything."

He rolled his eyes. "Here we go again with Selah's theory of being eternally bound by history." He leaned away from the table. "If everyone was the same as you, trapped in the past, studying musty old sculptures for an exhibit only a tiny percentage of people will see or care about, nothing would ever change in this world. You have to be the catalyst for change."

"Wow." I crossed my arms and gripped my biceps. "Nice to

hear what you think of my work."

"Hey, you were the one who said you should be doing more, something important, while you're here."

"I did," I huffed, glaring at him.

He ran his hands over his hair, making it stick up. It had grown shaggier the past several months.

We sat in stiff silence for a few minutes. Or hours. It dragged out like hours. The tension between us thick and spiky while we stared in opposite directions, neither making eye contact nor speaking. I poured the last of the water from my bottle into my glass, stewing over his words and how they made me feel. I was used to people minimizing my work and writing, but hadn't expected it from Kai.

With his hands resting on the crown of his head and his eyes closed, he finally spoke, "Is this our first fight?"

I waited for him to look at me before replying, "Possibly."

Chuckling, he rolled his neck side to side. "I'm sorry for what I said about the exhibit. It'll be hugely attended and important."

"No, it won't." I joined him in laughing. "But thank you for saying so. I'm sorry for what I said."

He shrugged. "You're probably right. I was spoiled most of my life. A few years don't change my position of privilege."

I leaned across the corner of the table to kiss his cheek.

"What was that for?"

"For apologizing."

"You aren't stuck in the past." He pulled my hand into his lap and entwined our fingers.

I laughed softly. "Oh, but I am. I'm stuck in a past which isn't even my own."

"You don't have to be."

"Be the change?"

He nodded, kissing the inside of my wrist. "Volunteer with Ursula. From what I've seen, the women in the collective mainly sit around and gossip. You'd fit right in."

He caught my hand so I couldn't slap him. "So violent. Afua was right to stop you. You might have unleashed real mayhem."

"I'll show you some mayhem," I said, letting my hand drop to his thigh.

"Will this be make-up sex?"

"I suppose."

He wiggled his eyebrows before turning to find a waiter. "Bill, please!"

FOLLOWING KAI'S ADVICE, I met with Ursula for a late lunch to talk about volunteering.

"Why the sudden interest in helping out?"

"It's not sudden," I defended.

"You've been here for months." She peered at me over her glass. "Did you and Kai break up?"

Laughing, I said, "No. Nothing like that."

"Are you sure? Why the sudden free time?"

"It's nothing bad, I promise. I realized half my stay is over and I need, no, I aspire to contribute with my remaining time."

"Tick tock?"

"A little."

"Why my group?"

I told her Kai's comment about the gossip and she laughed. "That's probably true."

"Honestly? I prefer women over kids. Most volunteering centers around children."

"Kids are terrifying. You should stay away from them for sure."

"Stop mocking me. Kids don't like me."

"I'm sure that's not true." She paused and studied me. "Okay, maybe it is true. You're scary."

I sighed. "So I hear."

"I'm joking with you. I'll bring you to the center tomorrow afternoon if you want."

The next day I met Ursula outside of the workshops for a tour. In a courtyard sat beehive-shaped kilns and molds along with piles of colored glass bottles waiting to be recycled into the glass beads. Under a thatched roof with open sides, women strung beads together to make bracelets and necklaces.

Everyone warmly welcomed Ursula, inviting us to sit and join them. I couldn't follow all of their conversations, but I laughed when I understood the gist of the subject. Kai had been right. They laughed and chatted away while they worked. The sound of their giggling reminded me of book club meetings with girlfriends where more wine was consumed than books discussed.

Quietly observing the group, I noticed a handful of the members were younger women, even teenagers. Shy smiles greeted me, and when I made eye contact with them they would giggle and turn away. I could relate to teenage girls; some days I still felt like one. One girl brought over her bin of beads and elastic to my bench. She showed me how to string the beads and then tie off the ends. My fingers weren't as nimble as the other women, but they encouraged me even after the beads from a bracelet broke free and bounced over the packed dirt of the courtyard.

A couple bracelets made and a wonderful hour spent with the women, Ursula finally dragged me away after the sky darkened.

"You enjoyed yourself?" she asked.

"Very much. When can I return? What can I do to help out?"

Smiling, she said, "Slow down. Come later this week. They liked you. We'll figure out how to use you best."

"My bracelets sucked, didn't they?"

She pinched her thumb and forefinger together. "A little, but I have hope for you."

I had hope for me, too.

NINETEEN

THE HAZY, LATE October sun bounced off the small domestic planes sitting on the hot tarmac at Kotoka Airport. Next to the giant 777s for international flights, they looked miniature and toy-like. Kai had arranged our tickets to Tamale, never telling me the plane flying there had propellers. He crouched when we boarded the minuscule plane. Even with four seats per row, the plane looked tiny by my standards.

"Remind me again how long we have to be inside this tin can?" I asked, taking my window seat.

"This plane is huge compared to ones I've flown in with some of my projects."

"Not helping."

His eyes crinkled. "Under an hour."

"And how long would it take to drive?"

"Thinking of changing our plans?" He stuffed my bag into the tiny overhead compartment. "Driving takes at least eight hours, typically longer."

I tapped my fingers on the narrow armrest.

"Selah?"

"I'm thinking."

He sat down and buckled his seatbelt. "We're not driving there. We'll drive back."

"How? We don't have your car."

"We'll hire one and visit Kumasi." He pecked my cheek.

"If we live that long."

"You're worse than Cibele. She's a much better flyer than you."

Rarely did he mention his daughter. They video chatted often, almost every day. Between us there existed some sort of unspoken rule about talking about her. We didn't. I wasn't sure if it was me or him.

"Thanks for the compliment." I wrinkled my nose at him. "Flying isn't something to be enjoyed. It's a means to an end."

He had the nerve to laugh at me. Interlacing our fingers, he said, "You'll be fine. Think of the views."

Once the little plane settled at cruising altitude, the view over Ghana was gorgeous. The deep green hills along the coast and Volta River faded to rolling, sepia-hued land as we headed north to the arid land closer to the Sahara.

KOFI MADE ARRANGEMENTS for us to have a driver meet us in Tamale and take us the short distance to Mole National Park.

If I had been excited about Mona Lisa, nothing compared to my anticipation about the elephants. To torture me, Kai scheduled a detour for us to visit the ultra-modern looking Larabanga Mosque outside Tamale. Dark spikes protruded from its fresh white stucco exterior, giving it a surreal appearance unlike any mosque or church I'd ever seen.

Cool.

Interesting.

We took tons of pictures.

Not elephants.

Leaving the mosque, I insisted on sitting up front with the driver to play Spy the Pachyderms as soon as we crossed on to the rough, unpaved red dirt road from the main gate of Mole leading into the park.

I scanned the brush and scraggly trees, awaiting a flash of gray or a tell-tale rustle. At one point I leaned so far forward that when Davis, our driver, hit a pothole, my forehead bumped against the front window. Rubbing the sore spot, I reluctantly slumped in my seat and told Kai, who laughed in the back, to shut it.

Davis stopped the car and I panicked, thinking I'd missed my chance to spot the first elephant. "Where? Where?" I shouted, my head turning almost three-hundred-sixty degrees.

Kai and Davis both laughed at me. "No, Mah-mee, not the elephants. Look …" He gestured out his window. "Warthogs."

Warthogs?

Seriously?

I hadn't flown inside a teeny-tiny plane to see warthogs. Still, I leaned over the SUV's console and observed the furry boars with their snaggle-tusked underbites.

"*Hakuna Matata,*" I greeted them with a wave.

"That's Swahili," Kai corrected me. "Wrong country."

"I assumed it was Disney-speak." I turned around to smile at him while he banged his head against his headrest and groaned.

"I'm kidding!" I laughed. "Okay, not the wild gray beasts I came to see. Onward, Davis!"

Davis peered at Kai through the review mirror as he put the SUV into gear and slowly moved forward.

We spotted a few kobs prior to arriving at the park's only hotel. Their elegant horns reminded me of antelope.

Warthogs, five.

Kobs, three.

Elephants, zero.

Davis dropped us at check-in with a promise to return three days later to drive us down to Kumasi and then home to Accra.

Three days for elephants. The odds were in our favor.

Our room didn't compare to Kai's luxury mini-suite or either of our bedrooms in Accra. Or even Ama's.

"Sparse," I said, looking around the bare walls and lack of decor, sniffing the vague smell of cleaning solution and maybe bleach. The king bed looked inviting. Until I sat on it. "Hard."

"Not what you envisioned?" Kai flopped down next to me. Or rather bounced off the extra firm mattress.

"It's fine."

"Uh oh."

I raised an eyebrow.

"I was married long enough to understand 'fine' means 'not fine, not even close to fine'."

"No, really. Three nights. It'll be grand." I gave him my best pageant smile.

"Don't make that face."

"What face?"

"That smile. It's scary."

I took on a serious expression. "Okay. Truth? It's not what I imagined."

"What did you imagine?"

"Tents for one."

"You? Sleeping in a tent?"

"Not a regular tent for camping. One of those safari tents like in *Out of Africa* or on a brochure for game preserves in Tanzania."

"Again, different country. Not Ghana."

"I know, but a girl has her fantasies."

"And you have a wild imagination," he whispered right as he kissed me.

His kisses made me forget about my safari fantasies. Serenaded by the hum of the air conditioner, we made love.

Delightful Double Dutch mind eraser.

"DO YOU HEAR that?" I shoved Kai's shoulder.

"What?" he grumbled from his side of the bed.

"Are you awake?"

"I'm speaking, so yeah, I'm awake. Now." He rolled over and threw his leg over mine.

"Listen …" I waited for the sound to return.

A thump, thump, and then a rustling noise sounded outside of our window. The noise carried over the whir of the air conditioner.

"What is it?"

"I have no idea. That's why I asked you."

Yesterday we fell asleep after sex, missing the prime afternoon viewing of the elephants down at the watering hole. We barely made it to dinner before the restaurant closed. From the thin line of light behind the curtains, it was now morning. And something thumped and rustled outside our window.

"Find out what it is." I pushed his shoulder again.

"Why me?"

"You're the man."

"Seriously?" He rolled his eyes at me before standing and padding naked across to the window. Pulling aside the curtain, he covered his nudity and peered out. "You need to get dressed."

"Are we under attack?" My voice betrayed my alarm. I covered myself with the sheet up to my chin.

"No." He laughed and grabbed his shorts. "Get dressed." Yesterday's T-shirt was pulled on and he stared at me. "Hurry up."

"Let me see out the window." I scrambled off the bed wrapped in a sheet toga.

He blocked me and spun me around to face my suitcase. "No, no peeking."

I dressed with whatever I found first and put on my sandals. "Ready?"

"Grab your phone," he instructed, heading for the door.

"Phone?"

"Trust me. We need photographic evidence."

I found my phone and followed him out the door of our little chalet to the strip of grass separating it from the long row of other rooms and pool.

Only the pool wasn't visible through the elephant.

The elephant who stood mere yards away, pulling up plants with his trunk and stuffing them into his mouth.

An elephant in the garden. Right outside our room.

He turned his wrinkled butt in our direction and his tail flicked side to side, but he didn't seem to notice or mind we were there.

"Quick!" I whisper shouted. "Take my picture with him." I handed the camera to Kai and then posed with my arms out, pointing to my new best friend.

"Okay, now me." Kai's voice sounded almost as excited as mine.

I snapped a picture of his beautiful, smiling face standing next to an elephant's ass.

"This is the best morning ever!" I continued whisper shouting.

"Why are you speaking like that?" he asked, using his normal speaking voice. "You're a very silly woman."

"Shh. Don't scare him away." I faced our breakfast guest and watched him meander down the row of plants, deliberately picking and choosing what to eat. Eventually he moseyed away from the hotel rooms and down the path to the waterhole, his breakfast buffet evidently finished.

Nothing would top that.

Or so I believed.

First day elephant count? Seven.

Suck it, warthogs.

Our afternoon walking safari brought us down to the waterhole where two families of elephants, a few antelope, additional warthogs, and countless birds intermingled. Thankfully, zero crocodiles had been spotted, although they were rumored to lurk in the murky, muddy water. Earlier in the day, another group had a python sighting. Kai and I met eyes, laughing at Solomon's warning. I said a small prayer of thanks, grateful for our room and door instead of a tent.

Later, while we sat on a terrace next to the hotel pool, sipping well deserved beers and watching the sun fade into a pink haze of a sunset, I counted my blessings. A sweet floral scent tinted the ever present faint smell of smoke.

Kai held my hand between our chairs, softly rubbing the edge of his thumb against my palm.

"Do you ever have perfect days? Days you don't want to end so badly it makes you sad?" I asked him, continuing to face the view over the flat plain and the watering hole in the growing shadows below us.

A soft, slow smile replaced his typical cocky grin. "I know exactly what you mean. Today is one of those days for me."

I beamed at him. "Me too. Thank you."

"I love making you happy, Selah."

There was that word. The one we'd danced around for months.

Falling in love was the last thing I expected to happen.

Kai was the last person I expected to fall for.

But I had. Somewhere and sometime over the past weeks, I'd fallen. Hard.

Those butterflies schoolgirls had in their stomachs took up residence in mine.

It was silly.

I didn't do love.

Or butterflies.

Kai kissed my hand. His touch anchored me in the moment. The here of a hazy pink sky and black silhouetted trees. The now of him.

I loved him.

I was screwed.

And not in a good way.

TWENTY

OUR BREAKFAST FRIEND didn't return the next morning. However, while we sat on the patio eating breakfast, a family of warthogs snuffled around the edge of the lawn. They reminded me of dogs—big, bristly, tusked dogs.

On our final morning, I cut my flat, bland omelet into tiny pieces, moving them around the plate, but not eating.

"No appetite?" Kai asked, touching my arm.

I shrugged.

"What's going on?"

What would I confess? My sadness over leaving the elephants? I couldn't believe our three months together were ending? I'd squandered the time and didn't savor every moment with him?

I'd fallen in love with him?

Who said those things over room temperature eggs and watery coffee?

"I miss real coffee," I said instead.

"Okay," he said, drawing out the 'a'. "I don't believe you."

I sighed. "Fine."

"Not fine." He ducked to meet my eyes.

I focused on dissecting my omelet. His hand covered mine and slowly moved my plate out of cutting range.

"I'm sad." I poked the table with my fork.

"I gathered as much." He placed my fork across the table with my plate.

"I don't want to talk about it."

"Are you sure?"

I met his eyes, feeling tears sting. Looking away, I scratched the side of my nose to distract myself from crying.

"Selah," he paused, waiting for me to look at him, "it's okay to be sad."

I nodded. "I really do miss amazing coffee. Hell, I'd settle for decent. I don't think I realized how much I loved it until it was gone."

He narrowed his eyes, but didn't comment. With a deep exhale, he kissed my temple. "I understand."

I moved away from him, dipping my face to swipe my eyes and clear my throat. "When does Davis arrive?"

Kai checked his watch. "Two hours."

"Good. Let's say good-bye to the pachyderms."

"What about the rest of the animals?"

"Fine. I'll say good-bye to the kobs and the birds, maybe even the warthogs, but the baboons who stole my mango? No way. They can go fuck themselves." I jerked my chin in a physical scoff to emphasize my point.

"Silly primates. No one gets between you and a tasty mango."

"Bastards." Anger was an easier emotion for me than sadness.

Kai held my hand as we walked down to the viewing platform. We didn't speak or talk about his departure next week. This time he wouldn't return after a few days. This time there wouldn't be reunion sex. His three months in Ghana were finished.

My funny, brilliant man would be leaving me.

The thought stabbed me under my ribs where my tiny, shriveled heart sputtered.

FOR THE TRIP to Kumasi, I sat in the backseat with Kai, needing to be close.

In my mind, a giant countdown clock ticked away the hours and minutes.

Or maybe it was a bomb, counting down to destruction.

I fidgeted in my seat, unable to find a position that would turn off my brain. We'd been driving for hours along the two lane road running south from Tamale. The sun sat close to the horizon on my side of the car. Unlike at home, the sun still rose at six and set at six. Every day. Now the rains had gone away, each day growing increasingly more arid than the last, but nothing else changed to indicate November began next week.

Davis listened to a Hi-Life music station, but none of us talked. I leaned my head on Kai's shoulder and pretended to be sleepy. He wrapped his arm around me, pulling me down to his lap. I giggled, imagining teenage Kai using this move to receive oral attention.

"You have a dirty mind," he said.

"So do you if you know why I giggled."

His stomach shook with amusement. "Nap. We have a couple hours until we reach our hotel."

I unbuckled my seatbelt and lay across the seat. He stroked my shoulder and down my side, keeping a slow rhythm until my eyes grew heavy. Surrounded by his scent and touch, I fell asleep to the hum of tires on the paved road.

Several consecutive bumps on the road jostled me awake. The car slowed when it drove over them, coming to a halt.

"Why are we stopping?" I blinked and struggled to sit up, but Kai pushed me down against his lap.

"It's nothing. This is normal," he whispered.

Because of the darkness outside, I had no idea of the hour. The headlights of Davis' SUV lit up the shadowy side of the road where an old truck parked ahead of us. I lay still, listening for some indication of why we stopped.

"Put this inside your bra," Kai said, slowly removing his watch.

"What? Why?" I asked, panic settling into my chest as my heart raced.

"Just do it."

I tucked the warm steel into my bra when voices approached the car.

"What do you want me to do, Mister Hendriks?" Davis asked.

"They'll probably ask for a dash." Kai shifted to remove his wallet, extracting a short stack of *cedis* and tucking it beneath me.

Dash? I'd heard of these roadblocks, but had never experienced one. The majority of the time, legit police activity, but sometimes, and often at night, roadblocks were set up to collect bribes—or dashes—from travelers, especially *Obruni*.

A flashlight illuminated the interior of the car. I shielded my eyes from the bright light. Kai reassuringly rested his hand on my shoulder. When the light moved away, it outlined a machine gun strapped over the shoulder of one of the men.

Machine gun?

Holy shit.

"Are we okay?" I whispered to Kai.

Something hard tapped against the driver's window. Davis didn't move to open it; the tapping and voices grew louder.

"Roll down the window," Kai instructed, sounding relatively calm in the face of machine gun wielding men on the side of the road in the middle of deepest, darkest nowhere.

I couldn't understand a word of what passed between Rambo and Davis, but Davis turned off the car, silencing the radio.

"These good men have asked to see your passports, *Pah Pah*." Davis used the familiar term of honor for Kai.

I sat up, adrenaline coursing through me.

Kai tapped my shoulder. "Take the passports out of your purse."

Inside the bag, I located the documents by feel, never taking my eyes from the armed man standing a few feet away. Kai took them from me and slipped half of his stack of *cedis* between the pages, then passed them to Davis.

From my position, I couldn't see what the man did with the passports or the bribe. He said something additional to Davis, who turned and frowned at us. "Mr. Hendriks and I have been instructed to exit the car."

"What's happening?"

"I don't know, but we should probably do as they say," Kai said.

"Are you kidding me? You're going out there with those men and their guns?" I asked, my voice screeching.

Kai kissed my forehead. "I'm sure it's nothing." Unbuckling his seat belt, he moved to open the door.

"Have you ever had to get out before? At a security check point?"

"No, but there's nothing to worry about."

Reports of random armed robberies came to mind. "What if this isn't an official roadblock?"

"I guess we'll find out in a minute." He opened the door. "Stay in the car."

I protested, fear icing my blood.

"I'm serious, Selah. Stay inside the car."

Helpless, I watched Kai and Davis walk to the front of the car where two men with machine guns flanked them. The headlights shone on the foursome, creating a terrifying tableau from my viewpoint between the front seats. Rambo used his machine gun to gesture, carelessly sweeping it from Kai to the front of the car and back. Inside the silent car, I couldn't make out what Kai said to him, only that he lifted his hands, palms up.

Was he defending our innocence? Against what charges?

The uniformed man to his right spoke to Davis, who appeared to translate for Kai. Kai's eyes met mine over the hood of the car, our gaze locked for a second as the end of the machine gun swung along the bumper. I couldn't read his expression when he bent down and out of my line of sight. Davis also bent forward and disappeared, leaving only the two uniformed men standing, their guns held in their hands.

I scrambled inside my purse for my phone to call 911.

My breath caught in my throat.

Did Ghana have its own version of 911?

I held my phone and prayed, closing my eyes and calling upon God, Buddha, Jesus, Mary, and anyone who had any power to help.

Please don't take Kai from me. I love him. I love him.

I love him.

My chest hurt from holding my breath. I exhaled and gulped air, waiting for the sound of machine gun fire.

Blood rushing inside my ears partially muted the voices approaching the car. I froze.

Where they coming for me next?

A thousand horrible things flashed through my mind, each more terrifying than the next.

I covered my face with my hands and peered through my fingers.

Kai and Davis stood in front of the hood, shaking hands with Rambo I and Rambo II.

What happened?

How were their lives spared? Did they beg?

I clung to Kai when he sat down next to me, tears pouring from my eyes.

"Shhh, sweetheart." He wrapped his arms around me. "Shhh, why are you crying?"

Davis started the car, shifting into gear while we rolled over the last of the speed bumps.

"I thought you were about to die. Both of you." I choked out the words.

"Oh my love, no. No," Kai whispered against my hair.

I sobbed against his chest. "I couldn't lose you. I didn't know what to do."

"Shhh. It's okay. You won't lose me." He tightened his hold on me, pulling me across his lap.

"But I will. You're leaving and everything will be over." I wiped my cheeks with my palms. "What happened there? How did you escape?"

"Escape?"

"From the armed robbers?"

"Oh, sweetheart." He chuckled. "It was a security checkpoint, not robbers."

"I didn't see a booth."

"The truck blocked it."

"But they had guns." I sniffled.

"Most have guns."

"And they made you kneel in front of the car at gunpoint."

"Is that what has you so upset?"

I nodded.

"They pointed out some damage to the underside of the bumper. It's hanging loose and could fall off soon."

All that for a loose bumper?

"Why did you take off your watch if you didn't think we were about to be robbed?"

"Because if they saw my nice watch, they may have asked for a bigger dash. Same reason I took out only some of the *cedis* from my wallet."

I leaned away and took a shaky breath. "We were never in mortal danger?"

Kai shook his head, his lips pressed together. "No, no mortal danger."

Feeling foolish, I shifted off his lap. "Oh."

"Come back." He tugged me closer to his side.

"I overreacted."

"Not at all."

"I thought about dialing Ghana 911."

"What's Ghana 911?"

"Emergency services."

His lips twitched.

I rolled my eyes. "You could have told me everything was okay."

His smile broke free. "I did. I said it was nothing."

I pressed my hand over my heart, willing it to calm down. "I believed we were all about to die."

"We weren't. I'm ninety-nine percent certain of it." He kissed my forehead and then my cheek.

Sighing, I rested against him.

"You won't lose me," he repeated. "I promise."

TWENTY-ONE

OUR RETURN TO Accra marked the beginning of the end, and in some ways the end of the beginning.

At dinner with our little group, Kai relayed the story of the checkpoint. Ama gave me one of her half hugs from her chair next to mine. It was too soon for me to find the humor in my overactive imagination and overreaction, but the others had no qualms about chuckling at my expense. Kai gazed at me with nothing but affection—only his eye crinkles giving away his suppressed amusement.

Tonight was our final group meal before Nadine and Nathan flew home.

My months with Kai now measured days and hours. I didn't attempt to quantify our remaining time any more than that. It hurt too much.

After the roadblock incident, or as Kai jokingly called it "the night we almost didn't die," he'd tried to soothe my jangled nerves by making love to me in Kumasi. Not for naught, but I couldn't turn off my brain enough to relax and enjoy it. I considered faking my orgasm to reward his efforts. Instead, I admitted defeat and assured him he could make it up later. I tried to fuck the fear out of my heart. It had worked for me many other times in my life, but failed me the night in a random Kumasi hotel. For some a near death experience drove them to sexual madness. I reacted by becoming frigid.

He held me after, spooning me. With his nose nuzzled behind my ear, his breath steadied and slowed.

I counted the ceiling tiles.

We needed to talk.

I dreaded saying those four words to him.

Nothing ever good came from those four words.

Now we sat amongst our friends, and I worried I'd missed my chance.

We raised our glasses in toasts to Ghana, to friendships, to staying in touch. I learned at twelve—after my first summer camp experience—that these pledges were rarely upheld. Still, I clinked my glass with others.

When the dishes were cleared, Kai softly spoke near my ear, "Let's get out of here."

Saying good-bye, I hugged Nadine tightly and shared an uncomfortable hug with Nathan. I willed myself not to cry and failed miserably. This was the end of our summer camp.

"I'll email you soon," Nadine promised.

I gave her a watery smile. "You better."

With a final wave, Kai put his hand on the small of my back and guided me away from the group. His hand felt beyond familiar now. It was part of me.

My breath caught when sadness laced through me.

"I'm sorry you're sad to say good-bye to your friends." He consoled me.

Sorrow added up to one percent of what I was experiencing. "How do you adjust to it?"

"Saying goodbye? I don't. Not really." He softly smiled at me. "Some are easier; some are more 'see you later' or soon. Others are forever, but you don't realize it at the time. Those hurt later when the truth becomes clear."

I sighed.

"We don't know when those forever good-byes will happen most of the time. Yes, if someone is dying and you visit them, you have closure. But life's funny. Often it's only after time passes when you realize something was the last one."

"For example?"

He pressed his lips together. "A simple example is a favorite restaurant you don't visit often. One night you decide to return, only to realize it closed a month ago."

I nodded my agreement. "Tonight was our last meal with everyone together."

"For now."

"But after tomorrow, some of us will be gone."

"True, but you never know if our paths will cross again."

"Okay, this was the last dinner with everyone together in Ghana."

"That's true."

His words didn't soothe me.

"And for us?"

"We'll have dinner again tomorrow night. And the three nights after."

I turned to gape at him and stopped walking.

He paused mid-stride.

"What?"

"You're so casual about this?"

"About what?"

"Argh! Are you being deliberately obtuse?"

"Are you finally ready to talk to me about what happens when I leave at the end of the week?" He glowered at me.

"Me?" I raised my voice.

"Yes, you."

"But you're the one leaving."

"I am aware of that. And you're the one avoiding any discussion of what comes next. Or feelings. Or anything other than what's happening today or tomorrow." He crossed his arms and leaned against his ancient Rover.

I huffed and crossed my arms.

He held up his hands. "I'm not saying anything you wouldn't agree is true if you would stop being defensive for a minute."

My eyes gave him a death stare. He might be right, but that didn't mean I would admit it. "Fine."

"I hate that word."

"Fine, you want to talk, let's talk, but not standing outside of the hotel."

He opened my door for me. "After you." His voice held an edge.

"Thank you." I climbed into the front seat and sat on my hands.

Judgement day was upon us.

I STOMPED INTO Kai's house, acting like a child. My defenses stood ready for a fight and brought along my hackles.

"Why are you pissed?" he asked, stalking after me to the living room.

"I'm not pissed."

"Then why are you acting like it?"

"I don't know!" I shouted.

"Okay, that makes sense." He walked into the kitchen. "Water?"

"Sure."

I flopped onto his couch and closed my eyes.

His weight shifted the cushion next to me.

"What if this is our forever good-bye? And we don't know it?" I asked, not brave enough to look at him.

His long, slow exhaled breath brushed across my arm.

I kept my eyes closed.

"Selah?"

"Yes?"

He moved closer to me. "Not opening your eyes doesn't make anything disappear."

"I had hoped for invisibility."

"That's not working either." His finger trailed along my arm.

Each hair stood up and begged for his touch. I sighed and peeked at him with one eye. "I'm out of my comfort zone."

His brow furrowed, and he stared down at his hand. "Me too."

"Really?"

He dipped his head. "Really."

"What do we do now?"

"We talk."

I scrunched up my nose. "That sounds very adult and mature of us."

"I tried it your way, and look where it got us."

"My way?"

"Deny and deflect."

"Oh. Right."

"Want me to go first?"

Did I? What if he told me he loved me? What if he told me this was a fling and thanked me for a good time?

Which would be worse?

"No!"

Startled by my vehemence, he blinked at me. "Okay, then. Talk."

I could talk only if I didn't lose myself in his eyes, so I stared across the room at the black TV screen. "Where to begin?"

"How about the beginning?"

My gaze skittered across the wall. "Well, when I was fourteen I had a crush on a boy named Mike."

"I didn't mean ancient history."

I tossed a throw pillow at him, which he caught easily. "It's important stuff."

He relaxed into the corner of the couch. "Okay, tell me about this Mike guy."

"Huge crush. He looked like Robert Smith—angst and red stained lips." I sighed.

"Maybe you still have a crush on him." Kai sounded annoyed.

"No, not at all. Everyone, including him, knew I had a crush on him. I acted sappy and lovesick around him. Doodled his name on my books and listened to The Smiths over and over while I pined for him."

I glanced at Kai from the corner of my eye. He waved me to continue.

"Two years later—"

"You crushed on him for two years?"

I nodded. "Ridiculous, I know."

"Okay. What happened?"

"Two years later we were at a party, and thanks to some help from Strawberry Hill—"

"What's Strawberry Hill?"

"Seriously? You didn't drink Boone's Farm at boarding school?"

"We drank beer from cans and cheap whiskey."

"Strawberry Hill is a strawberry flavored booze for teen girls that tastes like Jolly Rancher candies. Although I'm positive that's not their official slogan."

"Sounds terrible."

"I have a certain nostalgia for it."

"Is this important?"

"It is. Quit interrupting. Thanks to the booze, I threw myself at Mike."

"And?"

"We had sex."

He raised his eyebrows. "Just like that?"

"Pretty much. From the red lipstick stains on my chin, nose, cheeks, neck, and lips, there had been a lot of sloppy kissing, too."

"You don't remember?"

"Not a lot. It's vague and fuzzy. The actual event took place in a random dark bedroom and ended pretty quick."

Kai grumbled.

"I was fine with it. I'd wanted to lose my virginity ever since *Sixteen Candles*. And Mike was the boy I'd loved from afar for years. What could be better?"

"Did he love you back?"

"Not so much."

"What a jerk." Anger clouded his voice.

"Thank you for your misplaced chivalry." I smiled at him and continued, "Since we had done the deed, I figured he reciprocated my feelings, and it meant we were a couple. I floated home, little pink puffy hearts dancing around me. Monday morning I waited for him to stop by my locker. Or come sit with me at lunch. Or meet me after class."

He growled. "Let me guess. He didn't?"

"Nope. In fact, he stopped speaking to me."

"What a loser."

"I know that now, but back then, I was humiliated. Everyone knew we'd hooked up at the party. Right then and there I vowed to never confuse sex with love again."

"You were sixteen."

"I know."

"And you've stuck by that ever since?"

"Pretty much."

"You've never been in love?"

"I wouldn't go that far." I glanced across the room. "I learned life is easier if you don't allow yourself to be swept away."

"Easier, but empty."

"Maybe." I shrugged.

"What does this story have to do with us?"

I stared at him, willing him to understand so I didn't have to say it out loud.

His eyes met mine, and for five breaths he studied me. The crinkles appeared and his cocky smile dimpled his cheek.

"Oh."

"Oh," I echoed.

"Well, then." He rested his arm on the top of the couch.

I waited for him to speak, my heart racing and my breath shallow.

"I don't really see how we have an issue."

I quirked an eyebrow at him. "We don't?"

"None I can see."

"Fill me in."

"I love you, and you love me," he said without pretense, the same way someone would say the sun was shining or the time was eight o'clock.

I blinked at him, my mouth hanging open.

"That's it?" I asked.

"It's not all of it." He paused. "But it's a big part."

I managed to close my mouth. Crossing my arms, I huffed at him.

"What now?"

"That, Gerhard Kai whatever-your-middle-name-is Hendriks, was possibly the worst first I love you ever."

"I don't have a middle name." He grinned at me.

"That's not the important part!"

Tucking his knees under himself, he crawled over to my side of the couch. I leaned into the cushions when he rose over me. Shadows darkened his eyes into deep gray when he lowered his face closer to mine. I held my breath.

"The Dutch word for love is *liefde*."

I slowly exhaled. "Liefde. It kind of sounds like life."

He nodded. "Funny that."

"Funny," I whispered.

"I love you, Selah, my liefde."

My audible gasp filled the space between us. I stared up into his eyes, seeing nothing but love and passion in them.

"I love you."

I didn't say "too" because I would love him even without knowing whether he reciprocated. I loved him without expectation. I loved him.

TWENTY-TWO

IN MY LIFE, there had been good sex and bad sex. Sex with mind-blowing orgasms and toe curling pleasure. Times where getting off trumped everything else. Moments when the day's to-do list was written during the act.

Making love with Kai required its own separate category.

We'd had mind-blowing, toe curling, spine arching, put a porno to shame sex over the past three months. Looking back, we'd also made slow, easy love.

After saying "I love you" Kai scooped me off the sofa like I weighed nothing. Or was at least a much smaller woman. I protested, and he silenced me with a deep kiss. The man's strength and multi-tasking abilities left nothing to be desired.

He dropped me on the bed and stood gazing down at me.

"What are we going to do with you?"

"Make love to me?"

"Of course, but I meant in general."

He traced up my inner calves, parting my legs when he reached my knees, gently shoving the fabric of my skirt out of his way while his hands moved over my thighs.

I let my head fall back, reveling in his touch.

"I'll miss this." He kissed the soft skin of my inner thigh.

"It will miss you, too."

"And this." His fingers skimmed the lace edge of my underwear.

"So much." I squirmed when he slipped a finger underneath.

Lifting his eyes, his gaze locked with mine for a few beats of my heart.

His hand snuck below my shirt, gliding across my belly until he reached my bra.

"I can't bear to be apart from these." He cupped a breast

"Their longing will be unbearable," I moaned.

Without pretense or haste, he stripped me bare, and I did the same for him. My hands memorized his warm skin, marking each angle and dip of muscle and bone. I licked and tasted him, filing away every detail: his salty skin, his sweet, vaguely minty kiss. The skin behind his ear held his Kai pheromones—I could live inside that small patch of him for days. Other parts of him smelled musk, deep and pure man.

We lay together, tangled up in each other, our lust quiet for the moment, lost in our bubble. He buried his nose against the crook of my shoulder and placed a kiss there. I loved his lips. He reached out his arm and tore the condom foil with his teeth. I loved his teeth. I watched his nimble fingers ready himself. I loved his fingers. He rolled over me and aligned himself. I loved his weight on me. Silently, he entered me, inch by slow inch until his pelvis rested flush against my thighs. I loved the way he filled me.

I wrapped my legs around his hips and my arms around his ribs, wanting to consume him and never let him escape. The futility of desire washed over me while we moved together, rocking into one another with no space between where he ended and I began.

This wasn't about seeking release or even pleasure. Each gesture held the weight of our love and the coming loss. Heavy, so heavy, our eyes held emotions our kisses tried to soothe away. My eyes closed, seeking to avoid revealing my fears.

His mouth sought mine, licking and nipping. I wove my fingers into his hair, pulling enough to flirt with pain. He responded by sliding his hand around the nape of my neck and grabbing my hair. The pain focused me on the moment, taking me out of my thoughts. I opened my eyes. He arched over me, towering above, pressing me down and claiming me. Over and over our eyes met, then closed with the knowledge time wasn't in our favor.

On the fringes of perception, my orgasm began to escalate. I moved my hand between us, finding my clitoris and pressing down. Kai increased his thrusts while we sought simultaneous pleasure. He stilled and his release set off mine. I closed my eyes, relishing the pure contentment pulsing through me.

We had now. We loved. There was no promise of forever.

I wouldn't say I saw God that night, but angels might have sung. Or wept.

WITH KAI CURLED around me, his hand splayed across my stomach, the drama of last night faded with the morning light.

I'd had lovers before him. Many lovers. With no regrets.

Okay, a few.

But I'd never had love.

Not the emotion which crashed over me, causing my heart to clench. I gave into the undertow and let it pull me away from safety into its depths.

He loved me.

I loved him.

Such simple concepts.

He stirred behind me. I rolled my head on the pillow to look at him.

"Morning." He kissed my shoulder.

"When did you realize you loved me?"

He nipped my shoulder and rolled his hips against my butt. "Does it matter?"

"No, but I'm curious."

His hand came up and cupped my breast while his scruff tickled the skin of my shoulders. "I followed you to Ghana. That's everything you need to know."

I rolled over to face him. "You didn't love me in Amsterdam."

"No, but you intrigued me as no other woman has."

I smiled affectionately at him. "I do?"

"Mmm hmm." He bowed down to kiss the swell of my breast. "You're both the most fascinating and frustrating woman I've ever met."

I moaned when he nipped the skin near my nipple. "I'll take that as a compliment."

"You should." He brushed his whiskers across my chest, making me squirm. His hands held me so tight I couldn't escape his slow torture. "And you?"

"Me what?"

"When did you stop resisting my charms and fall in love with me?"

"My birthday."

He paused and chuckled. "All it took was dressing up as a pirate?"

I laughed. "Not the dressing up as much as the willingness to do it. I accepted I loved you when you almost got killed on the road to Kumasi. I prayed for you."

He lifted his eyes to mine. "You prayed?"

I slowly nodded. "To God and Buddha and a couple others. I figured I'd cover every base with Team Divinity."

"What am I going to do with you?"

I gave him the same answer from yesterday. "Make love to me."

THE THING ABOUT amazing sex was it could make you forget your name and lower your IQ temporarily, even make you forget, momentarily, about impending doom. If the zombie apocalypse ever happened, I would be the one having sex to distract me from reanimated corpses, not running through dangerous woods or venturing out of my bunker.

Sadly, after our morning in bed, in the shower, and again in the kitchen, we had to address the elephant in the room. The imaginary elephant. We didn't bring one with us from Mole. Sadly.

Standing at his kitchen island, making lunch with CNN on in the background, he brought up the inevitable.

"As you know, I'm leaving on Thursday for Kenya."

"Shh. Don't remind me."

He bumped my hip with his. Or given our height difference, he bumped my waist.

"I'm leaving, Selah. That hasn't changed."

Sighing, I jumped up to sit on the counter. "Okay, if you insist. Kenya. Thursday."

"Yes, and after there, I need to fly to Chicago for Thanksgiving with Cibele. Anita goes overboard with the meal. It's her favorite holiday, surprisingly."

"Should I be jealous you're spending the holiday with your ex-wife?"

He shot me a dirty look. "No. If it weren't for my ex-wife, we wouldn't be together."

"True." I stole a piece of chopped pepper from his pile. "I should send her a card. Or a basket of cookies as a thank you."

"I'll let her know."

"Why do you think she told me to call you? I mean, other than I'm super-hot and smart, and had location desirability."

He slapped my hand away from another pepper piece. I dodged him and tossed it in my mouth.

"She hated to see me alone."

"You had women fawning over you at the auction reception. How alone could you have been?"

"I didn't lack for company, but I was lonely." He held a pepper up for me to bite.

I frowned, imagining him always traveling alone. "It's weird she wanted to play matchmaker, though."

"Are you complaining?"

"No." I swiped another pepper.

"If you don't stop stealing food, there'll be nothing to eat for lunch."

"Fine." I grinned at him.

He rolled his eyes. "You're focused on the past again."

"I am?"

"Yes, trying to figure out the whys and hows of us together instead of facing the future."

"Okay, true. Thanksgiving brings us to three weeks. Then what?"

"That's up to you. When are you scheduled to fly home?"

"Second week of December."

"You could change your flight and come to Amsterdam."

"I promised my family I'd be in California for Christmas. They've been giving me grief over email about my sabbatical and being away for six months, especially my brothers and their spawn."

"Hmmm," he said.

"Hmmm?"

"I promised Cibele Christmas in Amsterdam this year."

"You want me to meet your daughter?"

"Of course. She'd love you. And you both love Robert Smith." He winked at me.

I blushed over my stupid Robert Smith lookalike story. "Why did I tell you such a ridiculous sad sack story?"

"You were emotionally open and vulnerable." He kissed the tip of my nose.

"Right. Remind me not to do that again."

"Never. I love your soft side." His hand moved near my middle.

"Do not poke the belly!" I squirmed away from him.

Laughing, he held up his hands in surrender. "So ticklish."

"I'm thinking Christmas sounds complicated. Where will you be in January?"

He wrinkled his forehead. "I'm not sure."

"You don't know where you'll be in two months?"

He shook his head. "Nature of my business. It's flexible, but difficult to make plans."

"I'll return to teaching in January. In Portland. The one in Oregon," I clarified.

"I'll come to you, then. I've never been there. You can show me the best places. Introduce me to the local customs."

"Or tie you to my bed and never let you leave the house."

His laughter made me laugh. "That works, too."

I reached up and tugged him down to me by his neck. "I'm not kidding."

His kiss told me he wasn't either.

OVER THE NEXT three days, I lost track counting my orgasms.

I filed each one away for future alone time.

Who needed porn when I had memories of Kai to revisit?

After the sun set Wednesday night, we joined Ama and Ursula for dinner.

Another last dinner.

In a little over a month, it would be my turn for a last supper.

How depressing.

I rallied and smiled throughout the meal by focusing on my tender body after our three day love-fest. Crossing my legs brought out a new ache, reminding me of our session standing in his shower. I even had bruises on my hips where he'd pulled me against him.

Cataloging the physical evidence of our love distracted me from the painful bubble resting inside the middle of my chest.

When not eating, I held Kai's hand. He rubbed his thumb along my palm in that soothing way of his. I concentrated on the touch and the energy warming my skin at the point of contact.

I didn't count the hours or minutes until morning.

I listened to the conversation around me, adding a chuckle or an affirmation when appropriate. I had no idea what they discussed.

I pictured how pretty Amsterdam would be at Christmas with holiday decorations and lights reflecting along icy canals. I wondered if it snowed.

While I sat, dwelled, and imagined, dinner finished.

The last dinner ended.

The final good-byes were spoken.

It was over.

We'd run out of hours and tomorrows.

Kofi drove us to Kai's place. With a promise to return in the morning, they wished each other well.

Inside the house, every sign of Kai had been packed away, returning the space to its neutral rental decor. On the bedroom floor, his luggage sat stacked in the corner—too few bags for the months he spent here—an entire life stuffed into suitcases.

Despite my best efforts to not cry in front of him, my eyes filled with tears. Over the past week, I'd moved my things back to Ama's. Besides the linens, which smelled of sex, and a couple of towels, there remained no sign of us—no proof we'd lived and loved in these now empty rooms.

Nothing tangible existed to touch and memorialize our love.

No talisman for me to cling to instead of him.

I sat on the rumpled bed, the linens balled and tossed into heaps from tangled limbs.

I lay in the mess, inhaling and closing my eyes.

When I opened them, I spied him leaning against the dresser, watching me. He ran his thumb over the corner of his lower lip and stalked over to the bed.

"What's going on inside of that big brain of yours?"

I blinked away the tears and sat up. "Memorizing things."

"What sort of things?" His hand swept my hair away from my face.

"Everything."

With a small, sad smile he reached for me, tugging me down with him to lay across his chest.

"Kofi will arrive before dawn tomorrow."

"I know," I whispered. Saying it out loud would make it true, but whispering meant it only existed as rumor.

"This isn't the end, this isn't forever," he said, his voice thick with emotion.

I cleared my throat. "It might be. We won't know until it isn't."

"Selah," his voice hitched. "You're one of the best things that has ever happened to me. I never expected you, yet here you are."

Hot, wet drops slid down my face. I tried to speak and tell him the same, but my voice stuck in my throat. My chest heaved while I attempted to hold it together.

He clutched me closer and let me cry. His own chest trembled. I couldn't bear him crying, so I closed my eyes and sniffled my own tears.

"Damn you."

A low sound rumbled through his chest. He was laughing.

"Damn you," I whispered.

"You curse at me a lot, don't you?"

"When you laugh at me, yes." I wiped my cheeks and below my eyes with my hands. "I'm having a moment, and you're laughing."

"I'd rather laugh with you than cry. Always." His kissed the top of my hair.

"Can we promise not to say good-bye? It feels permanent."

"What should we say instead?"

"Nothing. Can I ask a favor?"

"For you? Anything."

"Don't wake me in the morning. Let me stay asleep. Please?" My voice shook. "I'll wake up and think you've gone on one of your short trips to Volta. If I don't witness you leaving, I can pretend you didn't break my heart."

"Oh, my love." He tipped my face up to look into my eyes. My chin trembled, and I didn't try to hide the tears streaming down my face, or my pink nose. "I would never break your heart. Not intentionally."

I bobbed my head. If I opened my mouth, the ugly crying would begin. Instead, I kissed him.

"I love you," I mumbled against his lips

"I love you," he repeated, wiping my tears. "Don't ever doubt it. Don't ever regret loving me."

I gulped a breath and shook my head. "Never."

TRUE TO HIS promise, Kai slipped out of bed and into the dark morning. I woke at the sound of the front door clicking closed. My heart screamed at me to run out and say good-bye, and kiss him one last time. My mind kept me in bed, snuggled into the warmth, surrounded by his scent, eyes closed for as long as possible.

Finally, my bladder revolted and pushed me into the bathroom.

I love you. Always.

Written on the mirror with soap, his final words made me smile.

I ran to my bag in the living room to find my phone to take a picture.

A miniature wooden elephant sat atop my purse with a note:

Never forget.

TWENTY-THREE

KAI TEXTED ME when he arrived in Nairobi.

I replied with a picture of his message on the mirror.

That was almost a week ago.

He warned me his communication would be infrequent during this part of his trip. There was something else about Jeeps, the UN, and radio silence.

I didn't worry.

At first.

To distract me, Ursula invited me to the women's cooperative every afternoon. My beading still sucked, but I enjoyed their company and stories. It was easier to listen and not have to talk. The silence allowed me to wallow.

"You're worse than a lovesick teenager," Ama chastised me over dinner one night.

"I feel like a teenager," I said, pushing my *jollof* around my plate, but not eating. The spicy aroma I'd come to love repelled my appetite.

"You need to eat."

"I'm hoping one of the side effects of lovesickness is weight loss."

"You'll see him again. Kai always returns."

"I haven't heard from him in a week."

"He'll come back. Trust me."

Unable to stand my own company, I invited Emmanuela to join me on a short trip to Aburi to visit the woodcarvers.

While Kofi's car climbed the steep hill up to the little village, I stared out the window at the hazy gray sky and thought of Kai. Emmanuela offered me a Kingsbite chocolate bar; my sadness apparent even to her. Chocolate was the emo girl's friend no matter the country or location.

The chocolate helped and I smiled my thanks for her kind gesture.

When we arrived at the woodcarvers, sawdust and wood shavings lined both sides of the narrow road. Each carver had a compact booth with workspace in the rear and their wares out front. We walked amongst the booths, chatting with men and women, taking pictures and making notes on the contemporary versions of the sculptures at the museum.

Emmanuela held up a fertility figure with large breasts, wide hips, and a very round bottom. "Look, Dr. Elmore."

I chuckled. It was a mini-me. I immediately wanted to buy it for Kai. I held it up and negotiated with the carver. Although I could easily afford his initial offer of the equivalent of ten dollars, negotiating was most of the fun of buying in Ghana. We settled on eight dollars, and I tucked the doll inside my bag next to my elephant.

I showed it to Ama at dinner.

"It's the spitting image of you," she exclaimed.

"My head isn't that big, but isn't it odd?" I laughed. "I'll give it to Kai for Christmas."

She raised an eyebrow at me. "Are you joining him in Amsterdam?"

"No, he's spending it with Cibele."

"And?"

"And I wouldn't want to intrude."

"Intrude? The man loves you. He's invited you into his life."

"It's too soon."

"That's not for you to decide."

I furrowed my brow. "It isn't?"

"She's his daughter, if he's ready, then you should be ready."

"But what if she hates me?"

"She might. She's a teenager. They dislike everyone."

"Ugh. Sounds delightful."

"Don't give up until you meet her. She might surprise you. Hell, you might surprise yourself."

"Wouldn't be the first time this year I've surprised myself."

Her smile was warm and motherly. "Bless you."

"For what?"

"Look at you. You glow with love."

I blushed.

"When you arrived, you were shut off, compartmentalized, like your objects. Now, you're open and full of love."

I smiled at her.

"Many people come to Ghana, to Africa, to change things, to right perceived injustices, but Africa is ancient, mother earth, and she will change you even more."

"I didn't come here to volunteer or fix things."

"Probably the reason you've been affected so strongly. No one is the same after they visit Africa."

Her words were truth.

I would never be the same.

Nor did I want to be.

ON DAY SEVEN, I received a garbled voicemail from Kai.

There were issues with the project. He'd borrowed a satellite phone from a UN worker passing through the same village.

In hindsight, I wished I knew the details of his work and where exactly he was. Other than flying into Nairobi, I didn't know many details.

I asked Ama. She was unclear as well, again reassuring me he would be fine.

I forced myself to focus on wrapping up my project at the museum.

Each day I encouraged Emmanuela's chatter to keep my mind occupied. Every evening I watched CNN for news of Kenya and random missing Dutch men. There was never any mention of violence or kidnappings, but would there be? People were kidnapped every day and it never made the local news, let alone international.

With no word the weekend prior to Thanksgiving, I broke down and dug through my bag to find Anita's business card. Twelve days was a long time, and apparently, my breaking point. I emailed her for news of Kai. Whatever pride and misconceptions of strength I had left disappeared when I hit send. Yes, I was *that* woman—desperate, frantic, and needy enough to reach out to my lover's former wife—I had sunk lower than I ever imagined. Yet, it didn't matter, because I needed information to stop myself from tipping over the edge and falling into crazy.

At dinner, I told my kidnapping theory to Ama who frowned and rolled her eyes at me.

"He's fine."

"You don't know that. You can't know that."

"This is what he does. He goes to places where he's out of touch. And then he returns."

"You keep saying that. What if this time is different?"

"If it's different, then when we know, we'll deal with it."

Kai's word about forever good-byes haunted me.

In my room, I propped myself up on my bed with pillows and checked my mail for a response from Anita. Nothing.

Unopened messages from friends filled my inbox. I randomly clicked through them and caught up on the gossip at home. My sister-in-laws pestered me to confirm Christmas. Maggie invited me to her and Gil's holiday party. Quinn sent pictures of Lizzy dressed up as Tinker Bell from Halloween. Jo had tagged me in an old college picture on Facebook.

An hour later, I'd caught up on everything. I responded to Maggie, spilling my heart out all over the text box. Unloading felt amazing. I missed her.

I refreshed my inbox.

Anita had responded to my email.

I scanned the page for the words "dead", "killed", or "loss".

Hi Selah!

I'm happy to hear from you. I can't tell you how thrilled I am that my little introduction turned out so well.

Sorry about the whole Gerhard/Kai thing. It's too much fun teasing him. You should have known him before he had the stick removed from his ass.

You sound worried. One thing you should understand about Kai is he does this. He disappears into work sometimes and forgets people worry about him. Hell, he forgets everything.

That said, he's okay. He texted us when they returned to Nairobi last night.

He'll probably contact you soon. Feel free to yell at him about worrying you, but don't expect it to change.

Hope our paths cross again.

Happy Thanksgiving.

Anita

Last night? After almost two weeks without a word other than a garbled voicemail, he'd returned to the capital where cell service, and most definitely cell telephones, existed. Yet I hadn't received so much as a text in the last twenty-four hours. I had to find out from his ex-wife what he was really like.

Anger replaced the fear that had taken up residence inside my chest.

What the hell?

Tiny bubbles of rage percolated, blocking out any feelings of relief.

He might be alive, but I wanted to kill him for making me worry and behave like a ridiculous, pining girl.

I wasn't a moony teenager.

I didn't pine.

I didn't sit around waiting for the phone to ring.

Closing my laptop, I resolved to stop being whoever this woman was and return to being myself.

Strong.

Independent.

In charge.

I turned off my light. In the darkness, I gave thanks for Kai being alive, letting the knowledge comfort me. Traitor tears escaped. Maybe he hadn't called because it was over.

Ugh.

I was a mess. A hot mess as Quinn would say.

Stupid men.

Stupid feelings.

Stupid love.

Stupid elephant taunting me from atop my dresser.

I fell asleep chanting the lyrics of *I Am Woman*. My mother played that song non-stop during my childhood, and along with *Our Bodies, Ourselves*, it was the feminist foundation of how to be a strong woman—the kind who didn't cry over boys.

AMA AND I sat at the little table near the railing, which I'd first considered my own all those months ago. Since my resolution two nights ago, my anger created a barbed hedge around my heart. My pride acted as a super-hero cape, enabling me to leap to conclusions in a single bound.

I am Selah, hear me roar.

Writing in my notebook, I plotted killing off my Nordic pirate. Death by orgasm or during one. Or maybe I'd make him suffer longer. Pirates had many clever, creative ways of torture.

Ama took a call at the front desk and then returned, clapping like fool with a huge grin plastered to her face.

"You have a phone call!" she shouted.

"Who's calling me on the hotel phone?"

"Answer it and find out!"

I gave her a sidelong look before I walked to reception.

Fourteen days.

That's how long I waited to speak to Kai. Five of those days spent thinking he could have been kidnapped or dead. Two days stewing he hadn't bothered to let me know he was neither.

"Hi, love." His voice sounded happy.

To say I was livid would be a mild understatement. "Hi."

"It's Kai," he explained.

"I know."

"You don't sound happy to hear from me."

"I'm relieved you're alive and not held for ransom by terrorists."

"Why would I be held for ransom?"

"That's usually what happens when someone is kidnapped."

"Who told you I was kidnapped?" His voice rose.

"No one, but after almost two weeks with nothing, it was a possibility. Or death."

"In your mind you had me dead or kidnapped?"

I bristled at his amused tone. "Anything's possible."

"Selah." He sighed.

"What?"

"I'm fine. After I called you from the satellite phone, I lost my cell phone … well, a Jeep ran over it, and I didn't have your number memorized. Stupid of me, but I never wrote it down. I called Ama to get it. I'm so happy to hear your voice. I love you."

I paused, my heart and mind debating my response.

"Hello? Hello?"

"I'm here."

"You're mad."

"I am."

"I'm sorry. This isn't typical."

"I emailed Anita because I thought you could have been dead."

"You did?" His voice revealed his surprise.

"I did. How dare you put me in a position to have to email your ex-wife to find out information about you." Anger colored my voice.

He paused. "I travel frequently. You knew this. I traveled while I lived in Ghana."

"I know." I sighed. "It's different now. Anita told me you do this, this disappearing act, a lot. I loved learning about you from her. Things I should probably have learned from you."

The line crackled for a minute.

"What are you saying, Selah?"

"The past two weeks freaked me out. More than anything, they were torture."

"I'm sorry."

"You apologize, but it doesn't change things."

"Are you having second thoughts about us?"

My heart hurt. I nodded silently, knowing he couldn't see me, and tears stung my eyes.

"Selah …"

"Kai …"

"Please don't give up on us. It won't be easy, but I love you."

I found my voice, but it came out a whisper. "I love you."

"Let's not do this right now, please?"

"It won't become easier later."

He inhaled a deep breath. In the background, something hit a hard surface. "Don't."

With the tips of my fingers, I swiped the tears from under my eyes. "I love you, but I can't be this person. I've spent weeks consumed by you, losing my mind listing the horrible things that could have happened to you. Before you, I loved my life. It wasn't conventional, but it was mine. I had control and I liked it."

"Love—"

I cut him off. "No, don't. It hurts too much to say good-bye to you again."

"Then don't."

I bit the thin skin of my knuckle to the point of pain to stifle my voice.

"We're only at the beginning. We have plans for the future," he continued.

Ignoring him, I spoke again, "The other night I cried myself to sleep. I haven't done that since high school. Not over a boy.

"Oh, sweetheart," he whispered, his voice thick.

"And I remembered a saying my mother told me about fish and bicycles."

"What saying is that?"

"A woman without a man is like a fish without a bicycle." I spoke calmly. "Gloria Steinhem."

"What does that even mean?"

"A fish has no use for a bicycle."

"Ouch."

"It means even without a man, a woman will be fine."

"I've never said you needed me."

"No, but God help me, I wanted you."

"I love you."

"I know, but sometimes love isn't enough."

"It's everything."

"Not to overcome reality."

"I disagree," he argued. "Don't I get a say?"

"I'm sorry, but no."

"Stop. I'll change my ticket to Chicago and come to Ghana. I can be there tomorrow."

"If you fly here, you'll miss Thanksgiving."

"It's not even my holiday."

"But it's important to Cibele. I'm sure she misses you."

"It won't be the first time I've disappointed her, and probably won't be the last. I'm far from perfect."

"Don't be that father—the one who disappoints his daughter because of a new woman in his life. I'm not that woman, and never want to be that woman. Go, be with your daughter, Kai."

"Damn you, Selah. We are not over." Anger, frustration, and hurt overlapped in his voice.

The hurt sliced through me.

"I love you, Kai. There's a part of me that always will. Forever."

"I love you," he said, resigned.

"Good-bye.

"Selah—"

I hung up so he wouldn't hear my sobs.

TWENTY-FOUR

AMA HELD A Thanksgiving dinner for any ex-pats who wanted to attend. The veranda was filled with American accents while I processed the strange sensation of being around so many Americans at once. I texted my parents and sent a group email to friends, telling them how grateful I was for all of them.

I ignored the texts from Kai. The voicemails, too.

I suspected Ama gave Kai my cell number again. Meddler. Not that it mattered. He wasn't on the same continent anymore. I pictured him with his beautiful ex-wife and daughter, eating and laughing over a traditional meal—the wet dream of Norman Rockwell.

I finished my gin and tonic and asked Sarah for another.

"I think you've had enough," Ama warned.

"Now you're my mother?"

"No, but you've had enough. Eat something."

I shoved a forkful of greens into my mouth, acting petulant. No one should have to deal with me. This was why I was alone.

It might have been the three gin and tonics or something in the food, but my head reeled and my stomach gurgled. I put down my fork and sipped some water.

The water didn't help.

I dashed to the bathroom, sparing my shoes, barely, when I lost my dinner. Perhaps it was my ungrateful attitude, or maybe something I ate. Resting my forehead on the cool tiles of the wall, I let my misery loose and sobbed.

Cried out after several minutes, I splashed some water on my clammy face and attempted to appear less vomitus.

Ama frowned at my appearance when I sat down at the table. "I'm worried about you."

"Please don't. I think I drank too much gin on an empty stomach and maybe my malaria meds. Bad combination."

Her expression serious, she touched my forehead. "You're warm."

I waved her hand away. "I'm fine."

"You should take it easy. Otherwise, you'll end up in the hospital."

"I promise. I'm fine, but I should go home."

I said my good-byes. While Kofi drove me to Ama's house, his worried eyes met mine in the rearview mirror several times.

"I'm fine," I reassured him. "Too much gin. Same thing happened when I drank in high school."

He frowned at me. "You take care of yourself, Dr. Selah."

Ama checked on me in the morning. She brought me a bowl of clear broth and some dry toast. The gesture was lovely, but my stomach revolted after two sips. My head pounded from the gin hangover.

When I asked for additional blankets, Ama touched my forehead again and turned off the air conditioner.

"You have a fever," she declared.

"It's probably a stomach bug."

I slept most of the day, waking again when it was dark outside. It could be early evening. Or the next morning. The dry toast laid on the table. I tested a few bites, and then sipped from a fresh bottle of water.

And waited.

Nothing happened.

I finished the toast and water.

When I woke up, light peeked around the curtains. I hadn't been sick for hours.

Relieved whatever hell virus had been expelled, I dressed and left the room to find food.

Ama scowled at me. "You should be in bed."

"I'm fine. Hungry even." I grabbed some plain rice from her pot on the stove. "In fact, I'm setting out for the markets to do some Christmas shopping."

"You should stay in bed."

"I'm okay. Trust me?"

Her lips pursed with disapproval.

"I'll only be gone a couple of hours. I promise."

AFTER I SHOWERED and dressed, I felt more myself. A little tired and lightheaded, but overall better than I had the previous twenty-four hours. Except for the Kai-shaped hole, I felt almost normal.

I made a list of things to buy and left the house. With no Thanksgiving, there wasn't the Black Friday shopping frenzy. During the short walk, I spied Christmas decorations and fake trees complete with twinkle lights decorating several shops and hotels. Too close to the equator for real seasons, I still felt the chill of Portland's coming winter with the dry, dusty Saharan winds clouding the late November sky.

Makola was no more or less busy than any other weekend. Rebecca greeted me with a huge smile and handed me the parcel of dresses and rompers I'd had made for Lizzy. On top, she laid a little doll made of wax cloth as an extra gift. I thanked her and promised to recommend her to everyone.

I made my way out of the market. A strong scent of peanut butter overwhelmed me, and I couldn't catch my breath. I spun around, looking for the shortest route to fresh air, my head swimming.

In an open space at the entrance to the market, I sat on an empty crate, gasping for air. I closed my eyes and exhaled, counting to ten to calm my stomach and catch my breath.

Maybe shopping at the market wasn't the best idea, but I needed to buy these gifts before I returned home. I bought a bag of water and sipped it, awaiting the return of my balance. The craft market was only blocks away. I could make it there, find Abraham Lincoln, give him my list and finish everything in an hour.

Resolved, I trudged to High Street, hoping to locate Abraham without a long search.

Two young men greeted me near the coconut stand. *"Mah mee,* you need something? You are looking for something extra nice? We'll show you the best."

I'd been scoped by new shopping Sherpas.

"Thank you, but I'm looking for Abraham Lincoln. Do you know him?"

A look passed between them. "I know him, but his shops are not good. Our prices are better." His fib lurked behind his smile.

"Ah, thank you, but I promised I would shop with him." From the corner of my eye, I spotted Abraham's lanky form walking in our direction. "There he is."

Abraham glared at the pair, but greeted me warmly, "Dr. Elmore! You are ready to shop today?"

"Yes." I showed him my list.

"Very good." He turned his back to the other men. "What is the state capital of Oregon?"

"Salem. Oregon is where I live." I smiled at him.

"Excellent, what are you looking to buy?" He led me into the heart of the market.

In a handful of stalls, we haggled over prices on souvenirs that didn't scream tacky tourist. While standing at a table full of jewelry, the woozy feeling returned and sweat trickled down my neck.

"Abraham, I'm sorry, but I'm not feeling well and need to go home," I explained, looking for a place to sit.

"Here, Dr. Elmore." He pulled out a stool for me from under a table covered with beaded necklaces. "You rest."

I sat down and put my face between my knees for a moment until the feeling of passing out faded. "Will you buy me something to drink?" I reached into my bag for some *cedis*. "Anything cold, please."

He dashed off through the narrow aisle. I turned to the woman running the booth, an "Auntie" of Abraham's.

She gave me a sad look and gestured to my forehead. "Fever."

I nodded, wiping the droplets of sweat from my brow. "Yes, I think so."

Abraham returned with two Cokes and my change.

"*Me daa si.*" I thanked him.

I rolled the cold glass along the nape of my neck and focused on breathing.

"Abraham, I need to ask a favor. Do you know Ama's Hotel? Down High Street?"

"Yes, I know it."

"Can you walk there and tell them I'm here, and feeling very sick? Ama will send someone to pick me up."

"It is a short way, *Mah mee*. You cannot walk it?" He sounded concerned.

"No, I don't think I can." I wasn't sure if I could make the distance without vomiting. Or worse.

Abraham and his Auntie spoke quickly in Twi and then he left.

I tried sipping from the Coke, only managing to swallow one sip. I decided it would be better used to cool my skin.

The Auntie frowned at me again and repeated, "Fever."

Resting against the wall of her stall, I closed my eyes. Did she mean I had a fever or The Fever as in Yellow? Or Typhoid?

"You need Nibima."

I repeated the word, trying to commit it to memory.

When Abraham returned with Kofi, I sat slumped on a low stool, my whole skull pounding.

"Hi." I gave them a weak wave.

"Oh, Dr. Selah. You are very sick," Kofi said.

I shook my head. "No, I'm fine. A little woozy."

Kofi and Abraham helped me stand and guided me through the crowded aisles of the craft centre. I chanted under my breath, "Nibima-Nimibia. Nimbus."

"What is it?" Kofi asked, tucking me into the backseat of his sedan.

"The Auntie told me a word. Said I have Scarlet Fever." I frowned. "No, that's not right. Yellow Fever."

"Dr. Selah doesn't have Yellow Fever."

I rested against the seat. "She said I had some sort of fever." My eyes closed.

AMA'S HORRIFIED EXPRESSION greeted me when I woke to find we'd arrived at the hotel. The short drive couldn't have been longer than five minutes, but I'd conked out. Or passed out. She rushed over, put her hand on my forehead and promptly sent Sarah to find me a room where I could lie down. I would have hugged her if I hadn't been completely gross.

Time blurred together between trips to the bathroom and finally making a little pallet on the cool tile floor.

I hadn't been this sick for years. Either I had food poisoning or was dying.

I was positive it was the latter.

I alternated sweating and shaking with cold, using the thin towels to cover myself or wipe my sweat.

Ama returned and knelt beside me. The cool cloth she patted on my forehead soothed the burn. "You're going to the hospital."

"No," I whispered. "It's a stomach bug."

"No one else became sick. I think you have malaria."

"I can't have malaria. I always take my pills. Every week."

"Sometimes they don't work. You're very sick."

I rolled away from her. "Let me lie here a little longer and I'm sure I'll be fine. I've felt fine all morning."

"Sorry, my friend, but you need to go to the hospital. If you don't have malaria, you can tell me 'I told you so'. If you do, you can thank me for saving your life."

"But I don't want to go to the hospital," I whined. "Let me go home. I'll visit the doctor when I return home."

With an apologetic look, Ama indicated I wouldn't win this argument.

I sighed, and a tremor went through me. Maybe the hospital was the best idea.

"Okay, I'll go."

She stood and extended her hand. "Let me help you up."

I clasped her hand, pulling myself up to standing. The room swam and everything went dark around the edges. Her voice sounded far away and tinny. Blood pounded in my ears.

I prayed I wouldn't crack open my skull on the tile when I fell.

TWENTY-FIVE

BEEP.

Beep.

Beep.

I awoke with a dry mouth and pain on my left hand.

I coughed and my chest rattled.

That was new.

My eyes were glued shut. *Who would glue my eyes closed?* Slowly, I opened them, lash by lash. I blinked to clear my vision. The beeping didn't appear to come from me. White ceiling tiles came into focus while I lay there counting my breaths. A colorful floral curtain enclosed my bed, confirming I lay in a hospital, not Ama's house, or even the hotel.

The smell of bleach and antiseptic hit my nose.

I closed my eyes, the lids too heavy to keep open.

Beep.

Beep.

Beep.

BEEP.

Shoes squeaked on linoleum.

Beep.

Beep.

Soft voices.

A hand touched my arm. Warm fingers brushed my skin.

I swallowed around the sandpaper of my tongue and pried open my eyes.

Ama's soft smile greeted me. Surrounded by the sterile hospital setting, even her riotous rainbow scarf looked somber.

"Hi." I coughed.

She reached for a pitcher of water and poured some into a cup for me.

I sipped the cool liquid ambrosia through a straw.

"Thank you," I whispered.

"Nice to see you're awake."

"How did I get here?" I sipped and swallowed. "Where is here, by the way?"

"You're in a private clinic in Accra."

"I won't be able to say I told you so, will I?"

"No."

"Fever means malaria, doesn't it? Abraham's Auntie said fever. She told me a name of something that could help. An herb, maybe?"

"Fevers can mean many things, but you have malaria."

"Lucky me."

"Lucky indeed. The doctors say they caught it early."

"I don't feel lucky." I pouted around my straw. I looked down at my thin cotton hospital gown. "How long have I been here?"

"Two days. It's Monday morning. You woke up for a little yesterday. Do you remember Ursula and I visiting you?"

I softly shook my head. "No. I remember beeping and the ceiling tiles, but those might be from earlier today."

Ama's warm hand covered mine. "You gave us a big scare, but you will be fine. You're receiving the best care with excellent medicines." She pointed at the IV in my arm. Ah, that explained the pain. "It's mostly fluids to treat dehydration, but they decided to skip the oral drugs and move straight to the IV for fear of coma."

"Coma?" Could I have been that sick?

"You wouldn't wake up after you passed out on the bathroom floor. I screamed for Sarah and Kofi. We finally woke you up, but I swear your eyes focused in different directions. You kept mumbling about something. Nothing we said or did made you wake up and answer us."

"Yikes."

"Very scary." She glared at me. "Do not do that to me again. Ever."

"I promise," I said, giving her a weak smile. "What did I mumble about?"

She glanced away, interested in the wall behind my bed.

"Ama?"

"You talked about Kai."

I cringed. "What did I say?"

"Mostly his name. Over and over. You called him Gerhard a few times."

Internally, I crawled into a ball, hoping I wasn't talking about Kai's penis. "That's all? Only his name?"

She inhaled and exhaled slowly. "No."

"Tell me. How bad was it?"

"Pretty bad. You said at least you didn't soil yourself in front of him."

"Soil myself? I said soil?"

"No, you said shit." The corners of her mouth turned down.

"Can I die now?"

She laughed. "At least you said it to me, Sarah, and Kofi, instead of Kai."

I tried to pull the thin sheet over my face. "Kill me."

She tugged the fabric down from my face.

"Promise me you will never tell Kai this story?" I pleaded. "Please?"

"It stays between us. And you didn't soil yourself, in case you were worried."

"Oh, good. I'm happy I retained one scrap of dignity."

Ama's laughter triggered my own.

"Thank God for small graces Kai isn't here to witness this."

"Have some more water." Ama lifted the pitcher. "How are you feeling?"

"I'm pretty sure an elephant ran over me and is now sitting on my chest. Everything hurts."

"That's normal. Or so I hear. You'll feel better after a couple days."

"Will I have to stay in the hospital the entire time?"

"Probably."

"How will I afford these medical expenses?"

Her eyes focused on the pitcher. "It's all been taken care of. You don't have to worry about expenses."

"Who—"

A nurse swept aside one of my fabric walls.

"Hello, Dr. Elmore," she greeted me. "The doctor is coming to see you."

Ama had to leave while the doctor checked my vitals and chart. He kindly explained the gorier details of malaria and why it caused me to be sick, then assured me I would make a full recovery if I took my medications. He asked how long I planned to stay in Ghana.

"A couple more weeks."

"You should go home and recuperate," he said with a tone of authority.

"I have commitments here."

"You will have no commitments anywhere if you don't take care of yourself. I believe we caught the malaria early enough, but sometimes there are neurological complications. You will be better off resting at home with your family."

I had no family at home. Unless he meant my parents. Or brothers. No way would I move home.

I quietly sighed, and nodded.

"I'll check on you tomorrow during my rounds. Call the nurse if you need anything."

Ama stepped through the curtain. "What's the prognosis?"

"He thinks I should return home when I'm well enough to travel. He told me to go home to my family," my eyes filled with tears, "but I don't have anyone to go home to."

Her warm arms enveloped me in one of her signature hugs. "You're not alone. Your friends will be there for you."

"I live alone. I don't even have a cat anymore. Who will take care of me?"

Releasing me, she sat in the chair next to the bed. "Don't worry about that now. We'll help you organize your things and get you home soon."

I sniffled and wiped my wet face on the shoulder of my gown. "I'm feeling very tired."

I wouldn't think about what laid ahead until forced. Right now, I needed a nap.

"Sleep and don't worry about the details. We'll take care of everything."

We?

Fuzzy, warm sleep claimed me and I drifted off into oblivion.

LEAVING THE HOSPITAL was one of the happiest days of my life. People at home complained about sharing a hospital room with another patient. I shared a ward with at least four others.

I'd slept the sleep of the dead, or near dead, but it didn't erase my exhaustion.

Even days later, my world consisted of my bedroom and the hall bathroom. If I grew adventurous, I went to the kitchen, but that required a nap after I returned to bed.

I continued to take the new anti-malarial pills daily.

Otherwise, I slept.

Kofi was dispatched to the museum to collect my research. Ursula came over with a bag of bracelets and necklaces from the cooperative for me to bring home. I couldn't even be embarrassed when Ama and Ursula packed my things and discovered BOB.

A week of my life disappeared into a haze of the hospital, home, and sleep.

When he dropped me off at Kotoka, Kofi smiled and laughed when I snapped at the end of our handshake.

"*Mee daa si*," I said, thanking him for everything. "I'll miss you."

He frowned and held my hand while he said good-bye, probably embarrassed by my tears.

Now I sat in the departures lounge at Kotoka. Outside, the Harmattan winds colored everything brown, including the sky. Lively conversations took place around me. Missionaries and students chatted, puffed up with the pride that came with doing good work. I concentrated on not falling asleep and missing my flight. When I coughed my rattling hack, the couple next to me moved away. I snarled at them. Malaria wasn't contagious human to human. If I were being honest, I would have moved away from me, too. My skin had an eerie pallor—the best description for the vague green undertint I now sported. I'd washed my hair the night before and pulled it away from my face with a headband. No makeup, saggy yoga pants, baggie sweater—I created a pretty visual.

Not that I gave a flying fuck.

I coughed again and reached into my bag for a cough drop. My hand brushed against Kai's elephant. I didn't remember putting it inside my purse. Although, I didn't recall a lot about the last week.

Never had I needed my friends as much as I did after malaria. Ama coordinated with Maggie and my parents, keeping them informed of my recovery and return home. The woman should be a saint.

I missed her already.

The best part about the eleven hour flight to JFK was sleeping most of it. With a row to myself, I stretched out, not caring if I snored or scared the other passengers.

Clearing immigration and customs sucked away my energy, leaving me feeling dizzy and tired. Setting aside my dignity, I requested a wheelchair to make my connection to Portland. When we passed the now infamous sushi bar, I closed my eyes. One conversation with a stranger had changed my life forever. No wonder parents warned kids about stranger danger. Strangers were dangerous.

I enjoyed the wheelchair ride so much, I ordered one to meet me at the gate in Portland to take me to baggage claim. By far, it was the best part of having malaria—if there was anything good about having malaria.

I located several boring green dollars inside my wallet to tip the wheelchair pusher and thanked him, explaining I would be fine to sit and wait for my friends to meet me.

I sat at the end of a row of uncomfortable chairs with my back to the glass while I waited for the whir of the baggage carousel to call the awaiting passengers to stampede. The long wait for checked bags equaled a level of hell somewhere between never ending thirst and whatever punishment awaited murderers. I loathed it with a fiery hatred. Exhaling a long sigh of resignation, I looked around for Maggie's ginger hair and Gil's towering height.

With my dead cell phone and its charger packed inside of the still-not-arrived luggage and unavailable to help me, I sat and waited.

And waited.

I calculated with the time changes and layover, I'd been traveling for nearly twenty hours, almost an entire day. Another day of my life lost.

I closed my eyes. Maggie and Gil could find me when they arrived. My luggage might be the last to be picked up at this rate, sadly traveling around and around the carousel, all alone.

The sound of the motor grumbling to life and the clunks of the first bags hitting the belt woke me.

If I didn't stop sleeping, I would have to change my name to Selah Van Winkle.

I blinked and rubbed my eyes.

A familiar face stared at me from a few feet away.

Not Maggie's face.

Not Gil's face.

The last face I never imagined I'd see again slowly smiled at me and moved closer.

TWENTY-SIX

IN THE WORLD, there were people who enjoyed meddling in the lives of others. Some did it for their own amusement, or some sick sense of humor. Some had God complexes. Others, the majority, meddled from some sort of twisted place of optimism, love, and belief in the good in people and humanity in general. Missionaries fell under the latter group, doctors in the middle, and sadists in the former.

I suspected my friends fell both in the former and the latter categories. What they lacked were God complexes. Well, maybe not Quinn, or his doctor husband, but that was beside the point.

My friends, whom I loved dearly, were meddling meddlers who meddled.

Pot, meet kettle, I know.

I plotted their punishment. It would be fast and silent. They'd never see it coming.

Six-foot-something of dark blond and golden hued gorgeous man stood next to me, smirking.

He smirked.

How dare he smirk.

Our eyes met briefly. The familiar deep, oceanic blue undertow pulled me under his spell.

I blinked.

I closed my eyes and counted to ten.

When I opened them, Maggie and Gil stood next to the ghostly apparition of my very own Flying Dutchman. Maggie grinned while Gil awkwardly stuffed his hands inside his coat pockets.

"Welcome home!" Maggie embraced me with a warm hug.

"Can you see him too?" I whispered in her ear.

"Who?" she asked, still hugging me.

Malaria had snapped my brain's ability to rationalize.

"The man standing next to you."

"Gil?"

"No, the other one."

Maggie kept her arms wrapped around me, but turned to look behind her. She faced me again and whispered, "Wait. You don't know him? He isn't your boyfriend?" Her face scrunched up with confusion when she released me and took a step away.

"You can see him?"

"Yes, of course." She met my eyes and frowned, then looked at Kai.

"Is she going to faint again?" Kai asked.

"Again?" Gil said.

"When I surprised her in Ghana, she fainted."

"Maybe you should stop doing that," Gil said. He stepped forward to hug me. "This was all Maggie's doing. If you're mad, and I'm guessing by the look on your face you are, please note I'm an unwilling party to these shenanigans," he whispered.

"No way, mister, you're guilty by association." I squeezed him.

When Gil moved away, my vision centered on Kai for a moment.

Maggie stared at him, then looked at me. "He's gorgeous," she mouthed.

I rolled my eyes.

I had eyes, I didn't need reminding.

Finally, my gaze met Kai's again. He looked weird wearing wintery clothing. Weird, but still hot. I trailed my eyes down over his jacket, gray sweater, dark jeans and low boots, slowly returning to his face. Scruff covered his jaw and dark circles shadowed his eyes.

"You look terrible," I said.

"So do you." He grinned. "Really horrible, like death warmed over."

I ran my hand through my hair, and then smoothed down my travel rumpled clothes. "Fuck off."

Everyone, but me, laughed.

"You're definitely feeling better," Kai said.

"She's her old self if she's telling someone to fuck off. I'm thankful it isn't me," Maggie said.

I glowered at them. "Your turn will come, Maggie. Live in fear. Sleep with one eye open. You'll never know when or where, but I will seek my revenge upon you."

"Wow, you're cranky. Let's collect your baggage and bring you home." Maggie ignored my threats and gathered my things.

After I pointed out my bags on the belt, Gil and Kai walked over to grab them, joking together like old friends.

"When did that happen?" I asked her.

"The bromance?"

I nodded.

"It was love at first sight."

"And that was?"

"Yesterday."

I quirked my eyebrow at her.

"It's a long story, but your friend Ama called us after you collapsed. Kai arranged everything—the private hospital, the earlier flight home—all his doing."

"He what?"

"Who what?" Kai stood next to me, holding the handle of my largest suitcase.

"You?"

"Me what?"

"Are we playing a game of *Who's on First?*" Gil grumbled. "You stay here. I'll get the car."

"I'll come with you." Maggie trotted after him.

"One. Eye. Open. Marrion," I called out behind her.

"Someday you'll thank me!"

I met Kai's worried eyes. "You have a lot of explaining to do."

"I do? Speak for yourself," he scoffed.

I crossed my arms and glowered.

"Give me dirty looks all you want, but I didn't fly across the country, lose sleep for over a week, spend hours coordinating phone calls on two continents, worry about you being sick, and cut short my visit with my daughter to make sure you had help collecting your baggage." He sighed and mirrored my defensive position. "Will you listen to me now?"

"I'm not giving you dirty looks." I huffed. "And I've always let you explain yourself."

"Right. Like the time you broke up with me over the phone? And then hung up on me? Or those text messages you ignored? Like that?" His voice held an edge.

"Okay, bad examples, but to answer your question, yes."

"Are you only saying yes because I'm standing in front of you right now?"

He was probably right, but it would be cruel to admit. "Maybe."

His eyes squinted into tiny slits, and he exhaled through his nose.

I was mad at him, scared of him, and desperately wanted to crawl inside of him and never leave.

Instead, I stared at him.

Nothing says, "I love you and missed you more than air," like a good, old-fashioned staring contest.

"Thank you," I said.

"You're welcome." He gave me his signature shy smile and heaven help me, I smiled back. The dimple demanded submission. "We're not finished with our conversation. Don't think your thank you makes everything better."

"I—"

Kai cut me off. "Gil and Maggie are outside."

I wanted to apologize for being a bitch, but I wasn't planning to do it in front of those two. While Gil drove us to my house, Kai sat with me, keeping to his side of the backseat, but sneaking glances in my direction. I knew he snuck glances, because I caught him when I did the same. We still hadn't touched. Not a hug or a hand on the back or a brush of our thighs. Nothing.

It was maddening.

Maybe I repulsed him. I surreptitiously sniffed myself by turning toward the window and inhaling.

I smelled of plane and the smoky, spicy scent of Ghana.

Puddles of cold rain reflected Portland's twinkling lights shimmering on the wet road. Foreign and overwhelming, home greeted me the best way possible—with rain and cold.

Everyone piled out of Gil's car when we arrived at my darkened bungalow.

"What happened to Nicole?" Six months was a long time to be away and Nicole, a fellow professor, agreed to house sit. "She agreed to stay until Christmas break."

"She and the husband reconciled," Gil informed me. "When I called her last week to tell her you'd be coming home early, it wasn't an issue for her to move out. Apparently, they'd returned her things to their house over Thanksgiving."

The four of us walked up the steps to my front porch. I glanced around at my vintage patio set and porch swing—simultaneously familiar and unfamiliar. Everything looked exactly as it had when I left.

Everything was the same.

But I wasn't.

I gave Kai sidelong looks while Gil opened the door to my house.

In what world would Kai Hendriks be walking into my little Craftsman bungalow?

Not any world I imagined. Or dared to let myself.

Standing a little bit to the side of the three of us crowded at the door, Kai shifted from foot to foot.

Maybe he needed to pee.

He caught me staring at him. "What?"

"Nothing." I glanced away.

He sighed and straightened his shoulders. "I should go back to the hotel."

"Nonsense," Maggie said.

I shot her a look.

"Selah, invite him inside," she encouraged.

"Kai, would you like to come inside?"

He arched his eyebrow. "I wouldn't want to intrude." He stared at me, his eyes a mix of emotions.

"Too late."

"Selah!" Maggie scolded me.

"Kai, please come inside my house." I sarcastically grinned at Maggie.

"Is rude behavior a side effect of malaria?" she asked Kai.

He chuckled and shook his head. "None I've ever seen."

"Could it be a drug reaction?"

"Could, but I think it's Selah being Selah." He stepped away and smiled at me.

I sighed and ignored them, walking into my house. "When you two are done, wipe off your shoes before you come inside."

"That's what she said," Gil joked, laughing at himself. Maggie rolled her eyes.

I groaned. "Seriously? Does anyone still say that?"

A pair of table lamps lit the space, giving my entry and living room a warm glow.

Hello, house.

Inhaling, I smelled the familiar scents of home, dusty books, and cleaning supplies. Everything smelled overly antiseptic. Yesterday I was in Ghana. Now the past six months felt like another life. Or a dream.

It wasn't a dream because Kai stood in my living room, observing me and my life before him. Through an arch sat a brown leather couch where I graded papers and wrote under the patchwork throw laid on the arm.

Bookshelves filled with art books and novels lined an entire wall opposite the couch. A mossy green upholstered chair sat by a bronze floor lamp in my reading nook.

Kai peered into the dining room and the kitchen beyond. My three small bedrooms were up the stairs behind me.

"Your home is lovely. Very you," Kai politely complimented me.

"Thank you. I'd be polite," I stared at Maggie, "and offer you something to drink, but I don't know what I have. Tap water?"

"I'm fine."

Gil cut through the awkward by asking Kai to help him with my luggage. After a discussion of where it would go—the guest room—and their schlepping everything upstairs, there wasn't anything left to do but stand there and be uncomfortable.

"Well …" I said.

"We should let you rest. It's late. Or early for you. You must be exhausted," Maggie said.

I had no idea if Kai was supposed to remain behind or would leave with them. I looked around at their faces, then yawned.

"We'll let you sleep, love." Perhaps afraid I'd spook and trample him, Kai approached me slowly, the same way we did with the elephants. My mind tried to argue, but my body leaned into his open arms and melted into his hug. "We'll finish our earlier conversation tomorrow morning," he said softly, barely above a whisper.

The house smelled unfamiliar, but Kai didn't. His spicy warmth surrounded me and I inhaled deeply. His arms tightened around me for a brief second when he kissed my hair.

I stumbled, off balance and unsteady, when he pulled away.

I blamed the malaria and jet lag, but in reality, my body missed him.

My heart missed him more.

JET LAG SUCKED.

I fell asleep almost immediately after Kai and the Meddlers left. Thinking of climbing the stairs exhausted me, so I lay down on the couch to work up some energy.

Several hours later I awoke to the glow of the table lamps and smell of clean. It took a moment or two for my brain to process my location.

Home.

My clothes smelled of Ghana, but I was home in Portland.

Alone.

Maybe the whole thing had been a dream. Gil was the scarecrow. Maggie was the good witch. There was no heartless Tin Man or lying Wizard to be found.

I grabbed my purse and carried it upstairs. On the bench at the end of my bed, I dumped out its contents. After locating what I sought, I placed the little elephant on my nightstand.

I stripped out of my travel clothes, put on my favorite pajamas, and crawled under the duvet.

I could have slept for days, but knocking on my front door woke me only a short while later. Or maybe it had been hours. The gray sky outside concealed the time of day.

"Go away!" I shouted from my bedroom.

The knocking continued, and transformed into pounding.

I sighed and grabbed my favorite red silk robe. It smelled of soap and my old life.

"I'm coming," I called from the stairs. The knocking ceased.

"If you're a Jehovah's Witness, leave now." I peeped through the hole in the door.

There stood Kai, holding coffee cups and a paper bag.

"You're very persistent," I said after I opened the door.

He smiled in response. "Glad you're beginning to pick up on that."

I crossed my arms. "Why are you here so early?"

"It's almost eleven. And I brought you coffee." He held up one of the cups. "Large raspberry mocha."

The cup almost fell to the floor with how quickly I grabbed it from his hands. "Gimme."

He licked a spot of spilled foam from the side of his thumb. "And if you weren't in the mood for sweet, there's a large latte, extra shot, with skim milk."

"Gimme." I took that cup, too. "What's in the bag?"

"Can I come inside?"

"If it's food, yes."

"It is, but I'm not telling you until I'm inside."

"Fine." I grinned at him. "Entré!" I swept my hand to the side.

"You look beautiful in red. You wore red the night we met."

I blushed. "Thank you." I looked down to make sure I wasn't giving him a free show. Nope. My robe and pajamas covered me beyond modesty. Sexy? Not sexy.

I led the way into the kitchen and put the coffees on the table after sipping from both.

"Mmmm, good." I licked some foam from the corner of my lips. "Explain to me how the land of cocoa and amazing chocolate doesn't have decent coffee."

"Blame the British and their tea."

"I will. Think about the perfection of chocolate and coffee. They would rule the world."

Kai sat in one of the kitchen chairs, completely comfortable.

He looked like he belonged at my table, in my kitchen, in my home—in my life.

Shaking away any images of him doing naughty things to me on said table, I reached for the bag filled with croissants and *pain au chocolat.* "Sweet heaven. What sort of evil are you conjuring?"

He laughed, then opened the lid of the latte and sipped. "No evil. I figured you would wake eventually and probably wouldn't be able to function without coffee. You talked about it enough times when we were together, I knew your favorites. The pastries are only the beginning. I have groceries in the car."

"Car?"

"I rented a car."

"Groceries and a car? Do you plan to stay in Portland a while?" I asked, pretending my heart wasn't pounding away in my chest.

"Maybe. Things aren't one-hundred-percent right now, but I'm optimistic."

I raised an eyebrow at him. "Oh, really?"

He nodded and drank from his cup.

"Interesting. But just so you know, I plan on eating both the pain au chocolat."

"I figured." His dimple showed. "I ate mine on the drive."

"Clever man," I mumbled around the flaky, buttery mouthful of pastry.

After breakfast, I napped on the couch while Kai rummaged through my drawers. He said he put away groceries and then sat in the armchair and read the paper, but I didn't believe him.

He didn't leave.

I didn't ask him to go.

TWENTY-SEVEN

AT SOME POINT in a relationship, if that was what this was, swooning and palpitations at the sight of each other turned to comfort and vague reminders of what once had been a throbbing desire.

Throbbing desire. I made a note to use it in my next book.

For me, swooning and palpitations could be blamed on malaria. Or at least the residual medications and "possible neurological complications". Or so I told myself until Kai showed up Saturday for Maggie and Gil's holiday party. Somewhere along the way, my friends had turned into *that couple* who hosted themed parties. They insisted everyone dress in "festive wear" aka holiday sweaters. Not since Mark Darcy wore his reindeer jumper had my little black heart swooned over a man in ridiculous clothing.

Kai could wear wooden shoes, and I would probably swoon.

Images of him in eyeliner and my scarf flickered through my mind.

"Mmmm," I said.

"Mmmm what?" Kai asked.

"I spoke out loud?"

"Moaned out loud, but yes." He smirked. "I take it you like what you see?"

"Sure. Of course. Who doesn't love Christmas attire?"

"I'm especially fond of yours." He gestured to my chest where moose and deer fornicated in a red and white Fair Isle pattern picked out by Maggie.

"Big fan of moose sex?" I gave him a sidelong glance, grabbing my coat and bag.

"No, but I love where it focuses the eye. I'm a big fan of that area."

I coughed to draw his eyes away from my breasts. "Can we leave now?"

"After you." He swept his arm in front of the door and took my coat to hold out for me.

"I see your chivalry, Mr. Hendriks."

"Good. It's all part of my master plan."

"And what would that be?"

"Can't tell you."

"Sounds like a plan of evil."

"Maybe. Ready?" He held out his arm. "I hope there's mistletoe at their party."

"Part of the plan?"

"Of course."

At the party, he managed to corner me under the mistletoe four times. After kissing him chastely, he and Maggie giggled while I attempted to jump high enough to rip the vile greenery from its ribbon.

"I think the lady doth protest too much," she said, shooing me into the kitchen. "I can't believe I'm saying this, but you need to get laid."

"My how the tables have turned, haven't they?" I lifted my eyebrows. I'd said the same words to her over a year ago. "That's beside the point. Mistletoe kisses do not count as real kisses. For one, there's questionable forced consent." I stared at her smiling face. "Second, anyone can kiss you. Did you miss me dodging Elbow Patches Peterson with a cheek?"

"Who knew they still sold Aqua Velva?" Her giggles turned to guffaws.

"Aqua Velva sounds too close to Aqua Vulva, which is all sorts of wrong." I joined her giggling.

Wiping tears from her eyes, she focused on filling a tray with *macarons* and petit fours.

I stole a tiny cake from the tray and escaped across the kitchen to avoid her wrath. "Who serves petit fours outside of a tea room?" Delicious cake muffled my voice.

"I've been experimenting with a French baking book." She watched me lick my fingers. "You approve?"

I nodded and tried to sneak around her to grab a cookie.

Unfortunately, she shielded the tray from my grabby fingers. "These are for guests."

"I'm a guest. Look, ugly sweater and everything." I stuck out my chest. "You picked it out, and I'm such a good guest I wore it. Plus, I could have died recently. How sad would it be if you stood here alone, crying over the fact I never tasted your homemade *macarons*?" I batted my eyelashes at her.

"You didn't almost die."

"We don't know for certain." I pouted out my bottom lip.

"Okay, you win." She handed me a red cookie. "Have the raspberry."

"Mmmm …" I moaned.

"What are you moaning about now?" Kai's voice came from behind me. "You've been doing a lot of that tonight."

Instead of answering him, I swiped another cookie and held it up to his mouth. "Eat me."

A wicked smile crossed his face. "I thought you'd never ask." He opened his mouth and held out the tip of his tongue.

The moan was soft, and might have actually come from me, but I was pretty sure Maggie moaned.

I stuffed the cookie in his mouth—let him smirk with his mouth full.

"Mmmm …" He closed his eyes and licked tiny crumbs from the corner of his lips.

Maggie's hand clutched my wrist. She whispered near my ear, "How do you resist that?"

Not willing to take my eyes from Kai's glorious face, I whispered,

"Who said I ever did?"

His eyes opened and met mine. There was the smirk. "I've tasted better." His tongue peeked out again, and he ran the tip halfway along his top lip.

I held the edge of the counter, my legs proving unreliable.

"You two need a room." Maggie fanned herself.

Kai and I laughed.

"I think that's our cue to leave," he said.

"So soon? I'm sure there's a decrepit history professor or two lurking around who haven't yet attempted to floss my tonsils." I shot Maggie a dirty look. "What's with all the mistletoe everywhere?"

"It's festive."

"It's a cold sore outbreak waiting to happen," I snorted.

"And on that note, I'll grab our coats." He walked out of the kitchen.

"Be good to him. He's a keeper."

"Oh, great. Now you're on Team Dutchman?"

"I'm on Team Selah. Up until November, he made you happy. Happier than you've ever sounded."

"It's difficult to infer tone in email."

"And the smiling pictures of the two of you? Or the blush on your cheeks when you look at him?"

"Pfft. I haven't blushed since Bush. The father."

"You're flushed right now."

"Must be the booze."

"You're not even drinking."

Right. "Maybe Elbow Patches spiked my cranberry soda. I wouldn't put it past him."

"You're in love. Fight it if you want, but resisting doesn't change the truth."

"Hush your mouth."

"I will not. Don't shove him away, Selah. Or find excuses and flaws that aren't there."

Kai returned, saving me from further pep talks.

We said good night to everyone and headed home, to my home. Not our home.

There was no ours at this point.

WHEN WE ARRIVED at my house, I wasn't ready to say good-bye to Kai. Every day it became increasingly difficult to send him away at the end of the evening. I couldn't even remember why I had been adamant about him not staying at my house. Or in my bed.

"Come inside?" I asked when he stopped in my driveway but didn't turn off the engine.

"Are you sure?" His hand hovered over the key.

"Yes."

Silence filled the interior. We paused, waiting for what I didn't know.

"Selah …"

"Kai …"

"If I come inside tonight, I'm not returning to the hotel. I want you to know if we go inside, I'm staying."

I smiled at him in the darkness with only the street lights and my porch light for illumination.

"I'm sure."

The unsnapping of his seat belt echoed around us.

"Eager much?" I teased.

He growled and opened his door. "Coming?" he glanced at me.

"God I hope so. And soon," I mumbled softly under my breath.

"Come again?" He grinned.

My mind told me we needed to talk.

My heart told my mind to shut it.

My body ignored both of them and hummed with anticipation.

When we made it inside the house, he pinned me against the wall and crushed my mouth with his. In romance writing there was a trope about tongues battling for dominance. I never understood the appeal or the action until that kiss.

Battled.

Dominated.

Pillaged.

Massacred any resistance I still held.

I rubbed against him like a cat. Yearning for Shiva's multiple arms, my hands touched everywhere they could reach. They tangled into his hair, ran over his shoulders, inside his coat, under his sweater, and over his lower back before coming to rest on his ass.

When we broke apart, panting for oxygen, he asked, "Am I forgiven?"

"Less talking tonight. Talk tomorrow," I said between pecks across his scruffy jaw. I nipped the smooth spot under his ear and inhaled a big dose of his pheromones. Not that I needed them. "Upstairs."

He guided me toward the stairs. With a single smooth swoop, he lifted me into his arms and carried me up to my room. Normally, I would have complained about weighing too much, or not wanting him to hurt his back, but the way Kai held me made me feel light, even dainty. And I wasn't fool enough to argue.

When he set me on the bed, I fell into the soft down of my duvet. Staring up at him, I remembered our first night together at his hotel. We might have had sex seven hundred ways to Sunday between now and then, but now, this, felt like the first time all over again.

"You said no talking, but I'm not very good at following rules, so I'm ignoring your request for a second." His dimple appeared. "I love you, Selah. Not a temporary kind of love either. I didn't stop after our disastrous phone call, and I don't have plans to stop. Ever."

"I love you. Truly, madly, deeply," I whispered, lost in the depths of his eyes.

He shook his head and chuckled. "You just quoted One Direction."

"Pretty sure it was a movie title first." I sighed and rolled my eyes. "You know One Direction song titles?"

"Father of a girl who loves them. What's your excuse?"

"College students."

"Mmm hmm. Sure."

I wanted to kiss him to stop any further discussion of boy bands while I waited for the squishy feeling which usually accompanied my fear of facing Cibele, and her inevitable rejection and dislike. It didn't come. If Kai and I loved each other, we'd figure out Cibele. If not, there was always boarding school.

"Hey." He sat on the edge of my bed. "Sorry to ruin the moment with reality."

I patted the bed beside me, and he lay down. Propping myself up on my elbow, I gazed down at him.

"It's okay. She's yours and a part of you. I'm sure I'll love her."

He blinked up at me in stunned silence. Or in awe at my maturity.

"What am I going to do with you?"

I giggled and leaned over to kiss him. "I don't know, what did you have in mind?"

"You're the one who's been sick."

"True. I'm not my usual wild self."

"Maybe we should sleep. You need your rest."

"No way. You riled me up with those mistletoe kisses and One Direction references."

"I enjoy you riled up," he confessed, kissing me softly. "You rile me up, too. In all of the best ways."

My glance flicked to his jeans where there appeared to be evidence of riling.

Oh, hello, Gerhard.

Any other man bringing up a boy band and his daughter would have killed the moment. Somehow, Kai doing it only made me love him— deeply, madly, truly, and foolishly love him.

He pushed himself up on his elbows to deepen our kiss. I let him guide us, falling backward when he leaned over me. Exhaustion seeped into my bones and I swallowed a yawn, not wanting him to stop.

Sensing my mood, he slowed everything down to an agonizing pace.

Each piece of clothing, beginning with the hideous sweaters, was peeled off us and tossed onto the floor. He pulled off my shoes and toed off his, before gliding my pants down my legs and then his jeans.

The slow seduction didn't change once we were naked. He kissed down my body, nipping and licking patterns along my skin. Each touch reignited my nerves. I squirmed when he scraped his scruff over my hips. He held me down with his forearm while he went further south, teasing me along my upper thighs, and lavishing me with attention.

His tongue set the rhythm I loved, and his fingers found the spot inside me, providing backup. He forgot nothing during our time apart. If anything, this was the best sex we'd ever had. The knowledge we weren't beginning or ending only intensified every emotion and sensation until I shuddered and pleasure coursed through me.

My orgasm tingled the hair on my head before traveling down to my feet, which curled and flexed with gratification.

He kissed my stomach and gazed up at me. "That's my favorite thing in existence. Giving you pleasure. I'll never tire of it. Ever."

If I hadn't been lying down, I would have swooned.

"Come here," I beckoned him.

"Let me grab a condom," he offered, kneeling.

"No."

"No?"

"I'm clean. You?"

"Yes. Are you sure?"

I nodded. "Please? You won't get me pregnant, if you're worried."

"Why would that worry me? I know it's not really an option, but imagine the potential for world domination if we procreated." He crawled up my body until his face settled inches from me.

"Bite your tongue."

"I'd rather bite yours." He kissed me and tugged on my bottom lip with his teeth.

I reached for him, stroking his warm, smooth cock. "I never gave you your birthday present. Or wished you a happy birthday."

"No, you didn't. You broke up with me instead."

"I suck," I said, swirling my thumb over his tip.

He moaned and thrust into my hand. "Speaking of sucking ..."

He didn't have to ask twice. Means to an end or not, I loved all of him, and his cock in particular.

I slid down the bed to reacquaint myself with Gerhard. He appeared to have missed me as much as I missed him. Using my tongue, mouth, and the occasional gentle drag of my teeth, I further brought Kai to the edge when I cupped his balls. They tightened under my touch and he clutched the comforter, his hips rolling away while he held off his orgasm.

"Love?" His voice sounded strained.

"Mmm?" I hummed around him.

"That's about as much happy birthday as I can handle if you want to have sex now."

I didn't argue with him; my jaw ached.

He rolled over me and kissed me with no qualms about tasting himself.

We'd made love. We'd fucked.

I loved both.

Tonight we went slow. Each time the heat between us built up, we let it ebb, savoring our connection, never wanting it to end. We rolled over and then to our sides and back, never breaking apart. Finally, we crossed the line, unwilling and unable to hold off our orgasms any longer.

When he came, he whispered his love like a prayer.

TWENTY-EIGHT

KAI LEFT IN the morning to check out of his hotel and bring his things to my house. In Ghana, we lived together in all but shared mail. Now reunited, it would have been odd for him to be anywhere but my house.

His scent, and the smell of cooking, coffee, and fresh flowers replaced antiseptic and dusty smells which first greeted my return. The house smelled of life and love.

Over omelets, made by him, we talked the talk.

"Tell me again how you came to be my guardian angel?"

"I was still in Chicago Thanksgiving weekend when Ama called in a panic. I made a few phone calls and found a room for you at the private clinic under the care of the best doctor I knew."

"He acted very stern with me."

"You need a stern man," he joked, raising his eyebrows.

"No charming, more talking."

"Okay, charming later. If you were sick enough to be hospitalized, it would be best to bring you home as soon as possible in case complications arose later. I booked a ticket for you and had Ama arrange to get you to the airport. At that point, I feared if you realized I was involved and pulling strings, you'd refuse any help at all. I also knew you wouldn't say no to Ama."

"Devious."

"And true. Especially after the delightful speech you gave me over the phone about not needing me."

I lowered my head and poked at my omelet with my fork. "I was wrong," I said softly.

He lifted my chin with his finger. The lines around his eyes deepened with amusement. "I'm sorry. I couldn't hear you."

"I was wrong about not needing you. Apparently, I did."

"Did?"

"Do." I grinned at him. "No way can I make my own omelets."

"Are you okay with needing me?"

I exhaled and paused. "Yes, I think so. Maybe. But it will take a big adjustment, huge. I've been on my own since college. You can't crash into my life and not expect some collateral damage or unforeseen meltdowns over inconsequential things."

"Like leaving the toilet seat up?"

"Exactly." I laughed. "For the record, my ass hits toilet water once, and you'll be in big trouble."

"Noted."

"Most of all, even more than my newfound ability to admit I need you, is the overwhelming longing I have for you. It scares me."

"It scares me, too," he admitted. "But we'll navigate it together."

"By having a lot of sex?"

"That will probably help, yes."

"Now?" I asked, eyeing the table.

Turned out, my kitchen table had the right height and support for many different activities besides eating or reading the paper.

Over the next several days, Kai apologized multiple times for worrying me when he went off the grid, even showing me which satellite phone he'd ordered online. I accepted his apologies, knowing he would leave me again and again if we had a life together.

A life together.

The concept was strange, but I smiled imagining our future.

Ours.

There was the O word, and I didn't mean orgasm.

More than half of my life had been filled with I and mine. Now there was a we. And ours. Or at least the potential for it.

Kai still planned to fly home to Amsterdam for Christmas, stopping through Chicago to pick up Cibele. I had my family to appease in California.

The new year would return Kai to Portland and to me.

One rainy afternoon, we sat on the floor of my living room, festooning a Noble Fir Kai had brought home.

"Explain to me what happened at Gil's house when I hid in the mistletoe-free zone of the kitchen?"

"When I almost punched that old man in the tweed jacket for kissing you?"

Laughing, I threw popcorn at him. "You did not!"

"I thought about it. Instead, I glowered at him from across the room in a threatening manner."

I munched on pieces of popcorn.

"Are you stringing popcorn or eating it?"

"I'd rather eat it. It needs salt. And butter." I grabbed the bowl and headed to the kitchen.

"What will you use for garland?" he asked, following me and sitting at the table.

"Who needs a garland?" I waited for the butter to melt in the microwave. "Finish your story."

"Right. Gil introduced me to Warren Johnson, chair of the economics department."

"I know of him and his reputation of staring at boobs."

"Sounds like a typical economics guy."

"Weren't you an economics major?"

He smirked at me. "Anyway, he saw the articles about me, which made the rounds last year, and is familiar with my work."

"Articles plural?"

"Plural. Several ran in major US media outlets."

"They did?"

"You need to read more news and less smut, my love."

"Smut is better for the soul." I should have done a search for him online. Lust, love, and malaria had distracted me. "What did these articles say?"

"The usual stuff about walking away from millions to focus on microfinance and clean supply chains for investors."

I almost dropped the hot bowl of butter. "Millions?"

He sighed. "It's not as if I woke up one day and gave away all of my money, but that's how the press reported it."

"Millions plural?"

He nodded. "With a little m, not a giant M."

"You really are Robin Hood?"

"According to the press. Sometimes they call me the Pied Piper with the way I can convince people to do the right thing."

I poured the butter over the popcorn. *Millionaire.* "And you're kind of famous?"

He scratched his jaw. "I guess. Obviously not famous enough, otherwise you'd have heard of me."

Who was this man sitting in my kitchen?

"And it never came up in conversation … because …" I asked.

"It did. In Elmina."

"Yes, your epiphany, then I became distracted by long hair and bendy yoga images of you."

"Whose fault is that?"

Images of a younger Kai doing bendy yoga positions filled my mind.

"Hello?" Kai waved his hand in front of me.

"Sorry."

"Having perverted thoughts about me again?"

"Again?" I rolled my eyes. "You're very distracting."

"So are you with the way you're sucking butter off your finger."

I pulled my finger out of my mouth. "What does you being a millionaire, with a small m, have to do with Warren and Gil?"

"Warren turned fan boy on me and asked me to do a guest lecture on campus sometime in the spring semester, with an offer to teach a course fall semester."

"Fan boy? Warren Johnson fanned over you?" I found it hard to believe.

"The conversation involved a lot of arm touching and back-slapping."

"Okay, that's plain weird. Are you considering doing it?"

"Doing what?"

"The guest lecture."

"Of course. It's another way to justify to TNG relocating my base to Portland."

"Is being in Portland a long term thing?" I looked over his shoulder at a spot on the window.

"It could be. Lots of big money and foundations in the Northwest I could partner with or consult for. I'll keep my place in Amsterdam, but since I'll always travel for my work, home base can be anywhere. If you're asking."

"I wasn't asking."

"You were. That's okay. I like your need to know about my plans, and hopefully that means you want me here."

I walked over and stood between his legs, setting the bowl of popcorn on the table next to him. "I do want you, more than I'll ever admit."

His hands found their place on my hips, and he pulled me closer. "I'll always return to you." He kissed me. "Always."

OUR TIME TO part again grew closer and a nugget of fear settled into my belly.

I tried to smother it, but the voice that worried and created undue anxiety didn't respond to threats. Or Christmas cookies. Emotional eating only made my pants tighter. Kai would return in less than a month. In my bones and in my breath, I knew it. Yet the voice of doubt continued its soft whispering.

I shared my thoughts with Kai while we prepared dinner for Maggie and Gil. My energy level still hadn't returned to normal, so instead of a holiday party, it would only be the four of us. Kai volunteered to cook after my failed attempt at boxed macaroni and cheese. Apparently, you needed to set a timer or the water would boil away, leaving a soggy, gelatinous mess.

Gil and Kai hung out in the kitchen, reveling in their bromance while Maggie and I sat on the couch and eavesdropped.

"I told Quinn we'd video chat tonight. He's dying to show us Lizzy's latest trick and outfit," Maggie said.

"You know his ulterior motive is to get a gander at Kai, right?"

"Of course! He's completely transparent."

"He's seen pictures. Isn't that enough?"

"For Quinn? Never. He won't be happy until he can flirt with him in person. They'll be on Whidbey for their annual summer visit. You two should join us. You can meet Diane, John's girlfriend. He's completely smitten; it's adorable."

"Smitten lumberjack? That I would like to see." Kai and I hadn't planned months into the future. I had no idea where he'd be over summer. "I'd love to be there in July."

"Well, we'll put it on the calendar, and that way Kai can plan around it," she assured me.

"That feels very domestic."

"How so?"

"Having a shared calendar and making summer weekend plans in December."

"Welcome to life as a couple. It takes work and coordination sometimes."

"Ugh. The work word." I scowled.

"You can complain, but I bet you wouldn't give it up at this point."

Deep male laughter carried from the kitchen.

"Never." I smiled.

THE NIGHT BEFORE Kai left for Chicago and then Amsterdam, we exchanged gifts.

He loved the sculpture I bought for him in Aburi. He rubbed her curves with the same adoration he gave mine.

Finally, I was allowed to open the shipping box, which had arrived two days earlier from Amsterdam. Inside it sat the beautiful Ashanti comb he had purchased at auction.

I gaped while I gently lifted it from the tissue. "How?"

"I remembered how much you loved it. Your eyes lit up when I showed you the catalogue."

My brow furrowed. "You bought it for me?"

"Don't hate me, but no. I did buy it for my father. However, when I told him about you, how we met and that I wanted to give it to you for Christmas, he sent it the next day."

Tears filled my eyes. "I can't accept it."

"Why not?" He frowned. "Don't you like it?"

"It's too much."

"The money?"

I nodded, swiping my errant tears.

"Selah, I want you to have it as a tangible reminder of where we began. This brought us together. Think of all the elements and powers at work to make sure you ate airport sushi, chatted to Anita, agreed to meet some crazy man, went to an auction viewing—"

I cut him off with a kiss. "It's impossibly implausible. The whole thing."

"Yet here we are." He kissed me and swept packing peanuts and tissue to the side, laying me down on the rug.

I made sure the sculpture was safely out of range as things became heated.

"I love you," I whispered against his lips.

"Always."

EPILOGUE

SIX MONTHS LATER...

"IS this outfit okay?" I asked, attempting to close the clasp of my necklace.

"For flying?" Kai's fingers moved mine out of the way and smoothly attached the two ends.

"For what comes after flying." I stared at him through the mirror. "Meeting Cibele. And Anita."

"Again. You've already met Anita."

"Not really. She was some random, pushy supermodel in JFK last year."

"She's still pushy." Kai smiled lovingly at me through the mirror. "And you look perfect."

I studied my black dress and wedge heels. The thick strand of beads added color, but it was kind of a somber look. "Do I look like I'm attending a funeral?"

"Not with that cleavage." His eyes focused on my chest while his hands snuck around to touch my breasts.

"Is it obscene?"

His fingers squeezed me. "More than obscene."

"Don't start what we can't finish. We don't have time."

He hissed. Or exhaled. I couldn't tell.

"You look beautiful and appropriate. Stop worrying."

Other than flying first class, our flight to Chicago was uneventful. Blessedly, Kai had enough money and mileage points for neither of us to ever fly coach again. I sipped my wine and looked out at the puffy spring storm clouds over the flat land of the Plains.

A humid cab ride later, we arrived at the Ritz where our room overlooked Navy Pier. I loved Chicago and couldn't wait to visit the Art Institute the day after tomorrow. If I survived tomorrow.

Saturday was Cibele's graduation from junior high school.

Kai wanted her to come to Portland for spring break, but I hadn't been ready. I had plotted faking a relapse to get out of it. After confessing my planned deception, Kai took her to Mexico instead with the excuse sunshine and warmth were better than gray and cold in Oregon.

When I attempted to avoid this weekend, he'd put his foot down. That was how I found myself having a panic attack in Chicago. My present to the daughter I hadn't even met laid on the desk. I sat on the bed and stared at it, willing it to have magical powers of instant approval and connection.

"What are you nervous about?" Kai sat next to me and laced his fingers with mine. "She'll love the gift."

"You think? It isn't too old lady trying to be cool?"

"No, you'll win major points." He kissed my hair. "Ready?"

"No," I sighed.

"It isn't the firing squad."

"Sure feels like it."

"Based on your personal experience with firing squads?" He tugged me to my feet and kissed me resoundingly, thoroughly, and lovingly.

"Let's stay in and have hotel sex."

"We can do that later." He tucked a lock of hair behind my ear. "You're beautiful. Intelligent. Amazing. Mine."

I nodded. "Remind me later?"

"I'll do better than remind you. I'll show you." He slapped my ass.

"That stung." I rubbed the warm spot.

"Good. Now, let's go."

We arrived first at the restaurant and sat along a banquette. Whenever someone entered, I glanced at the door.

"Stop staring and order something to drink," Kai said.

I pretended to peer down at the menu, but kept one eye at the front of the restaurant.

Anita was impossible to miss. If anything, she looked taller and abundantly super-human beautiful, exceeding my memory of her. Her height blocked out the person following behind her until they reached our table.

"Hello!" she greeted us warmly.

Kai stood up to greet them, and I did the same. Or tried. My hip hit the table and caused my water glass to wobble and slosh liquid on the white tablecloth.

"Selah!" Anita hugged me, tightly, the way old friends do. I peeked around her arm. Kai hugged a slim teen girl, the tips of her hair a soft pink. "I'm so glad to see you again, especially under such happy circumstances."

I mirrored her joyful expression, and then stepped away. Kai released Cibele and turned her to face me.

The moment of reckoning was upon me.

The look of love he gave her, and then me, as he introduced us melted my heart and my nerves.

Deep, sea blue eyes met mine, and a sweet, shy smile full of silvery braces greeted me. "Hi."

"Hi." I gave her a little wave. We smiled shyly at each other for a moment before Kai invited everyone to sit down. Cibele sat across from Kai and Anita opposite me. His hand rested on my leg, and entwined with mine, the contact calming me.

I assumed our evening would have been awkward with silence, and perhaps a few death glares from an angry teen.

At some point, I would learn to not assume anything when it came to Kai.

"You saw Nirvana live?" Cibele squealed and bounced while I told stories about seeing shows in Seattle.

"And The Cure." I smiled at her.

"I want to see one of their concerts, but my parents say I'm too young."

"I went to my first concert at fourteen."

Cibele looked between her parents expectantly.

"We'll talk about it," Anita replied. She gave me a soft smile. "Maybe you could go with Selah."

"Oh em gee." Cibele rapidly listed ten bands she wanted to hear live. I recognized the names of four of them.

"Also, I had the same pair of Doc Marten's as you do."

"Really?"

"Really. Speaking of concerts and clothes, I brought a graduation present for you." I reached for the box on the banquette next to me.

"You didn't have to," Anita said. "Say thank you, Cibele."

"Thank you, Selah."

"You haven't opened it yet. You might not like it." I fidgeted with my bracelets.

Kai's hand gave me a reassuring squeeze.

Cibele gasped. "Is it really vintage?"

"It is. It was mine."

"You were at this show?" She clutched my old *Head on the Door* concert T-shirt to her chest.

"I was."

Kai leaned over and whispered in my ear, "You just became the coolest adult she's ever met."

I rested against him, smiling while I watched Cibele study the cities on the back, chattering away about songs and vinyl albums, and much to her parents' amusement, boys who liked vintage music.

Later, Anita and I found ourselves standing at the bathroom sinks together.

"You really made her week with your gift." Our eyes met in the mirror.

I shrugged. "Kai told me how much she loved The Cure."

"It's perfect." She smiled and smoothed down her hair. "I'm happy for you and Kai."

At a loss for words, I stared at her.

"You're probably thinking this is all very strange."

"A little." I turned to face her. "Can I ask you something?"

"Sure."

"I've asked Kai, but I'd love to hear your version. Why did you encourage me to meet him last summer?"

"Ah." She laughed. "I've been waiting for this moment."

"You have?"

"Of course. It's not typical for an ex-wife to play matchmaker. We're not very typical, though. We've known each other half our lives. Our history together is long, and Cibele ties us together for the future, however long that might be." She reached into her purse for a lip gloss. "Last spring, I found a lump in my breast. I don't know if Kai told you. He didn't know until Thanksgiving."

"Oh, no." My heart rate increased. "I'm sorry."

"Turned out to be benign, but it scared me. I thought about death and what dying would mean for Cibele as an only child and two parents who travel too much."

I gaped at her. "You didn't think I'd be a good mother, did you?" Fear laced through my words.

Her laughter echoed inside the tiled space. "Oh, gosh no. When we met, I liked you, and I have an excellent sense about people because of my work. No, I realized how different you were from the women Kai had dated after the divorce. I won't go into details, but will say the majority of them could be summed up in a single word: gold-digger."

"Really?" I raised my eyebrow.

"That's another reason why I told you his name was Gerhard. Kai Hendriks holds a certain caché in many circles."

"I'm discovering that."

"Long story short, my brush with cancer scared me into action. More than anything, I want Cibele and Kai to be happy. I figured if nothing else, you would have been something different in his world. Maybe you would have had coffee, conversation, and never seen each other again, but it might have been enough to remind him he deserved better. He's a good man, but he's not my man." She gazed happily at me. "He loves you."

"He is a good man," I agreed. "And I love him. More than anything." Overcome with emotion, I hugged her. Her love for Kai was real and present, not tinged with bitterness or jealousy. "Thank you," I said after stepping away.

"You're welcome." Anita smiled at me, grasping my hand. "We're not promised long lives, or even tomorrows, so we must love the lives we have now."

WEEKS LATER...

"Try it," I held the spicy tuna roll to Kai's mouth.

"I'd really prefer not to develop food poisoning on a transatlantic flight." He closed his lips tightly.

"Fine, more for me." I took a bite. "Mmmm," I moaned. "So good. The best thing I've had in my mouth for a long time."

He arched an eyebrow. "Oh, really?"

"Mmm hmm." I licked soy sauce from my lips.

"You're ridiculous."

I held up a piece with my chopsticks. He rolled his eyes, but opened his mouth.

"Mmm, it is good."

"Told you so." I popped another bite into my mouth and defended my plate with my chopsticks. "Order your own."

"So, this is where it happened?" He looked around the sushi bar.

"Right here. We should buy plaques for these two stools." I gestured behind us.

"What would the plaques say?" He stole another piece of my sushi.

"Don't trust a Dutch man not to steal from you." I moved my plate further away from him.

"Selah ..."

"Kai ..."

His dimple appeared and worked its voodoo juju.

"Let me think." I tapped my chopsticks on the plate. "Something about talking to strangers. Or living in the moment."

"The secret of health for both mind and body is not to mourn for the past, nor to worry about the future, but to live the present moment wisely and earnestly."

"That's profound."

"It's a quote from Buddha."

"I love it when you get all namaste on me."

"I don't think namaste means what you think it does."

"Oh, it does." I grinned at him.

"What am I going to do with you?"

"Take me to Amsterdam?"

"Already doing that."

"How about visiting some Greek islands?"

"That, too."

"Be by my side when the sculpture exhibit opens in New York?"

"Wouldn't miss it for the world."

"Hmmm ... I'm out of ideas."

Dark North Sea eyes met mine.

"I have an idea."

My heart fluttered at the look in his eyes. I set down my chopsticks and focused on him. "What sort of idea do you have?"

"It's a big idea. Huge, really."

I blinked at him and waited.

"Marry me."

"Yes," I whispered before I could think my way out of it. I might have been a cynic, but deep down I believed in happily ever after.

"Yes?" His eyes widened.

"Yes. Why are you shocked?" I lifted my chin with a smug grin.

"I … I expected … I don't know what I expected, but a simple yes wasn't it."

"I can give it further thought, if you'd be happier. Consider the pros and cons, do a survey, design a research project—"

He narrowed his eyes at me.

"Maybe I'll discover I prefer only missionary position."

"No!"

Giggling, I wrapped my hand around his neck to pull him close for a kiss.

"Yes?" he asked against my lips

"Yes."

We kissed at the sushi bar in the middle of JFK airport without a care to who saw or judged.

We had our now, and I wouldn't miss a minute of it.

Forever and always would come later.

ACKNOWLEDGEMENTS

Writing and publishing a novel doesn't take place in a vacuum. Life keeps going on around me while I live inside my head, writing about my imaginary friends and their adventures. Not that I'm complaining. Being a romance writer is the best profession—I get to fall in love over and over with each new book.

Huge thanks to my husband and favorite travel companion, who rarely complains about a lack of homemade baked goods while we chase this dream together.

Special thanks to friends and family, who continue to support me despite cancelled dinners, slow replies to texts and emails, and general writer craziness. To the Lost Girls, who are the best friends a person could have, thank you for all the great adventures.

The past year of publishing has been an incredible journey. I've been blessed to meet many wonderful authors, bloggers, agents, publishers, and readers. The Indie world is a supportive community that feels like a big family. A big thank you to Heather Maven, who beta-read MP as it was written, giving me the feedback and the support needed to make this story the best it could be. Thank you to Kelly, Dianne, Marla, and Nadine for pre-reading; your honesty and enthusiasm were invaluable. Amanda, thank you for your help and input regarding all things Ghana. It was important for me to get those details right to honor the country and it's people. Thank you to Melissa Ringstead and Jenny Sims for polishing drafts and correcting my sins against grammar. (Any remaining errors are my own.)

Thank you to Sarah Hansen for a gorgeous cover and to Angela at Fictional Formats for making the inside of the book beautiful. Many thanks to ARC readers and bloggers, who shared their early enthusiasm and love for this book, including Vilma, Denise, Kandace, Lisa, Neda, Tiffany, Cindy, Diana, Hootie, Dympna, Becca, Stacy, Jessica, Denise, Daiana, Charlene, Mandy, and Missionary Sue. Special thank you to my agents, Flavia Viotti Siqueria and Meire Dias at Bookcase Literary Agency, for believing in my work and wanting to bring it to the rest of the world.

Biggest thanks of all to the readers who bought this book. I appreciate your support of Indie authors, including me. Thanks in advance for writing a review, telling a friend about MP, or reaching out to let me know you enjoyed *Missionary Position,* or any of my other books. Hearing from readers is the best part of publishing!

Happy Reading!
xo
Daisy

ABOUT THE AUTHOR

Before writing full time, Daisy Prescott worked in the world of art, auctions, antiques, and home decor. She earned a degree in Art History from Mills College and endured a brief stint as a film theory graduate student at Tisch School of the Arts at NYU. Baker, art educator, antiques dealer, blue ribbon pie-maker, fangirl, content manager, freelance writer, gardener, wife, and pet mom are a few of the other titles she's acquired over the years.

Born and raised in San Diego, Daisy currently lives in a real life Stars Hollow in the Boston suburbs with her husband, their dog Hubbell, and an imaginary house goat.

She has published three novels, *Geoducks Are for Lovers*, *Ready to Fall*, and *Missionary Position*, along with a Pirotica novelette under the pen name Suzette Marquis.

To learn more about Daisy and her writing visit:
www.daisyprescott.com

Or find her on social media:
Twitter: @daisy_prescott
Facebook: https://www.facebook.com/DaisyPrescottAuthor
Pinterest: http://pinterest.com/daisyprescott/
Instagram: http://instagram.com/daisyprescott
Google+: https://plus.google.com/u/0/+DaisyPrescott/posts

SYMBOLS

The symbols that appear in this book are Adinkra from the Asante tribe. These graphics can be found throughout many areas of Ghana and West Africa on buildings, fabric, carvings, jewelry, and metal castings.

"Love never loses its way home."
Represents the power of love.

"Change or transform your character."
Contains the Morning Star symbol (new start) inside the wheel representing movement.

Special thank you to http://www.adinkra.org for the graphics and definitions of these symbols.

Made in the USA
Charleston, SC
12 July 2014